Learning Goals
and
Dancing Poles

Book Two of the
Marchfield Middle Series

By M. Jayne LaDow

To my family, both blood and chosen:
You're the rocks that keep me grounded,
and the inspiration I occasionally trip over.
Love you all!

Chapter 1
Val

Winter Carnival.

Marchfield Middle's annual carnival was the stuff of legend. Held in the dead of winter when the snow has turned brown, and the air smells cold and crisp. By this point, the holidays were long forgotten, and spring break wasn't even a glimmer on the horizon. The carnival was THE Friday night event for the town, so the pressure on me and all the other teachers was at crisis-level.

Cue the laughter, cotton candy, and decorated booths doused in loud, pumping dance music.

Our school transformed into a wonderland for one night. We scrambled to decorate booths, vying for the coveted Best Decorated Award, of free lunch from any restaurant in town.

It was a cutthroat competition. Last year, fellow teachers, Frank Zamuda and Dee O'Malley, had won with a fog machine, an inflatable fire-breathing dragon, and fancy, rented knight costumes. Teachers will do anything for free food.

In the six years I'd been teaching at Marchfield, I'd never won. Creativity wasn't my problem, but who had the time and energy to teach, grade, and spend hours designing and crafting a booth? In other words, I'd make an effort, but I wouldn't get my hopes up.

The name of my assigned booth this year was The Rat Race, inducing nightmares of scurrying feet, twitching whiskers, and skinny naked tails for a full week. Even after assurances from our principal, Mr. Kline, that no live rats would be present, my apprehensions were still high.

I sketched out three huge posters depicting rats driving colorful racecars around a track, riding thoroughbred horses, and my favorite, rats in Marchfield P.E. sweatsuits running around a track.

Gathering tape, scissors, and my costume, I made my way to the gym. It was a madhouse of activity as teachers scurried like, well rats, setting up their booths.

I waved to my bestie, Audrey, and her fiancé, Oz. They were in charge of the Duck Pond this year. Oz filled the plastic baby pool with a hose while Audrey set hundreds of small rubber ducks afloat, so even the littlest kids could win a prize.

The two of them had a one-night stand last year which turned into months of drama, arguing, and eventually love. Google Perfect Couple and their engagement photo would be the first hit. They have plans to marry next October.

As the maid of honor, I should be thrilled for them. And I was... when envy wasn't painting me green.

Truthfully, I felt old watching them kiss and cuddle all the time, and a little sad at being the odd woman out, and I yearned for something more.

Shaking off those sneaky, selfish feelings, I hustled over to my booth set up on the opposite side of the gym and dumped my supplies on a plastic chair.

"Thank God, you're here." Brian Beckin, our Student Activities Coordinator, jogged over. We'd dubbed him Mr. Khakis because he always wore tan shorts and a Marchfield Middle shirt.

I curtsied. "If I had a nickel for every time you said that, Brian. I'd be rich."

"You're late," he chastised me in a loud voice.

I struck a pose with my hip cocked. "'A wizard is never late, nor is he early. He arrives precisely when he means to.'"

Brian gaped at me in silence.

"*Lord of the Rings?* Seriously, Brian, do you live in a hole?" I teased.

Face blank, he said, "We need to do a walk-through of the game."

A huge five-lane race track dominated the long cafeteria table. In a bin, furry, battery-powered rats stared up at me with beady eyes. Six inches long with hard bodies under worn fur coats. They even had skinny, bald tails. I repressed a shiver of horror.

"The directions are here." He pointed to a large poster by the starting line.

"Players choose a rat and a lane," I read out loud. "When the Starter..."

He pointed at me dramatically. "That's you."

"Thanks for clearing that up, Brian," I chuckled. "When The Starter begins the race, the mechanical rats will race to the end of the track."

Brian flipped a switch on the bottom of a rat. Its red eyes glowed brightly. He set it into the track where it trundled toward the finish line.

"Won't they all finish at the same time?"

"Watch," he said.

The rat stopped. Its whiskers twitched, as if smelling something delicious as it reared up to 'look' around. The moment passed and it continued forward again.

"It takes two minutes to finish a race," Brian told me as he returned the rat to the basket. "They're all programmed differently, so you will have one winner every time."

Picking up another rat, I joked, "How does a rat stay fit?"

Brian rolled his eyes. "How"

"He does mouse-ercise."

He groaned. "Awful." Pointing to a box tucked under the table, he continued, "Winners choose a glow-in-the-dark necklace or neon-colored, sticky rubber wall-walker."

"Got it."

"Don't feel sorry for the losers and give away all the prizes like you did last year."

He made it sound like it was a criminal offense. "Aye, aye, Captain."

The clock ticked closer to start time. I glanced around. The entire faculty seemed to be in the gym, working on their booths. A giant board hung over the bleachers proclaimed Marchfield Middle as the 2023 Girls Soccer Champs, and the scoreboard's countdown clock started with twenty minutes before the doors opened.

The gym was noisy, and everyone seemed busy. No one wandered around unaccounted for. "Is anyone working the booth with me?"

"Yeah. He's moving some cartons of water for me..."

A panicked shout went up.

"The damn thing zapped me" Marnie McCuistion yelped, shaking her fingers.

Turning, Brian and I watched sparks fly out of the Alien Operation game. A loud buzzer blared and a small trail of smoke wafted in the air above the booth.

Without a word, Brian ran toward Marnie and disappeared into the crowd.

Assuming Brian had everything under control, I turned back to my booth. Stacked, gray bleachers made a wall across the back, perfect for my posters. Unfortunately, they needed to be higher than my five foot seven inches could reach.

Clearing the supplies from the chair, I set the back rest against the bleacher wall and climbed up. Balancing the poster and tape dispenser, I rose on the tiptoes of my super cute Prada black leather booties and reached high over my head.

I had one corner of the poster attached to the bleachers when the chair wobbled. Dropping the tape, I grabbed for the bleachers, but they slid out, pushing against the chair with a thump.

Time slowed down, voices and music blended together, strange and discordant. The chair screeched loudly against the wooden floor, the world tipped, and I lost my balance.

My nails scraped along the smooth surface of the folded risers. Perhaps, like Alice falling down the rabbit hole, I might go on a grand adventure. More likely, I would be Humpty Dumpty, broken in a million pieces.

I would be the cautionary tale on OSHA's mandatory training module next year, *'Never stand on a chair: Dangerous slips and falls,'* brought to you by Val Bellini, teacher who fell off a chair.

One minute, I hurtled toward disaster, and the next, I was frozen in midair. Strong hands wrapped around my waist from behind, pulling me into a hard chest. My glasses were gone, but his strong body anchored me.

"Oof." I squeaked.

My imagination took over. Superman, in red flannel, held all one hundred and forty-five pounds of me with ease.

My hero's other arm came around me. His spicy cinnamon and citrus scent flooded my senses. He slowly lowered me to the floor, and I slid down his body, past his trim belly and his belt buckle to the very satisfying bulge beneath it. The bulge grew, pressing into my back. Was that my tape dispenser or was someone happy to rescue me?

Ready to play Lois Lane to his Superman, I fantasized about reaching up and curling my hand around my mystery man's neck, dragging his head down for a cinematic kiss, brushing across the sinews of his neck as I ground my hips back against his Man of Steel.

Fly me to the moon Superman, and I'll show you a good time.

Unfortunately, Lois and I always find trouble.

He released me before the heels of my fashionable booties were flat on the floor. Unbalanced, I shot my arms out wide and my flailing right fist met flesh with a crunch.

I'd punched Superman in the nose.

"Gah." My rescuer yelled, backing away.

"Oh my God! I'm so sorry. Are you okay?"

My rescuer Evan Shurden, the school's technology teacher, was more Clark Kent, endearing and sweet, than Superman.

His narrow brown eyes capped with dark eyebrows, and his straight black hair was gathered into a man bun. His attractive brown skin gleamed under the fluorescent lights, highlighting the sharp angles of his jaw and the warmth in his eyes.

Pinching the bridge of his nose, his lips quirk at my lengthy inspection.

Audrey rushed over with several other teachers close behind. She rescued my glasses, handing them back. "Are y'all okay?"

Should I take a look at his nose? Playing doctor wasn't really my thing. If he was bleeding, I'd pass out on the floor.

"No lasting damage," He assured Audrey. "How about you?"

Evan gave his nose one more pinch and grinned at me. With my glasses back on, I noticed the dimple that creased his left cheek. A fire began to simmer in my belly. Dimples scrambled my synapses. I wanted to press my lips against his. Rub my breasts against the hard muscles my butt already knew.

I nodded slowly, wondering if I'd somehow hit my head. "Thanks for saving me, Superman."

He winked. "Always happy to help out a damsel in distress."

Conflicted between irritation and lust, I reverted to my teacher voice. "Modern women don't appreciate being labeled as damsels."

Audrey raised an eyebrow at me. Without a word, she led the others back to their booths.

Lifting his palms toward me in surrender. "I didn't mean anything by it. I'm just glad I caught you before you hit the ground."

I couldn't rip my eyes from his chest. His shirt clung to his muscular abs, and the sleeves stretched tight over his shoulders and arms. My irritation burned up as flames of desire rolled through me.

I swallowed hard, jerking my head up to meet his eyes. "If you hadn't, I'd be filing workman's comp forms and going to the hospital.

"I'm sure it wouldn't have been that bad, Ms. Bellini."

"Call me Val."

"Nice to meet you."

A memory clicked of another terrible faculty icebreaker. Evan and I'd been grouped together with some other faculty members and Mr. Kline gave us three tennis balls and a prompt: demonstrate a teacher's daily responsibility.

"We've met. We won that game together."

"You mean *you* won. I just watched with my mouth hanging open. Where'd you learn to juggle?"

"I wanted to be a clown when I grew up. I dreamed of running away with the circus."

"Yeah? Like a sad clown? They kind of freak me out with those face paint tears."

"Heck, no! I'd have busted out of a tiny car last with ten dogs doing tricks."

"So you learned to juggle. Did you train your dog?"

I laughed at the absurdity. "No, my parents are not-pet people. Too messy. Too fun."

He nodded solemnly like I'd told him something unspeakably sad about my childhood. "I'll let you train my dog, Cocoa, if you want. She's sweet, but stubborn."

"Such a sweet offer, but those dreams are long gone. All I'm left with is a teaching degree and superior juggling skills."

Evan's eyes crinkled and the dimple reappeared. The deep laugh rolled out, full of humor and joy, and I immediately wanted to make him laugh again.

I warned him, "Don't get me started on my world record in the hula hoop."

I'm a teacher, but in my soul lives an awkward teenager. A dramatic only child.

When a dark, handsome, sexy man laughs at my jokes? It's an aphrodisiac.

Poets wrote odes about a lover's eyes twinkling, but I'd never experienced it in real life. Watching Evan's whole face light up and his eyes sparkle with mischief, I finally understood.

A microphone somewhere squealed with feedback, and suddenly I remembered we were in the school gym. I made a show of picking up the tape and poster off the floor. Would he take the hint and leave me alone to recover my composure?

"Um, Thanks again, Evan. I just need to finish hanging these decorations and get the booth set up."

He gestured to me to hand him the tape as he took the poster from the floor. "I'll help you hang those."

"I promise not to get on the chair again. Besides, you probably have to get back to your booth."

"This is it."

He stretched his arms up to position the poster. His T-shirt lifted to expose a delectable slice of brown skin at the base of his spine,

"Oh." I fumbled with the tape, sticking two pieces together before finally handing him a strip.

We worked together efficiently despite my current state of hormonal immaturity. I scolded myself for objectifying him.

Finally finished, I glanced over to see Audrey and Oz walking over, holding hands.

"You guys ready? Jess told us to give everyone a ten-minute warning." Audrey darted her eyes between Evan and me in wordless conversation, begging me for a quick chat.

"I need to put on my costume. Come help me, Aud." I threw my backpack over my shoulder and yanked her toward the girls' locker room.

"Whoa, girl!" Audrey jogged beside me ready to gossip.

Rows of gray lockers lined the walls of the dimly lit girls' locker room. Scattered refuse, dirty socks, a water bottle, and a pair of ratty sneakers lay on the floor. The whole place smelled of body odor.

I inhaled, letting the teenage miasma cool my overheated body.

I rounded the corner toward a line of curtained dressing rooms and pulled the fabric closed behind me.

"What's up between you and Evan?" Audrey asked.

I took off my work outfit and pulled on a white T-shirt and jean overalls without answering.

Audrey persisted, "Earth to Val, come in, Val."

I shoved sneakers on my feet and exited the stall. Setting my glasses on the edge of a nearby sink, I stepped up to a dusty mirror. Using the face paints from my backpack, I drew whiskers on my cheeks with a pencil.

After drawing a black spot on the tip of my nose, I put my glasses on before meeting Audrey's eyes in the mirror.

I stuck out my tongue and crossed my eyes. "He's too good-looking."

Refusing to snicker at me, she crossed her arms over her chest. "He keeps sneaking peeks at your butt."

He couldn't have! "What? When?"

She tilted her head, like an animal smelling fresh meat. "Are you interested in him?"

"No." *Maybe...*

Audrey clapped her hands and did a little victory dance, she could read me better than anyone else. "You do!"

I shook my head, not sure who I was trying to fool. "I enjoy the package, but it doesn't matter. I can't do anything about it."

"You could if you wanted to."

"Maybe in six months or a year. Once I get Mom and Dad to back off about marrying me off to Logan." If Evan knew about all the crap I delt with on that front he'd be gone in a flash.

"I don't like Logan. Something about him gives me the creeps." She shuddered.

"Aren't you glad you haven't known him all your life then? Anyway, I need to extricate myself from my parents' weird marriage obsession Goal one: get rid of Logan, Goal two: figure out what's going on with my parents, Goal three: ..."

What was goal three? I was already a successful teacher, so it wasn't career oriented. Maybe buy a house? Start a 401K? A vacation! Just me, some books, and the quiet sound of the waves on the shore. It sounded lovely-and depressing. A year ago, I'd have dragged Audrey away with me on a girls' trip. Now I was alone.

I needed a fling. Release the tension. A sexy man, a dozen Big Os, and I'd be all better.

Audrey snorted as if she could read my mind. "Get laid? Find your true love?"

I pursed my lips. "Just because that worked for you doesn't mean I should jump Evan's bones in the courtyard."

"Well, he couldn't keep his eyes off you. You should explore that."

I frowned gesturing to the baggy overalls and painted on whiskers. "Wait 'til he sees me in this outfit. It's a cold shower. The antithesis of sexy."

"It's your *If You Give a Mouse a Cookie* costume. You're totally adorbs."

I threw my hands up in the air in frustration. "I'm wearing a rat costume, Audrey. He couldn't see my butt if he tried with these overalls on."

"What's your underwear situation?"

I glared at her. "None of your business."

She hung her head. "Granny panties, huh?"

"Shut up."

"Comfort over style, I got you."

"You're being ridiculous."

"But he wants what you got, nonetheless. Did you rub across his baloney pony?"

I slapped a hand over my mouth and nodded.

"Oh my God, this is fantastic!"

While she cackled like a hyena, I pulled my long, wavy brown hair back into a ponytail, put on my mouse ears, and straightened my glasses. It was almost time for the doors to open.

Audrey tucked a strand of hair behind my ear. "Where's your tail?"

"I'm not wearing a tail."

She snickered, "I bet Evan would like some tail."

The next three hours would be loud, hot, and insane. There'd be no time for flirting or wondering whether Evan Shurden checked my tail out.

Despite all my protests to the contrary, my hormones sang a siren's song, and my heart pounded at the thought of him. Thirty minutes ago, I'd been fine, and Evan hadn't even been a blip on my radar.

Okay, he'd been a blip. A small one. The you-stay-in-your-hall, and-I'll-stay-in-mine kind, where I didn't think about him very often. I'd been fine with that.

I straightened my shoulders and took a deep calming breath. I needed to keep my head in the game.

Chapter 2
Evan

I took one look at Val six months ago and wanted her.

The faculty had gathered in the library on the first day of school in August. I sat at the front table with five other new teachers as the veterans walked in.

Wearing jeans and a flowy green top that showed off her tan skin and dark brown hair, she lit up the room. She gave out hugs like candy, and her laugh was a husky punch to my gut.

I'd never experienced such an instant attraction to someone before. The world narrowed in until she was all I could see and hear; her sashaying walk, her tinkling laugh, and the bounce of her breasts.

She sat down at a table, leaning over to whisper something to a redheaded woman. The urge to jump out of my seat and walk over compelled me, so much that I missed the principal introducing me.

Mr. Kline had leaned over to make eye contact. "Evan? Did I pronounce your name correctly?"

"Evan," Shayla Osgood, a new reading teacher, touched my shoulder and gestured to the principal.

My face felt hot as I stood and turned to acknowledge the staff's welcome, and I purposely kept my eyes far from the table where she sat.

***

I shook away the cobwebs of the memory, only seven minutes before Marchfield Middle's doors opened and hundreds of kids swarmed in to play games, win prizes, and eat until they exploded. I needed to get my head in the game.

Brian had asked me yesterday to help run the Rat Race game I agreed without asking questions. I should have asked who I'd be working with, perhaps then I could have avoided her.

Sometimes she wore boots that zipped up the back past her knees. I'd spent more than a few minutes on my planning break fantasizing about Val's legs. In those boots with her legs wrapped around my hips as I pushed up against my classroom door.

It was probably the boots' fault she toppled off the chair. And Val's torturous slide down my body was too reminiscent of my fantasy. I needed to clear my head and get my body under control.

Val and I were two professionals.

Surrounded by impressionable children.

"Evan, are you okay?" Oz Tayor asked. When Val and her friend Audrey hurried away to the locker room. They left Audreys fiancé in their wake.

I took a deep breath and let it out slowly. Searching for something to say to Oz that would ease my awkwardness, I said, "You're one lucky guy." I nodded the door that Audrey closed.

"Hell, yes, I am.".

I liked Oz. He was Marchfield's algebra teacher and girls' soccer coach. As war vet, he still kept his blond hair military buzzed. His language was not rated G in the teachers' lounge, but he had a great sense of humor around the kids.

The school gossip was pretty juicy about how he and Audrey got together. Some of them involved him making out with her in the school's back garden. I wasn't sure what to believe.

"I've heard the rumors. Someday you'll have to tell me how it all went down."

He nodded. "Buy me a beer sometime."

Oz's best friend and science teacher, Bobby Nooney, walked toward us. Her short black hair and elfin smile drew you in, but her confident swagger announced she was tougher than she appeared.

"Hey, need anything before this shindig starts?"

Oz shrugged. "We're waiting for Val and Audrey."

"I'm waiting for Mel, too," Bobby said. "My wife's got me wrapped around her little finger."

Oz snorted. "You love it."

"I really do." Bobby grinned ear to ear, blushing. Maybe she wasn't so tough.

"How long have you been married?"

"Two months. December 27th. Best day of my life."

I grinned at her, slipping into my mother's Cherokee language, "Gvlielitseha." *Gil-li-le-chi-ha*, congratulations.

Bobby beamed at me. "Does that mean 'Whoa dude, you hit the jackpot?' Because I did."

Her cheer was contagious. "Pretty much."

"I knew it. I have a natural affinity for languages." Bobby clapped me on the shoulder. "How's your first year going?"

"It's going well. I really like it here. The kids are like sponges."

I loved teaching technology. This class combined aspects from shop class with computers, robotics, and other disciplines. My classroom was in the basement, but I liked to think of it as starting on the ground floor of my Maker career.

Oz groaned. "Easy to say when you're teaching them to build birdhouses. Try convincing them to learn algebra. They're less like sponges and more like rocks."

"I tell them it's all about math. Measure twice, cut once. They get whiny about it, but they know their formulas."

"They'd better."

Temptation kept me glancing toward the locker room as Val appeared. I zeroed in on her, and the conversation lagged.

Despite being made up like a rat, Val Bellini was hot. I imagined unhooking those thin straps and letting the material skim down her body to the floor. I wondered what kind of underwear she wore, and I pictured her commando.

Her long, dark Italian beauty captivated me. She usually twisted her brown hair on top of her head in a way that screamed intellectual femininity. It made me want to drag my lips along her neck.

Bobby caught me staring and smiled knowingly. What was it with these two reading me so well?

The buzzer sounded on the countdown clock, and Bobby shouted. "Battle stations, people."

Audrey took Oz's hand. "We'll come back and check on you guys later."

Hurrying into the booth, Val bent to pick up the bin of rats, and my eyes returned automatically to her butt. I almost groaned. I counted to ten while imagining swimming in an icy river to banish my hard-on.

The unmistakable sound of children heading toward us was deafening. A sea of children poured into the gym waving tickets, their feet thudding on the wooden boards as they ran in every direction. Their excited voices echoed off the high ceiling.

I grabbed a hole-punch to notch tickets as our first racers lined up to choose their rats. When the first five had their rats behind the starting gate, Val shouted, "On your mark, get set, go."

She lifted the gate, and the rats were off. The mechanical racers scurried and paused like actual rats. The tech guy in me wanted to take one apart and study its programming.

Kids screamed, cheering on their mechanical rodents excited by the carnival atmosphere or from sugar highs. Even the most morose teens smiled, darting from booth to booth, having a great time.

When the gray and brown rat in lane four, the happy winner, walked off with a glow stick necklace.

The line formed ten deep to play, and Val and I fell into a rhythm. I punched the tickets and lined up the kids. She supervised the selection of the rats, the race, and the prizes.

The first hour flew by. The never-ending line of children racing mechanical rats, the winning and losing became surreal. By the end of the second hour, my stomach growled and my head ached from the constant noise. My patience began to fray from a long day of teaching and the inane repetition of the game.

I checked my watch and wanted to slump to the floor. We had an hour left.

"You guys need a break?" Bobby and her wife, Mel Driver, appeared like magical fairies. Mel, a guidance counselor, had been one of my first friends at Marchfield.

"Yes! Yes!" Val shimmied out from the booth, and I was right behind her.

"Bless you," Val kissed Mel's cheek. She raced off, bee-lining for the physical education office located on the opposite side of the gym and disappeared inside the door.

Mel turned to me with twinkling eyes. "What about you, handsome?"

"Why didn't you tell me you married Bobby in December?" I hugged her, teasing. "All this time, I still thought I had a chance."

Mel patted my arm. "I didn't want to break your heart. Besides, I heard from Bobby you might be interested in someone else."

"Guidance counselors shouldn't gossip." My eyes cut to Bobby, who was grinning like a fool.

Mel winked at me. "It's not gossip. It's just an old married couple placing bets on young lovers. Make me proud, Evan. I've got my money on you."

Before I could say anything, Bobby interrupted, "The kids are getting restless. Take your break, Evan. We've got this." She and Mel slipped into the booth and started the next rat race.

Seconds later, I was alone with Val inside the office.

She slumped in a metal chair with a plate of food. Near her a table, loaded with sandwiches and chips, sat in the middle of the small space. The sound of the crowd and music was slightly quieter, and I sighed in relief.

I grabbed a cola from a cooler and swallowed it in one gulp. Picking up a turkey on rye, I tried to pace myself and not to gobble it down.

Checking my phone, I noticed I'd missed six texts from Yona who lived back home in North Carolina with her two kids.

4:35 PM
Yona: Hey, can I call you?

5:02 PM
Yona: Guess you're busy tonight.

Yona and Noah and I had grown up together. We used to play all day on the mountain behind our houses. Noah and Yona fell in love in high school. When we graduated, they married and started a family. I went to college, but we stayed tight.

After college, Dad had a heart attack while working on a house. Even though I had a teaching job lined up in Martinsville, Virginia, I took over the business instead. It felt like a sign, a calling to step in and help.

I rented the house next to my friends for eight years. Their twin girls, Jacy and Fala, wrapped me around their little fingers

Then, last June, the unthinkable happened. A drunk driver plowed into Noah's truck, killing him. Yona was inconsolable, and the girls seemed like sad shadows of themselves.

The wound punched a gaping hole in my heart. Not only had I lost my best friend, I wished I had done something, anything, to prevent it. I still didn't know what I should do, how I should help.

Once again, I debated quitting the teaching job I'd accepted in Marchfield, but I needed a fresh start, something different. So, for the first time since college, I was out on my own. But every time I started to feel at home, Yona would call, and the guilt of leaving would rush in.

5:13 PM
Yona: It's nothing super important.

6:20 PM

Yona: Jacy is doing great in school. She's got a B in Algebra and an A in science.

I felt an ache in my chest. Jacy loved school. She'd transferred all her grief into hard work and learning.

6:26 PM

Yona: It's Fala I'm worried about. She has a D in English and is failing World Geography. I have a meeting with the school Monday. I was hoping you could give me some tips on how to handle it.

Like Noah, Fala learned better with her hands. She's always disliked everything about school except P.E. and electives. And now, it was growing worse.

7:14 PM

Yona: Oh, and thanks for the money you sent. I wish you wouldn't, but I appreciate it.

Sending Yona part of my paycheck every month helped me feel better about taking this job.

Mental note: call tomorrow.

Val stretched out her legs and groaned. "I feel like a starving rat, fresh off a shipwreck."

Tongue-tied, I watched her legs and desperately tried not to slip back into my fantasy.

Fuel was thrown on fantasy and the fire grew when she moaned, swallowing some of her icy soda. The sound sent flames racing down my spine, and I bit my lip to stop the echoing groan from spilling out.

Her mouse ears were now askew, the lines of her whiskers smudged, and the little black spot on her nose called to me to kiss it.

I wanted to pull her onto my lap, feel her breath, hot on my face. Would her rosy lips taste sweet like cotton candy or tart like cherries?

I spoke without thinking. "You're so beautiful."

Fuck! I'd stepped right across friendship and gone for the pickup line.

I wracked my brain for something to say that would make me sound less perv-ish. "I mean as a rat." *What was wrong with me?*

Her brown eyes popped open, and I panicked. "Ignore me. I'm tired, and I don't get out much."

She studied me with her dark, bittersweet chocolate eyes smooth like mousse. Once I got a taste of her, the craving might never stop.

If she didn't slap me, I would do it myself.

When she giggled, I let out the breath I'd been holding. The soft sound turned into a full belly laugh, and the tension eased from my body.

Her peals of laughter became infectious, and soon my chuckles joined hers. In minutes, we were both clutching our sides with tears in our eyes.

"Thanks for the compliment. This has been a really long day, and it struck me as funny."

She picked up her wrap and took another bite, and we ate in silence.

I took a second sandwich from the tray and leaned back in my chair, groaning. "Do we have to go back out there?"

Val sighed. "It's the right thing to do."

Neither of us moved.

I closed my eyes. "Five more minutes?"

"Sure," she agreed, and we sat in the quiet until she asked. "You have anything fun planned for the rest of the weekend?"

"One of my college buddies is in town this weekend. I'm meeting him for dinner tomorrow."

"What college did you go to?"

"Virginia Commonwealth. You?"

"James Madison."

"Great school. I know some people who went there. Have you always lived in Virginia?"

Val smiled. "Nah, my parents live in Richmond now, but we used to live in Greenville, South Carolina, near my Gran." From her tone, I could tell she remembered Greenville as her childhood home.

"I grew up in North Carolina, near Asheville."

"I miss the mountains sometimes." A faraway look grew on her face. "The air just feels different there. And there's always something to rest your eyes on."

"I know exactly what you mean. Mom says it's the altitude."

"Don't get me wrong, I love Marchfield, but the ground's so flat." She smiled, but it was tight, almost pinched.

"Is everything okay?" I asked.

She blinked, "Oh sure. I'm just a little homesick. I haven't thought about the mountains in a long time."

"Why not?"

"We used to live close to Gran. I'd explore the woods and streams, drawing the plants and animals. I picked wild raspberries, and we made jam and sat on the porch in the evenings. After she died, my parents sold her house, and we moved to Richmond."

"I don't know what I'd do if my parents moved. I need periodic doses of mountain air to live."

"Maybe that's my problem. There's not enough air in Virginia."

I sensed that her unhappiness wasn't only about missing the mountains. A pallor of sorrow settled around her like fog. The desire to jump to her rescue flooded me.

I opened my mouth, and the words tumbled out without planning. "I'm heading home for my *Elisi's* ninetieth birthday party over Spring Break. It's going to be huge. Not just family, but like the whole town. You could come with me. Get some of that mountain air."

Val gaped at me, and my face felt hot. Why would she want to go to my grandmother's party? We were virtual strangers. This was weird. She wasn't my girlfriend, not even my friend.

"That's very kind," Val started politely. I knew she was searching for a way to turn me down.

"Just think about it," I interrupted her. "I need to bring someone, or my mom will try to set me up with every single girl in town."

"I'm sure there are lots of women who would love to go with you." Val said softly.

I couldn't read her tone or face.

And I sure couldn't tell her she was the only woman I'd thought about in six months, so I shrugged.

Val pursed her lips, then opened her mouth as if about to say something. I leaned forward in my chair, but the speaker in the ceiling crackled. The principal's voice boomed loudly, ruining any chance of hearing what Val wanted to say.

"Thank you all for coming to the Winter Carnival. If you have any unused punches on your tickets, please use them now. We'll be closing in twenty minutes."

I met Val's eyes as she stood. "We should get back out there." Whatever she'd been about to say, she wouldn't share it now.

"Okay." I stood and threw our trash into the bin.

Noise crashed over us like a wave as we stepped into the gym. The music started again, and Justin Timberlake's *Can't Stop the Feeling!* pumped through the sound system.

All the teachers squealed and clasped their hands over their hearts. In unison, the staff turned toward Audrey and Oz where he spun Audrey around and began dancing with her.

Despite a long line of kids waiting to race at the booth, Bobby grooved with Mel.

I bumped my fist with both of them. "Thanks for giving us a break." They waved and disappeared into the crowd that had formed around their friends.

"What's happening?" I asked Val.

"It's Oz's dateposal song."

I tried to parse out that information while I punched tickets and got the kids lined up to race. When I glanced up to tell her we were ready to start, I caught Val staring longingly over at the crowd. "I've got this. Go dance with your friends."

"Are you sure?" She took in the long line of students waiting. I could tell she felt bad leaving me.

"Go," I repeated, nudging her out of the way to start the race. "Have fun."

She didn't ask twice or glance back. Slipping out of the booth, she ran over and joined the flash mob of teachers dancing.

Zane Treliane, an eighth grader in my class, handed me his punch card for the next race.

"What's going on over there?" I asked, nodding toward the celebration.

He shrugged his narrow shoulders. "Mr. Taylor asked Ms. Fremont out last year by doing a dance on the field to that tune."

"Really?" I watched Oz shake his hips.

"Yeah. Did you see him ask her to marry him this year while wearing a dress? Y'all teachers are weird."

I handed Zane a sticky wall-walker, and he took off in search of his friends.

Deciding to call it quits ten minutes early, I passed out prizes to all the kids left in the line. I took down the posters and straightened up the booth.

Then I helped Brian clear the gym and the hallways while the rest of the teachers danced.

Chapter 3
Val

"What?" I barked into my cellphone as I fumbled for my glasses on the nightstand. Who would dare call me on a Saturday before 9:00 AM?

"Valentine, it's Logan. I've made reservations for us tonight at Chez Riche for 7:00."

I sat upright, my mind whirling. I hadn't seen nor heard from Logan in five months. Not since my father's sixty-fifth birthday party.

I hadn't missed him.

I didn't even try to filter my reaction. "Whyyy?"

"I missed you."

Liar. He only popped into my life whenever one or both of our mothers pressured him. The last time he spontaneously turned up at my apartment, he'd come with a ring and a list of reasons why we should marry. It topped the list to please our parents, followed by we would make a cute couple. The list went on to include me being able to quit my job, move closer to my parents, and focus on charitable work.

I'd thrown up a little in my mouth.

And now he was back again after weeks of silence. "I doubt that very much."

Without missing a beat, Logan said, "I'll pick you up at 6:30. Don't be late this time, Valentine."

Irritation bloomed like algae in a red tide of frustration. I hated the way he said my name, and his smug satisfaction of knowing I loathed it made it ten times worse.

Mom gave birth to me on Valentine's Day. She and Dad could have named me Venus or Aphrodite. Or Susan or Nancy. But no, my creative as dust parents named me Valentine, a cutesy name I despised.

When I started middle school, I asked everyone to call me Val, but Mom and Dad flat-out refused and Logan's parents followed suit.

I dragged myself back to the present with difficulty.

"I have other plans." He didn't need to know my plans involved staying in, grading papers, and reading *The Princess Bride* for the thousandth time while eating a pint of *Cherry Garcia*.

In a deceptively charming tone, Logan coaxed, "Cancel them. Chez Riche has the best chef in southeast Virginia."

"I have a headache."

"Why are you so difficult? I'm inviting you to a nice dinner."

"You haven't told me why."

"The 'rents are making me crazy. Our moms blindsided me yesterday."

Logan was the spoiled son of Arwin Stephenson, owner of Stephenson's Department Store and the Richmond SuperSonics football team. Mom and Dad met

Arwin and his wife, Ginnifer, in high school. They met weekly to play cards and took several trips together every year. Their dreams of us marrying began when we were born only months apart and continued to this day.

I sighed, a long hissing breath into the phone. "Okay. I'll go to dinner with you, but only to make a plan to handle our parents."

"Absolutely."

"I mean it. No talk of marriage or babies, or I'm out of there."

"See you at 6:30."

He hung up before I could say I'd rather drive myself, but I let it go. It would lead to another civil disagreement, and I couldn't bear it.

Because I was awake, and didn't want to grade a hundred C.E.R. paragraphs about the purpose of local government, I drove into town in my sweet red Mini-Cooper. I called her Betty Boop; she was my first car, and I loved her even though she was in the shop more than I'd like.

After stopping by the grocery store for cereal and a loaf of bread, I walked over to Kick Ass Coffee for a mocha latte.

The chilly walk through Marchfield's cute town center eased away the rough start to the day. Dirty piles of snow clumped in shady areas, but the sun warmed my face.

The brick storefronts from the early 1900s lined Main Street. These renovated shops were transformed into storefronts with big front window displays.

I passed Pie in the Sky, the yummiest pizza place ever, and Sharky's Pub, where the school held happy hours once a month. Pat's Bakery smelled temptingly of cinnamon rolls.

Share with Your Buds, the flower store across the street, enticed me with colorful blooms. A few boutiques catered to mature women. Dina's stocked clothes for the younger crowd. Main Street also included a vintage record shop, a hardware store, and an indie bookstore.

But it was The Shoe Box that caught my attention. The display window showcased last year's Prada line. The bright colors and needle-thin heels called to me.

Designer shoes were my Kryptonite. My mom fostered the obsession on trips to Paris as I was growing up, and I'd never grown out of it. Now my favorite hobby was scouring for the best deals. As a teacher, I had to be careful with my money, but browsing the walls of discounted fashion gave me joy.

"Hi, Val." Taj, the shop owner, left the hardwood desk and hurried over. "How are those 2020 Louboutin boots working out for you?"

I did a jig, showing off the supple black leather boots. "I love them, and they go with everything."

Taj grinned. "I love your bag."

The small, brown cross body was one of my recent finds. "Thanks. I got it on sale down the street at North and Main. Did you know they create their products by hand? I was lucky to get this one at half price last year."

"You know, I have a pair of heeled booties that would match it perfectly." Taj bustled off to a shelf near the back of the store, returning with a pair of gorgeous brown leather ankle boots. Soft with delicate stitched accents and a chunky two-inch heel. I envisioned myself wearing them with my favorite jeans.

Unable to stop myself from trying them on, they were like gloves for my feet. Warm, comfortable, and damn, they made my legs look great.

"How much are they?"

"Two-fifty." She said.

I frowned. "I was hoping they'd be more like one-fifty." I slipped the boots off and returned them to the box.

Taj walked over to the cash register. She picked up a printed list, scanning it. "Actually, they are slated to go on sale soon."

I perked up. "Oh, yeah?"

"Would you buy them if they were marked down to one seventy-five?"

I could eat ramen every night for a while. "I'll take them."

"The boots work perfectly with your style."."

She rang me up.

The machine beeped, and Taj's eyebrows pinched. "It says your card's declined."

"What?" I gaped at her, embarrassed and confused. I paid the bill last week. "There must be a mistake."

"I'm sorry, Val."

"I'll figure this out and come back. Can you hold the boots for me?"

All the way home I worried. Had my account been hacked? My stomach tied up in knots, I immediately checked my online accounts.

Everything seemed fine. My last payment went through, but the red banner at the top ominously stated my account had been frozen. The bank's automated voice told me wait times were longer than normal, so I hung up.

My dad helped me set up my accounts and credit when I started college. His name was still on the account, but I paid all the bills. Dad also oversaw the investment account Gran set up in my name before she died. I wondered if he'd gotten an email or letter that I hadn't.

Picking up my phone, I called him.

"Hello, Valentine."

I pictured him at home in what Audrey dubbed the Gray Palace. Decorated in a severe style meant to be posh, my childhood home was the opposite of cozy or comfortable. Most likely he sat at his desk in the den, riffling through files, and checking the T. Rowe Price Index.

"Hi, Dad."

He sighed heavily, and I pictured him rubbing his eyes under his glasses. "I'm up to my neck at work, Valentine. Can this wait?"

That's the way it always was with Dad. Work came first, then golf and pickleball. I was somewhere down the line, but Dad was in no way a family-first type of guy.

"A store declined my credit card today. I checked online and everything looks fine, but I wondered if you'd heard anything."

I heard the *tap-tap* of his pen on the desk. "I canceled all your cards this morning and put a hold on the financial account your grandmother gave you."

I knew better than to respond with *what the hell?* Instead, I counted to ten, and tried to sound casual.

"Oh? Why?"

"Your mother and I want you to marry." I heard him rustling papers. A door clicked open in the background.

Despite my inner desire to scream, I kept my voice even. "I don't understand how these two issues are mutually exclusive."

"Since you're thirty and you're almost past your childbearing years, you must marry."

Well, that's fucked up. "Women have babies into their forties, Dad. I don't think my reproductive health is the real reason you did this."

"We've spoken to you about this many times, but you never listened."

"Oh, I heard you, Dad. I just never thought you'd sink this low."

"Is that Valentine on the phone?" My mother's voice sounded far away. "Let me speak with her."

The sound of the phone passing hands crackled loudly in my ear. "Hello, Valentine?"

I sighed. "Hi, Mom."

"I'm happy to hear your voice."

"I called because Dad canceled my cards."

"You can get new cards after the wedding when your name changes. When are you moving home?"

Did she think I'd drop everything and marry Logan tomorrow? With effort, I managed to keep my voice calm. "Mom, I'm not changing my name."

"Logan's proposing tonight. Your father will reinstate your cards when you've agreed."

"I'm not marrying him. I don't love Logan."

She cajoled, "I want you to be supported. A woman needs a man to look out for her. Despite all that feminism you learned in college, I want you to be safe."

My parents sent me to James Madison to round off my education and polish my resume as a good wife. It cracks me up how much that backfired. I majored in history restoration and political science, with a healthy dose of women's rights. I marched with the Me Too Movement and advocated for gun control. Then I did something they could never forgive. I took a job two hours away as a public school teacher.

Mom's voice rose into a nasally whine. "All of my friends have grandchildren."

"You're only fifty-eight, mom. There's time."

My Dad's voice cut in. "Valentine, you're thirty, and you've never had a boyfriend for longer than two months. It's time to get serious about life and—"

The calm surrounding me frayed as I bit out, "And do what you want?"

"Honey," Mom coaxed. "You know Ginnifer and I have always wanted you and Logan to join the families, but if there is someone else..."

Dad laughed, the sound snide and bitter. "If you've had any other recent proposals, please let us know."

An image of Evan asking me to visit Asheville amidst all the chaos of the Winter Carnival appeared.

I banished the image. "Excuse me, Father, I didn't know I'd time-traveled to the middle ages. You can try to lock my credit cards in a tower, and chain a dragon to the money Gran gave me, but I'm not marrying without love just because you demand it."

Mom wailed, "Valentine."

I hung up, turned off my phone, and threw it across the room. It hit the wall with a thud as I collapsed into a chair.

***

By 6:30, I'd showered, changed into a black and gray sweater dress with tall black boots. The heels, a spiky four inches high, guaranteed I would tower over Logan.

When he texted me from his car at 6:36, I was waiting for him smugly.

6:36 PM
Logan: I'm here.

6:37 PM
Me: You're late.

6:39 PM
Logan: Are you ready?

I debated turning on Season Four of *The Handmaid's Tale* and just letting him sit out there for an hour, but I wanted to get this over.

Logan's deep blue Jaguar was meant to impress, but I remained unmoved. At least it was warm inside. The weather had turned cold and windy. Clouds obscured the stars and moon. A storm approached.

The sharp edges of his face made him look a bit like Benedict Cumberbatch, but Logan didn't have his movie star charm. Logan probably spent more time on his slicked back blonde hair than I did. Today it glistened with gel, short, and styled like a serious businessman.

He leaned across to kiss me. I quickly angled my face so he couldn't kiss my mouth.

I kissed him once on the lips on Christmas Eve when were seventeen. I'd tried to talk myself into having a crush on him and wanted to see if the juice was worth the squeeze.

Catching him shaking the presents behind the tree, I'd tapped him on the shoulder. When he stood, I dove in like an Olympic diver, fast and with my eyes closed.

My kiss lacked finesse, and I smashed my teeth into his with a sharp-sounding crack.

Jerking away, my face glowed hot with embarrassment.

Logan pulled me back and chuckled, making me feel ten times more embarrassed. "Can't leave me hanging like that."

His lips were wet when they met mine, and mouth opened wide. He forced his tongue into my mouth, sweeping it from side to side.

Like kissing a thirsty dog.

He broke away laughing. His hands skimming down my bare arms, thumbs brushing along the sides of my breasts. "You wanna play peekaboob back here?"

Disgusted, I broke away from him, trying to hide my disgust.

Now, I placed a hand on my roiling stomach, wishing I'd gone with my instincts and just stayed home.

"Is this a bad episode of a reality dating show? I'm not kissing you."

"Charming as always, Valentine."

We drove to the restaurant in silence. Soft jazz spilled out of the speakers. The throaty engine of the car roared to life. I tried to relax, but an undercurrent of tension kept me on edge.

Chez Riche was tasteful, expensive, and pompous like Logan. Crisp white tablecloths with votive candles graced every table. A pianist played romantic ballads in one corner. My tan Italian skin drew rude glances from the older men.

He held my chair for me, then positioned his own too close for my liking.

A waiter in a tuxedo brought a place setting for Logan. "Our specials tonight are Boeuf Bourguignon and Lamb Chops with a Cognac Dijon Cream Sauce. May I start you with a bottle of Château Mouton Rothschild?"

"Sounds perfect. I'll have the beef and the lady will have the lamb chops."

I shook my head. "I'm sorry, this lady does not eat fluffy babies. I'll have the Greek salad, thanks." When the waiter left, I picked up my wineglass and took a big gulp.

"You're missing out on a delicious culinary dish."

My smile resembled a shark's. "I'm capable of making my own decisions."

"I'm aware," he bit out like a petulant eighth-grade boy. He leaned back in his chair, slouching casually and showing off his black Armani suit.

"Let's just get this out of the way. My mother says you're going to ask me to marry you tonight. Save us both the drama and don't."

"Valentine..."

I interrupted him. "I won't marry anyone who insists on calling me Valentine. That name is what my father calls me, which would be a huge turn-off in bed." I took another swallow of wine.

"But I prefer Valentine."

"Call me Val, or I'm leaving." I crossed my arms over my chest.

He mocked me, also crossing his arms over his chest. "Why are you so cranky?"

I tipped my glass and swallowed the rest of the wine. I knew better than to drink on an empty stomach, but when the waiter appeared at my elbow, I didn't stop him from refilling the glass. It felt like a sign.

"Why are we here?"

He slid his hand over his shiny hair. "To talk about our families' expectations and how we plan to deal with them."

I agreed with that. "They want us to marry and have kids."

"Yes." He nodded, his face blank.

"You don't love me. I don't love you."

"Does it matter? The benefits outweigh the negatives."

"How?

"You wouldn't have to work."

"I enjoy working."

"You'd be able to buy all the designer shoes and clothes you want."

"Not that it's any of your business, but my closet is full of carefully curated bargains, steals, and gifts. Besides, it's full. I don't need more."

"I would buy you a new luxury car in a suitable color."

"I love Betty Boop. Leave her alone."

"Your father tells me it's in the garage more often than not."

"My father has loose lips."

His calm, rational, emotionless eyes sent a chill up my spine. "I desire children. I assume you do, too."

Would he talk like that in bed?

"Orgasming can increase a woman's ability to conceive by fifteen percent, Valentine.

Open your legs wider, Valentine, so I may impregnate you.

I understand you aren't in the mood, but your ovulation calendar says today is your peak fertility, Valentine."

The thought alone made me want to gag.

"I have enough kids now. A hundred and twenty-seven of them."

"Your students are not the same as a baby with our genetic markers. A baby that belongs to both of us."

"Stop." My harsh tone drew the attention of several diners. "For the last time, I'm never having babies with you."

The hand resting on the tabletop fisted, his knuckles turning white. "Will you just listen?"

"I've done nothing but listen. You're the one who needs to check his hearing."

"Marrying will solve many issues of which you are unaware."

I knew something was going on and now we were getting to the good stuff. "What issues?"

"I'm not at liberty to say."

"So you just want me to trust you?"

"We've known each other forever, isn't that enough?"

Hell no. He didn't know me at all, but I knew him. Logan loved one thing in this world. Money. He wanted a mansion in the right neighborhood, and all he needed was a pretty, well-connected wife and two kids.

"You don't want me, Logan. I'm a huge pain in your ass. You'd be much happier with another woman."

And that's when it hit me. Mom and Dad wanted me to marry and have kids. They'd prefer Logan, but Mom offered me a loophole during our conversation.

"I have a boyfriend," I blurted out. "It's very serious."

Logan's eyes widened in surprise. "What?"

"His name is Evan." I fluttered my eyelashes. "We're in sweet, sweet, romantic love. So, you can see why I will never marry you."

"What does he do for a living? Is he rich?"

"He's rich in many ways." I measured Evan's worth in personality, sex appeal, and humor. I didn't know his monetary worth, and I didn't care.

"So he's poor. Your father will never approve."

"I don't know how to say this in a way you will understand. You and I will never marry. No matter what Dad says."

Logan's face darkened. His fist pounded down onto the table. The unexpected violence caused me to jump. The room became quiet around us.

He leaned forward, his snarling face so close to mine, I could smell the wine and his pungent aftershave

I shifted away from him. I'd made him angry before, but his transcended beyond Logan's casual insults and passive-aggressive taunts.

"If you want to keep using the money your Gran gave you and your credit cards, you'll agree to marry me."

I laughed despite myself. "Both you and my parents think I'm stupid and helpless, but you're wrong. I've already opened new accounts and already registered a complaint with the bank."

"You're missing the point. There are other factors at stake here."

"Then answer me. Why do I need to marry you?"

"Your father and I need this…"

And here we were again. This fiasco was circling back in on itself, and I'd had enough. I slid my chair back from the table, but he grabbed my hand. He yanked on my wrist, pulling me back down.

"Understand this, Valentine," he hissed in my ear. "The decision is out of your hands, and you need to accept it."

I met his furious eyes with my own. "I won't."

His fingers tightened on my wrist, bruising the skin, but I didn't glance away. With my spine straight, I let him see the steel of my resolve.

Seconds ticked past as we waged a silent war.

Finally, he released my wrist, dropping it as if touching me repulsed him. He stood, tossing his napkin on his lap. "I've had enough of you tonight."

I tucked my arm in, ignoring the pain, and glared up at him. Letting him see the absolute fury inside me.

"Don't call me anymore or drop by unannounced. I'll get a restraining order."

The waiter materialized by our table. "Can I get anything for you, sir? Miss? Your food will be right out."

Logan gave me a long glare filled with distaste, then turned to the waiter. "I'm afraid I have to go. The lady will take care of everything." He straightened his suit jacket, picked up his phone, and stalked out of the restaurant.

A sense of victory swept over me. For the first time, Logan walked away first. I wanted to stand up and dance like Rocky Balboa with my arms above my head. I remembered my favorite line from *Rocky*.

It ain't about how hard you hit. It's about how hard you can get hit and keep moving forward. That's how winning is done.

Glancing down at the bruises forming on my wrist, worry seeped into my internal celebration. Was he done for good, or would he be back? How much more violent would he get? He'd mentioned other factors at stake. What were they, and how did they connect to my father?

The waiter set my salad on the table in front of me. "Shall I box up the gentleman's meal?"

I wanted to say he could serve it to the alley cats, but reality came crashing down. Logan had left me stranded with no car or credit card.

Chapter 4
Val

I parked in front of Audrey's house on Sunday evening, letting the engine run.

Taking a few minutes to gather myself, I flipped open the mirror on the back of the sun visor. The circles under my dark eyes from the stress of last night's debacle were hidden under a layer of foundation. My natural color seemed a little washed out, but overall, I looked okay for not having slept much.

Knowing I'd see Audrey today, I'd avoided texting her. I wanted time to sweep the nastiness of yesterday under the rug before facing my friend.

Mom and Dad drilled the rules into me, and now I lived by them.

Don't whine about your problems.
Smile under pressure.
Don't make a fuss.
Don't blow things out of proportion.

I snapped the mirror shut, and I sent Audrey a text.

6:15 PM
Me: I'm here.

6:16 PM
Audrey: Be right out.

Pulling my puffy coat tighter around me, I turned up the heat in the car. Dressing in white short-shorts and a tank top was silly for March. So I'd added a long sleeve Henley for warmth and to cover the purple bruises on my wrist. My Uggs kept my feet warm now, but four-inch Dolce & Gabbana stilettos waited in a bag in the backseat.

Audrey's front door opened, and she waved. Dressed in booty shorts and a clingy sky-blue tank, the outfit showed off her short, curvy body. She wrapped a feather boa around her neck like a scarf and shrugged on her coat.

Long tan arms caught her from behind her as Oz yanked her back against him. The expression on her face was priceless as Oz explored her sexy attire.

I honked the horn.

Audrey slapped Oz's hands, his brawny arms like tentacles around her waist. When he let her go, she rushed out the door and scurried over to Betty Boop's passenger side. The cold air whooshed in, giving me goosebumps and making my teeth chatter.

"Shut the door!" I yelled.

"I'm trying! My feathers are caught on the seatbelt. You wouldn't want me to choke."

"If you don't close the door, I might."

Audrey giggled as she finally closed the door with a satisfying thunk. Oz stood in the doorway, shirtless and barefoot, and he grinned when she blew him a kiss.

"Your man needs to control his trouser rocket," I snarked as I put the car in drive and started down the street.

"He promised to start the countdown when I get home."

A pang of jealousy seized my heart. After last night, I decided never to marry or fall in love. I had no trust left in my heart after the betrayals I'd suffered.

Though, I wouldn't turn down a short fling with a handsome man. Evan was wiry, tall, and handsome with all that silky black hair down to his shoulders. I bet I could put a satisfied smile on his lips.

Lost in a sexy daydream, I almost crashed the car when Audrey asked, "How was your Saturday?"

Oh God, here we go.

"It…" I broke off, searching for the best adjective.

"That good, huh?" she wiggled her eyebrows. "Tell me more."

"The opposite of good. It sucked hairy balls."

She gasped, "Oh, no, what happened?"

"My loving parents are fucking with my money. Dad was the co-signer on my credit card. I never thought about it because I pay my own bills, so I guess I left him on the account, and now he's closed it."

"Shit." She shifted over to stare at me. "That sucks. Are you okay?"

I wanted to scream, *Of course, I'm not okay,* but what was the point?

"I have new cards coming, and an appointment with the bank on Tuesday."

"Well, that's good. How did your date go?"

I needed to tell her. She'd see the bruise, but I tried to keep it light.

"I lost my temper. He grabbed my arm." I shrugged. "And then he left."

I slowed to a stop for a traffic light. Twilight darkened the sky ahead of us. Audrey's life felt so picture perfect compared to mine. How had I become the mopey friend with all the problems? That wasn't who I wanted to be.

Audrey's eyes narrowed. "Did he hurt you?"

"I have a bruise, but it's nothing."

"Show me." The demand in her voice was unmistakable.

I shrugged out of my coat and pushed up the Henley. My face heated at the sight of the four purple marks around my wrist where Logan's fingers had dug into my skin.

"Holy fuck, Val! Why didn't you call me?"

"I would have, but Phil and Maria Henderson were there."

"Who are they?"

"I coached their granddaughter, Shelly, in acting a few years back, and now she's going to the University of Virginia for a theater management degree. They invited me to their table and covered my dinner."

"I'm sure Logan ordered a two-hundred-dollar bottle of wine and some ridiculously expensive meal."

My blush deepened. "More like three hundred."

"Shit."

"Phil and Maria finished the bottle and didn't blink at the cost, and I sent them a check this morning."

She crossed her arms over her chest. "I'm glad they rescued you, but Logan deserves to die. No one puts hands on my bestie and walks away."

The light turned green, and I put my foot on the gas. "I love you, Aud. You're my ride or die, but I don't think this calls for his death."

"I'll be the judge of that." She crossed her arms over her chest. "How'd you get home?"

This part of the story, I knew would make her laugh. "One of the waiters at Chez Riche is Frank Gilespe."

"Oh my God." She leaned back in the seat. "Is he old enough to drive?"

"They don't stay thirteen forever. He's a college sophomore, and he gave me a ride. On his motorcycle."

She gaped at me, her arms falling to her sides. "Holy shit."

"That's right, I rode with the wind in my hair and my sweater dress bunched up around my thighs with the former middle school terror."

I merged into a left turn lane while Audrey sat in stunned silence. Crossing Route 44, I drove up to our destination. "And today I'm going to bust my ass pole dancing."

Nondescript from the parking lot, Polar Vortex was floor to ceiling windows on the back. Once used for children's dance classes, the renovated building held a pole dancing gym.

I parked the car and reached into the back seat for my shoes. Audrey didn't move. The scowl on her face grew, and her hands fisted in her lap. "This conversation isn't over."

Oh yes, it was. "Let it go for now. We don't want to ruin Mel's party."

I slipped out of the car, hustling as fast as I could through the parking lot. If asked, I'd blame it on the chilly temperatures. It had nothing to do with escaping the Audrey Inquisition.

Walking into the brightly lit foyer, I took off my coat and hung on a hook by the door. Slipping off my Uggs, I sat on a little bench to strap on my heels.

When I stood, I felt ten feet tall and sexy as hell. With Audrey by my side, we sauntered into the adjoining pole room.

A group of our friends gathered at a table at the side of the room, sipping champagne and eating snacks.

"I love this music!" Audrey seemed torn between concern for me and wanting to dance to *Pony* by Ginuwine. I grabbed her hand, spinning her around until she laughed.

Mel rushed over. We were here to celebrate her tonight. Rainbows of sequins poured over her. She sparkled from her tiara to the tips of her ROY-G-BIV toes.

"I'm so glad you're both here. Your slutty shoes are to die for, Val."

"I love your sparkles, Mel, but you can't pole dance in sneakers."

"It's my birthday. I'm thirty-five and queer, and I can do what I like."

I clapped. "Preach, sister."

Laughing, Mel handed Audrey and me glasses of champagne, and I pressed a kiss to her cheek. "We'd have been earlier, but Oz is a caveman."

"That sounds like my brother." Stella gagged as she slung an arm over Audrey's shoulder. Oz's little sister wore tight neon pink shorts and a sparkly crop top. Leg warmers scrunched around her calves, and her feet were bare.

"My son is no fool." Diane, Stella and Oz's mom, smiled. Classy as ever, she wore tennis whites which glowed neon green under the blacklights.

"I didn't know you guys were coming," I hugged them both.

Stella hugged me back. "Bobby invited us. We're her chosen family."

Only months ago, Oz had walked his best friend down the aisle while Stella and Diane cried happy tears. Bobby's family had refused to come to the wedding. Why anyone wouldn't support Bobby because she was queer, I'd never understand.

I squeezed Stella's hand in agreement as Bobby joined us in loose navy shorts and a green tank top.

"You guys talking about Oz? I invited him to wear his spirit dress and come grip the pole with us."

Oz famously wore drag during last year's Tricycle Basketball fundraiser.

I shrugged, "He wanted to come, but my car's too small for both him and his size fourteen heels."

Sixth-grade English teacher, Rachel Bright, joined the laughter. Wearing black leggings and a quintessential teacher shirt with a rainbow made of tiny handprints. She was new to Marchfield, but fit in with our crowd.

"Where did he get those red heels?" she asked, winding a loose strand of hair around her finger before letting it spring back.

"I bought them for him," Stella said. "At Big and Tall Queens in Dover. We buy some of our accessories there for the Opera."

"You should get some for Keith. He dances every year in flip-flops." Dee O'Malley added. Her three-inch heels, sparkly pink shorts, and loose top showed off her curvy postpartum body. Her eager face glowed with excitement at getting away from the kids for a girls' night.

A tall, black woman with miles of curly black hair and biceps like rocks entered the room. "Ladies, y'all are looking sexy tonight. I'm Starlight, and I'd like to welcome you all to Polar Vortex for Mel's thirty-fifth Birthday Pole Party. Are y'all ready to get nasty?"

Mel grabbed Bobby and kissed her hard before shouting, "Heck, yeah."

Starlight glanced at me. "You might want to take your glasses off before we start."

Stowing them in my bag, I arrived back, just as she said, "Pick your poles, ladies, and let's learn how to ride."

Forty-five minutes of pole dancing flew by like a comedy montage.

We started with the sexy back slide, which started innocently enough in a spin like kids do around street signs. It ended by leaning back against the pole and sliding down low.

Bobby sank to her knees, joking. "I knew all my limbo dancing would pay off someday."

Starlight offered a suggestion on my form. "Grip the pole between your butt cheeks."

Shock rolled over me and then I let go of the pole and tumbled onto the floor, laughing my butt cheeks off.

When I recovered, I walked my hands back up the pole. "Hey, Starlight," I called over to her. "How do teachers afford their own dancing poles?"

Her lips curved up, waiting.

"They stack a chain of dry-erase pens together."

The group dissolved in giggles.

We perfected our Speed Bump by lying on the floor with our butts in the air.

Starlight gestured to Dee. "That's it! Really fuck the floor."

I couldn't breathe. I'd never expected pole dancing to be so hilarious.

We followed along through Flamingo Pose and the Front Hook Spin.

Things were going pretty well until Starlight told Oz's mom to "open your legs wider and put your vagina on the pole."

Diane blinked and said, "I beg your pardon?"

Her tone was so proper and haughty, I fell to the floor again, laughing.

Without grace or balance, we learned Hips Dips and added a Pole Sit to our dance routine.

"Audrey," I yelled as I wobbled slowly around the pole. "How is a man like a dancing pole?"

My bestie's grip slipped, and her hands made a farting squeak against the metal. "How?"

"They're both long, erect, and stiff."

Starlight rolled her eyes. "Form ladies, we're naughty girls, not messy ones."

This place was better than a comedy club. Audrey and I collapsed on the floor in hysterics.

"Get back on the pole." Bobby pointed her phone's camera at us.

"My make-up's a mess."

"Don't care," she said, clicking pictures of us pretending to know what we were doing.

The grand finale of our performance was a Stag Spin. Picture a very sexy male deer, one back knee hooked over the pole and the other leg bent at the knee, spinning slowly while his front hooves grasped the pole.

Sexy, right?

I grabbed the pole, ready to give it my best shot. Using my momentum to spin, I twirled up, but my grip slipped.

I put my feet down, and my fuck me heels, which had supported me all night, turned on me like traitorous bitches.

My left ankle rolled under my weight. I heard a pop. Pain vibrated through my foot, and I crumpled to the floor with all the grace of a moose on roller skates.

"Ow, fuck!"

I was surrounded in an instant by my glittery, scantily clad friends.

"I'll get some ice," Starlight said, walking quickly toward the back office.

"It doesn't seem too bad," Rachel said, peering down at my rapidly swelling ankle.

Audrey gently unbuckled my shoe and eased it off my foot.

"Can you wiggle your toes?" Dee asked as Bobby retrieved the first aid kit from its mount on the wall.

Satisfied that my toes could move, Bobby rolled an ace bandage gently around my foot and ankle. When she finished, Mel handed me two ibuprofen from the kit and a bottle of water.

Rachel elevated my foot on a pile of our coats. "Those heels were literally killer, Val. "

I smiled. "What's a pole dancer's favorite movie?"

My friends shot worried glances at each other.

"It's *Twister.*" I burst out laughing. "Just like my ankle."

"Is she hysterical?" Diane asked

Between gales of laughter, I puffed out, "I beg your pardon?"

And then all of them collapsed on the floor like speed bumps, laughing with me.

When Starlight returned with the ice, she stopped just inside the gym. Hands on her hips, she rolled her eyes at us, giggling endlessly.

"Come on ladies," she gathered the rest of the party. "Val's our audience now. Let's put it all together and strut our naughty stuff."

One by one, my friends dragged themselves off the floor to return to their poles. Starlight helped me into a chair, elevating my ankle on top of the coats on another, and left me icing my ankle.

The music started. Britney Spears' voice, sultry and seductive, sang *I'm a Slave 4 U*. The lights lowered, and the show began.

Offbeat and unsynchronized, the women began to move.

Bobby danced as if it were an aerobics routine.

Audrey was so limp and flexible; she could barely get off the floor.

Mel and Rachel were so stiff, they might as well have been virgins skipping around a May-Pole.

As the song ended and they dropped to the floor in sexy speed bumps, I whistled, screamed, and applauded. These women were my little posse of naughty girls.

Starlight joined me. "Well done, a couple more sessions, and you'd be working the pole like champions."

Mel high-fived everyone, and Bobby took everyone's photo with their pole.

Starlight came over to me. "If it still hurts tomorrow, you should go to the doctor."

I nodded. "I will."

She helped me stand, and I limped over to the table where Mel cut thick slices of birthday cake.

Audrey pulled my chair over so I could sit while everyone chatted around me.

Audrey, Stella, and Diane made plans for a spa day in Dover during spring break.

"You should come too, Val," Diane extended the invitation.

"I may have other plans," the words just popped out as the memory of Evan's invitation to his grandmother's party invaded my frontal cortex. "But I'll let you know." Maybe I'd take him up on it, just to see the mountains.

Bobby handed out black paper bags to everyone. As we prepared to leave. "Make sure you get your goody bags."

"What's in them?" Audrey asked.

"Oh, life's little essentials," Bobby chuckled. "Lube, condoms, dental dams, glow sticks, and sex dice."

"Wow," Diane exclaimed. "I'll be prepared for anything."

Stella's pink face turned red. "You can't give my mom dental dams and sex dice."

"I'll take your bag too for acting so prudish," Diane teased.

Dee took a bag and hugged Mel. "Brian is going to love this. Sorry I have to run, but I have to help put the kids to bed."

Listening to them chatter about their plans for condoms and glow sticks made me lonely. Everything in those bags would expire before I used them.

Though it wouldn't stop me from imagining locking Evan in my classroom. Tossing the goody bag to him, I'd challenge him to a. competition. How many items could he use on me in twenty minutes? Bonus points for multiple orgasms.

I was busy creating a rubric to judge his performance when Mel asked, "What about you, Val?"

"Uh," I stalled. "I beg your pardon?"

Mel snickered. There's nothing like an inside joke.

"What do you have planned for the rest of the weekend?" Mel's hopeful expression indicated she thought I'd be out partying all night long.

She seemed expectant. Like she hoped I had a naked man waiting at home to pleasure me. I hated to burst her bubble.

Tucking the goody bag into my purse, I took the time to find my glasses and put them on before answering. "Laundry, grading papers, grocery shopping, and I promised Starlight, I'd see the doctor tomorrow if my ankle isn't better."

Mel's face fell.

I shrugged. "You mean that's not how every teacher spends a holiday?"

Audrey helped me limp out to the car. My ankle hardly hurt, but she insisted on driving me home. We sat in silence while I stared out the window. I sensed the sidelong glances she threw at me, but I ignored them.

As she parked Betty Boop, I asked. "What's up, Aud?"

"That's what I wanted to ask you."

"Ha ha, beat ya," I snickered.

"I'm worried about you."

Sobering, I promised, "I'm okay."

"You had a traumatic dinner last night, and today you almost broke your ankle."

"You're exaggerating." Sure, it hadn't been a great night, but it had ended well. I was still in one piece.

"Am I?"

She helped me limp over the curb and followed me inside. I couldn't stifle the groan that escaped as I fell onto my couch. She flicked on the lamp.

Opening my fridge, she returned with a glass of iced tea.

"Thanks, Aud," I said, taking a sip.

"I'm gonna call Oz. I'll sleep over and we'll catch up on our shows, eat ice cream, and drink wine."

It sounded so much like something I would offer to do. When life gets you down, I'm the friend everyone leaned on. Call me if you're sad. I'll bring donuts and mimosas. I'm at the top of everyone's emergency contacts.

But, when I'm sad or broken-hearted, I turn off my phone, sit in the dark, and hide. Audrey was my best friend, but I wanted to lick my wounds alone.

Putting my brave face on, I said, "You don't need to stay. My ankle barely hurts." I bent over to remove my Uggs, wincing as the boot slid over my sore ankle.

"Liar."

"I'm fine. Besides, you promised to show off your moves to Oz."

She cocked her head to the side, studying me. "You should tell me what's bothering you."

"Nothing." I shrugged.

My philosophy on life was simple. If life gave you lemons, juggle them until you think of a joke. Then, while everyone is laughing, go hide in a corner. But I was too exhausted to spin my problems into a joke.

My bestie plowed on. "Tomorrow's a holiday. We can meet everyone for brunch, and Oz and I will have lots of time after."

I wouldn't win this argument with her. When Audrey made up her mind, there was no talking her out of it. I would need to juggle the lemons a while longer.

Pasting on a happy face, I refused to let the sullen, cranky side of me out. My bestie wanted to spend time with me, so I should be dancing on the ceiling. This time was precious.

"There are clean sheets on the guest bed already. I'll put on my jammies. I'll find some for you while you call Oz."

Audrey clapped. "We haven't done this in forever."

The hurt, angry part of me whispered, *whose fault is that?* But I bit the words back. If there was one thing I'd learned over the years, it was no one liked a pouty bitch.

Chapter 5
Evan

I dreamt of Val with her crooked mouse ears, the sound of her voice dancing across my senses: wicked, husky, joyous, and naughty. The details of the dream turned erotic. The softness of her tan skin brushed against mine. The press of her mouth on mine, her tongue sweeping in to tease me.

Dream-Val slid down my body, generating heat and electricity. The line of her shoulder, rounded yet strong, yielded to the creaminess of her breasts, drawing me closer.

Val slid up my body, her tongue and teeth teasing my skin. Her pink tongue licked across the stubble on my chin, leaving a sultry trail...

Cocoa propped her short brown legs on my chest and whined softly. Her wet tongue lapped at my chin. Irritated, I rolled away from her.

Falling back into the dream almost immediately. Val's hands traced the eagle tattoo that stretched across my left pec and bicep. Her mouth followed her hands down my body, stroking, teasing, pinching.

She peeked up at me, and the shadows behind her eyes alarmed me. I needed to discover her secrets, but no matter how I reached for her, she drifted farther away.

I moaned.

Cocoa barked. And barked again.

I cracked my eyes open to dawn's light as it crept under the shades. She barked again.

I rubbed my hand over my eyes. Flopping onto my back, Cocoa put her front feet on my chest and licked my face.

"Okay, girl, okay." I pushed the dog away, debating if I had time to jerk off before taking her out.

Cocoa ran on a strict clock, and I was already an hour late. She ran for the door. Stopping to check that I followed, she whimpered.

I pulled old jeans over my boxers and found a clean t-shirt in a drawer. Following her down the hall to the front door, I clipped on her leash and stepped outside barefoot.

Fridged wind hit me like a slap. Any lingering thought of masturbation withered and died in the frosty air. The sun struggled to get above the horizon.

The dog charged off the porch to smell the bushes by the walkway. Older than my almost ninety-year-old *Elisi*, my house was more postage stamp than a mansion.

It needed a ton of work inside and a new roof, but I couldn't turn down the price. Dad said she had good bones, and he would know after spending more than forty years renovating houses like mine.

"Hurry up, girl," I called from where I shivered on the new brick steps I'd laid last fall.

Cocoa tossed me a diva glance over her shoulder. She had a system and wouldn't be rushed.

In the quiet neighborhood around me, I could hear car engines in the distance and a dog or two barking. I loved living in this town. The people, the school, this street. It felt like it had been built for me.

Many American streets were jammed with cookie-cutter houses on top of one another, but not in Marchfield. Small houses nestled on large lots, allowing for big gardens and lush yards. There were no huge Victorians or colossal mansions. But what they lacked in size, they made up for in creativity.

An architectural dream, or perhaps nightmare, houses of every style lined the block. A Cape Cod sat across the street next to a small Tudor. The house next to mine had Doric columns stretching up to the second story. I'd bought a Craftsman, complete with a gabled roof and pedestal stone columns.

Finished with her business, Cocoa's medium-sized body scrambled back up the porch stairs. After lapping some water and breakfast, she curled up in her bed to chew on her squirrel toy.

I could go back to bed, but I knew I wouldn't sleep. My teacher's backpack hung on a hook by the door, reminding me of ungraded assessments and computer work I should do.

Resigned, I filled a big mug of coffee and sat on the couch with my laptop. Cocoa jumped up next to me, resting her head on my belly as I graded last week's assignments and loaded tomorrow's work onto Google Classroom.

An hour later, my butt was numb, so I grabbed my duffle to hit the gym.

I'd noticed Firehouse Fitness the first time I drove into town. Some retired firemen started the gym in a repurposed firehouse. The shiny fireman's pole graced the center of the space. I loved sliding down after using the bench press and free weights on the second floor.

There were only two other cars in the parking lot outside the gym, so I parked my navy blue 2020 Toyota Tundra near the door. Inside the locker rooms, I changed into the sweats I'd brought and headed toward the machines.

"Yo, Evan." Dakota's dark hair grayed around the edges, but he could press two hundred and fifty pounds. He owned half the gym and was part Cherokee like me.

I nodded hello. "*Osiyo.*"

We spent more than an hour on the machines. By the time we finished, more guys came into workout. I wiped down the equipment I'd used and hit the showers.

I headed out to my car as my phone rang.

"Hey, Yona. How's it going?"

"Sorry to bother you, Evan." I pictured her sitting at her kitchen table, twisting a lock of her long black hair around her finger.

"You're never a bother. What's up?"

"Jacy and Fala came home with permission slips today. I guess their class is going to Washington, D.C."

"That sounds fun." My stomach growled with enough force to shake the car. I hoped she couldn't hear it.

"It does, but it costs sixty dollars. Each. I don't have an extra hundred and twenty."

"No problem. I'll Venmo you later today." I heard cheering in the background and guessed the girls had been listening.

"You're the best, Uncle Evan," Fala called out.

Jacy asked, "Do you want to chaperone, *Agidutsi?*"

Yona shushed them. "Uncle Evan lives far away. He can't chaperone your trip."

"I want to hear all about it later. I've got to get some food now. I'm starving."

Yona laughed. "You haven't changed. Still a bottomless pit."

"Love you, Uncle Evan!" Jacy shouted.

"We all do," Yona added.

Guilt rose up in my chest. I lived five hours away with a house, dog, and a job I loved, dreaming of a woman like Val. All the while, Yona and her girls had no one. I loved them and wanted to be there for them, but at the same time Yona deserved to find someone she could fall in love with again.

When I'd been there at Christmas, Yona had mentioned possibly moving closer, but she was reluctant to uproot the girls from the only home they'd ever known.

Unlocking my phone, I sent the money for the field trip, plus some extra. It seemed the least I could do.

My stomach complained again. I remembered I didn't have much food left in my fridge, so I called the local breakfast place, Egglectic.

The owner, an older woman named Marta, took my order of a Southwestern Omelet, a bagel and cream cheese, and a side of hash browns, promising it would be ready when I arrived.

I merged into light traffic heading into town. Despite being a small town, Marchfield supported about fifteen shops on Main Street. Last week, I'd stopped in a specialty wine shop called Grapes and Gifts and bought my mom a birthday present. Wrapping the glass cardinal sun catcher and bottle of wine in pretty paper, the proprietor, Direde Gilbert, added a bow and my card to the package and shipped it for me. No Wal-Mart in the world would do that.

Located at the end of Main Street on Delancey Avenue, Egglectic stood out. Painted in pastel yellow, a giant chicken mural stretched across three outside walls. It was impossible to miss. Even the entrance resembled a huge chicken egg. A paper sign on the door fluttered in the breeze:

Please excuse the scramble.
When construction is done,
We'll be sunny side up!

I waited while Marta helped an older man pick out a piece of pie.

"That slice of apple smells as sweet as you, darling," he said with a wink.

She winked at me and said, "If you want some of my pie, Harold, you'll have to earn it."

He smiled. "I like a challenge, Honey."

Shaking her head, she slid an apple pie out of the case. At least five inches tall, the apples covered with brown sugar crumble. The smell alone brought me a step closer.

Slicing a piece for Harold, Marta put it in a to-go container and rang it up.

"She's a mighty fine woman," Harold muttered; his eyes glued to Marta.

"A real sweetheart," I agreed, deciding to add a slice of that pie to my order.

Harold touched my arm, his face serious. "Don't let a good woman go, son. You think you're doing it for the right reasons at the time, but you end up alone."

My eyes met his. Was he talking about Marta? I debated asking, but he'd gone over to pay.

And then I heard her. Val's husky, naughty laugh. The siren's song that haunted my dreams.

Scanning the restaurant until I found her sitting with Audrey, Oz, Bobby, Mel, and Keith. I recognized the woman by Keith, but didn't know her name.

I hesitated. I wanted to walk over to see Val, talk to her, breathe her in. But it didn't seem fair to Noah or Yona. Why should I be happy when Noah was gone?

Harold nudged my elbow with his. "Go get her, man."

Just then, Val seemed to sense my presence and swung around, her deep chocolate eyes on me from halfway across the room. Her wide lips were curved in sultry invitation, and her fuzzy red sweater dipped low in the front, exposing smooth skin from her neck into her cleavage.

My mouth watered.

"She's beautiful," Harold winked. "Remember what I told you."

She waved to me, beckoning to join them, and my feet moved before I realized it.

"Hey, Evan." Jerking my eyes away from Val. I nodded to Bobby, and she grinned. "Pull up a chair."

"Sit next to me." Val shifted her chair over closer to Audrey so I could squeeze a chair in between her and Keith.

We were so close our shoulders brushed. The guilt and loneliness from the morning washed away in her presence.

"Do you know everyone?" She asked.

I glanced around Keith at the pretty woman with golden brown hair. "I've seen you around school."

"I'm Rachel. I've seen you around, too."

Keith tossed me a hard frown before saying, "I teach next door to Rachel this year." His arm came up to rest on her shoulders.

Rachel flushed red and shrugged Keith's hand off her shoulder, refusing to acknowledge him.

"What are you up to on this glorious school holiday, Evan?" Audrey asked.

Everyone at the table turned toward me. They were a tight-knit group, and I was the new kid trying to find a seat in the school cafeteria.

Forcing myself to relax, I said, "My dog woke me at dawn. So, I got my school stuff done and went to the gym."

Marta approached the table. "Want your order here instead of to go?"

"Sure," I answered, glancing around the table. "Unless you guys are getting ready to leave?"

Marta laughed. "Nah, this table won't leave until we close." She glanced at her watch. "In twenty-six minutes."

I dug into my food while the others lingered over tea and coffee.

"That smells yummy," Val nodded to the rapidly disappearing food on my plate.

"You should have ordered more," Audrey said. "My treat."

"I didn't want anything until now," Val responded. She bit her plump lower lip, then ran her tongue along her teeth. Her warmth radiated toward me, and I leaned closer as currents of desire zipped through my body.

Unable to help myself, I reached for a tendril of hair that escaped her ponytail. Rubbing my fingers over the tendrils, I didn't hear Keith the first time he spoke.

"Evan, what gym do you use?" Keith repeated.

I forced myself to focus. "Firehouse."

"I love that place. It's great how they kept the pole."

The three women at the table exchanged glances and burst out laughing.

I raised my eyebrows in question, and she patted my arm. Her index finger slid along the outline of the eagle's wing that peeked out from under my shirtsleeve. She leaned in to whisper, "We took a pole dancing class last night."

The touch of her warm fingers against mine stole my breath. Coughing, I sipped some water at the image of Val sliding down a slick pole.

Bobby snickered. "Val tried to do a Superman pose that became more of a Drowning Dolphin and sprained her ankle."

Was that code? Following this conversation took all my concentration. "Are you hurt?"

Val shook her head. "Not really."

"Audrey said you might need a walker." Oz scowled.

"I might have exaggerated." Batting her eyelashes, Audrey patted his hand. "I have some tricks to show you later."

Oz grabbed her hand and pulled her onto his lap. I heard him whisper to her, "You can use my pole any time, Red."

I wasn't the only person who heard his words. Mel laughed. "You don't have to pick Audrey up in restaurants and bars anymore."

"That's how they met," Keith explained to Rachel.

"Audrey picked Oz up in a bar." Mel smiled.

"And took him home to do horrible, nasty things with him." Val chuckled, but I felt her hot gaze on me.

"But he fell asleep on her after," Bobby snorted.

"She wore me out." Oz lifted Audrey's hand and kissed her knuckles.

Keith shook his head. "One time, we went to Barrel to throw axes and found Oz and Audrey making out on the bench."

"And then they more than made out outside of the school." Bobby teased.

Audrey blushed pink. "Stop it, you, guys."

Val nudged my shoulder with hers. Her eyes glittered bright and full of fun behind her green glasses. I imagined lifting them off, my palms on her face, tracing the seam of her mouth with my tongue.

Val shifted in her seat and winced when her foot knocked against mine. Without thinking, I found her hand under the table.

"Are you okay?"

She nodded and squeezed my hand. Her fingers danced across my wrist and down onto my knee and to cup the inside of my thigh.

My gaze met hers. A single question reflected in mine.

Are we really doing this?

My heart raced and my body eagerly responded. The last time I saw her, I fumbled the ball by moving too fast. Now she was taking it to the next level, and I was running to catch up.

She squeezed my knee, her nails drawing little circles on the inside.

I'm caught up.

I placed my hand over hers, my thumb gliding across the top, then gently over the underside of her wrist. She sucked in a breath of air, releasing it with a whoosh.

My hand found her knees and slid up her thigh. The soft fabric of her leggings tantalized me. It would be so easy to slide my hand up under her blue skirt and delve into her heat.

The conversation around us continued, but I only heard my pounding heartbeat. My chest hurt from the pressure of holding back a groan. Val's fingers escaped mine, trailing up the inside of my thigh, dancing closer to my balls.

Her simple touch destroyed me. I wanted to throw her over my shoulder and carry her to my cave. She brought out the Neanderthal in me.

Her pretty pink lips parted. The tattoo of her pulse, light and quick, showed at the base of her throat. Our gazes locked. Her green glasses enhanced the challenge that gleamed in their depths. Her fingers ran lightly across the seam of my jeans, brushing my balls,

Squirming in my seat, I grabbed her wrist. Bringing her hand to my knee. Her face shone with naughty glee as I grappled for control.

Val turned to the group. If they knew what she'd been up to, no one let on. "I need to get going."

"I'll take you." Audrey wiggled to get off Oz's lap, but he held her tight.

"Thanks, but Evan says he'll take me home."

Marta brought us our checks. "I'll take them at the register."

"Can I buy your meal?" I asked Val.

She searched my face with mistrust.

What bastard hurt her?

"Yes, please," she said, her voice soft. "I appreciate it."

The women exchanged hugs, whispering before everyone moved to the counter to pay.

We joined the line at the counter, standing silently side by side behind the others.

Audrey waved as she and Oz left with the rest of the group. "Call me."

And then Val and I were alone.

With Marta.

I tapped my card.

Val squeezed my bicep. "Meet me by the back exit. I need to use the restroom."

"Sure," I said, watching her skirt swish over her butt.

Minutes later, I walked toward the restrooms and prepared to wait. But she popped out of the doorway almost immediately.

Taking my hand, she led me across the hall through an empty room. The smell of fresh paint hung in the air.

Tarps lay on the floor and over tables. Tools, cans of paint, and brushes littered the floor.

A door at the back of the room stood open, and Val tugged me toward it. Flicking on the light switch, Val closed us inside a large walk-in storage area. Shelves of tablecloths, napkins, and utensils lined the walls. A workbench sat against the back wall.

"I waitressed here the summer after college before I started at Marchfield Middle. They're doing renovations in this room, so I thought we might..."

She bit her lip nervously, but there was nothing shy about her when she sealed her cherry lips to mine.

Chapter 6
Val

Flirting with Evan lit me up like a candle. Sitting close enough to brush against his biceps sent sparks arcing across my senses. I barely followed the conversation for wanting him, and the tent in his pants spoke volumes about his feelings.

And that's when it happened. A plan- wicked and delightful- popped into my head to scratch the itch that nagged me since the Winter Carnival.

Of course, I mentally drew the pros and cons chart first. I wasn't walking into this blind. The pros were topped with Evan's delicious body and the awesome tremors of passion it sent careening below my belly button. Also, it was an awesome "fuck you" to my parents and Logan. A subjugation of all the stress and anxiety they'd thrown at me. My sexual rebellion.

The cons were insignificant by comparison.

Trying to appear casual, I told him to meet me at the restroom and hurried away. But instead, I slipped into the room across the hall. When I'd worked here six years ago, we'd used it for parties, but Marta closed it for renovations.

Paint cans, boxes of flooring, and light fixtures littered the floor. Tiptoeing through the debris, I bee-lined for the closet I remembered from when I'd waitressed here the summer after college. The door to the walk-in stood partially open. I flipped the overhead light on.

More of a small room than a closet, the space was designed to store linens, decorations, and other items. Built-in wooden shelves make the whole space smell of fresh cedar. They were stuffed with folded tablecloths and napkins. Wreaths and votive candles lined the higher shelves. A sturdy wooden table spanned the back wall of the closet.

The thought of bringing Evan here and having my way with him triggered a flood of desire. I'd never had sex in a public place before, but the naughtiness made the ache in my core throb in anticipation. Feminine power roared through me.

And yet, a flicker of uncertainty whispered in the back of my mind. Was I rushing things? What if someone discovered us? My wicked certainty crumbled around the edges.

When I woke up this morning full of serenity and inner peace, I was determined not to allow my family to narrate the drama anymore. I would make my own, and if Evan was willing, I'd start with taking him to bed.

Pleased that my ankle barely hurt, the stress and weariness felt lighter on my shoulders.

When we'd met everyone for breakfast, I brushed off the nagging feeling of loneliness. All my friends had found love. Even Keith, the ultimate player, seemed captivated by Rachel.

Personally, I needed a boyfriend like a hole in my shoe and had zero energy for the pandering and pretense. I spent enough time pleasing people, and I couldn't handle adding a needy boyfriend into the mix.

But that didn't mean I couldn't have a bit of fun. A pop of pleasure without the strings. I needed to make it very clear to Evan I wasn't interested in a relationship. This was just sex.

Footsteps sounded in the hall. Whirling around, I dropped my bag inside the door and hurried through the maze of cans and boxes to peek out into the hallway.

Evan sauntered toward me. His hair tied back from his face, showing off his high cheekbones. Anticipation gleamed in his eyes as he swaggered toward me. His long legs were encased in worn denim, and his flannel shirt clung to the contours of his body.

Hunger banished all doubts, and I rushed to meet him.

"Hey, Gorgeous," he breathed. His eyes hot on my face. Leaning in, his hip brushed against mine. His head bent close until his forehead rested against mine. Hesitating for a moment before tugging me close.

I clung to his shoulders as his mouth devastated mine. His lips and clever tongue nipped and teased, leaving me thirsting for more. I took his hand, leading him into the party room.

"Where're we goin'?" His husky, masculine tone was filled with enticing promises.

Stopping just inside the threshold of the walk-in closet, my lips curved in sultry invitation which I bungled by speaking.

"I thought, if you wanted that is, we could maybe..."

He stared past me into the space, lit by a single overhead light. When he met my eyes, the wicked gleam delighted me. I trailed my hands down his abs, feeling him suck in a breath.

Taking his hand, I stepped back, pulling him in. He closed the door behind us and embraced me.

Evan's hands grasped my hips, drawing me against him. My sensitive nipples grazed his front. My tongue tangled with his. The friction burned between us stole my breath.

Strong arms lifted me, and I wrapped my legs around him. My hot center met the steely length under his fly as his large frame braced me against the door.

The pain of the last few days vanished in a river of heat and fire. I was free. A woman who reveled in her desires.

Smiling against his lips, I spoke sassily. "Wanna butter my biscuit, Evan?" The breathless, husky sound of my voice was soft in my ears.

Continuing to rain kisses over my face and neck, he said, "Are you propositioning me, Val?"

The feel of his unshaved cheeks made me squirm. I twisted to suck his earlobe between my teeth and biting gently. "Maybe."

"Maybe?" His teeth nipped my neck, trailing fire across my collarbone.

Air hissed from my lungs, my breasts heaving against his chest as I gasped, "Yes, Evan. Please..."

"Thank God." Shifting his weight, I tightened my grip on his hips with my knees and thighs as he moved deeper into the tiny room.

Digging into his hair, I loosened the leather band, setting his silky hair free. Tangling my fingers in the strands, I buried my nose into it. Savory and spicy, his scent reminded me of wood smoke and thick pine forests.

Lowering me onto the cool surface of the table, he stood between my parted thighs.

I moaned as his calloused hands slipped under my red sweater. His smile turned wolf-like as he gently traced the lacy edges of my scarlet bra. Palming the globes, he squeezed.

I relished the pressure, tossing my head back and pushing the hard pebbles more firmly into his hands.

"You're so beautiful," he said gruffly.

I arched up, blindly reaching for his shoulders. The soft fabric of his flannel was cool against the heat of my palms. I wanted Evan with a hunger I'd never experienced before.

He bent his head to my cleavage, and I gasped. He found my hard nipples under the fabric, fingers plucking and pinching, sending bolts of sensation zinging straight to my pleasure center.

My hands raced down his shoulders, across his chest, and down to the button of his jeans. I longed to strip him naked.

The heat of his cock seared through the fabric of his jeans as I lowered the zipper, revealing his yellow boxers.

A half chuckle, half wheezing gasp escaped me. "Is that a banana in your pants, or are you just happy to see me?"

I slipped my hand into his boxers and wrapped my fingers around his cock. Evan groaned deep in the back of his throat, his hands groping along my leg and under my skirt. He slipped his fingers beneath the lacy edge of my panties and found the wetness between my legs.

"Evan," I cried, shifting closer. Hooking my knee around the back of his thigh while I continued to stroke him.

Outside, a door opened. Voices spoke about tips and laughed. Dishes clanked, and a cart on wheels rolled down the hallway.

Evan whispered softly in my ear, "We need to be quiet."

I gave him a naughty smile as my fingers squeezed his balls. "We can try."

Lifting me slightly, he grabbed a fistful of satin.

I trailed my mouth to his ear. "I dreamt of you and woke up dripping wet for you."

The sound of tearing fabric filled my ears as my panties fall away.

His hot eyes met mine. "Did you come?"

I released his cock as he slid me back from the edge of the table.

"Yes," I whispered.

Parting my legs, he knelt, teasing his way up my inner thighs. I hooked my ankles, my black heeled boots tight around his shoulders. My stretchy skirt was bunched up around my waist, and I sucked in a breath, holding it as the rough hairs of his unshaven cheek made me wild.

"Did I do this in your dream?" His mouth found my clit. His tongue tasting, circling, swishing. The rhythm drove me higher. His fingers spread me wide, sliding in and out as his mouth ravaged me.

"I'm coming," I moaned.

Evan buried his face between my legs, driving me up and over the edge, riding the waves of my orgasm along with me.

I rode the sensations, biting my lips to hold back the screams of pleasure.

Pulling me off the table, he turned me. His cock strained against the roundness of my backside.

"Shit."

I tossed a glance over my shoulder at him.

"I don't have a condom."

"I have some." I stood, running my index finger along his shaft and relishing his grown of impatience. Knowing he was watching, I sashayed to the bag I'd left earlier.

Pulling out the sparkly bag full of naughty gifts, I found a purple packet.

Glancing at the packaging, Evan rolled his eyes. "It says it glows in the dark."

I ripped open the foil. "Beggars can't be choosers."

"Who gives out condoms as party favors?" He asked, then groaned as I rolled it over the engorged head. "Never mind."

His fingers found my core again, sending desire shooting through me again. Tasting my lips, he stoked the fire inside me.

He bent over the table, his broad cock pressing against my opening, teasing me.

"Tell me you want me," he whispered, his breath hot against my neck.

I pressed my hips back, rolling my center over him. "Take me, Evan."

He groaned and pinched my nipples. His hard cock plunged into me, stretching and filling until we were one body. His movements, the pressure took me higher, close to another climax.

His hand slipped between my legs, stimulating my clit. Passion coiled tight inside me before releasing, shattering into a thousand pieces.

Biting the base of my neck, he growled as my inner muscles squeezed him. Reaching between my legs, I squeezed his balls.

"It feels so fucking good," he panted into my ear.

"Show me," I demanded.

His teeth closed on my shoulder. Thrusting deep, he came with a muffled shout. My pussy pulsed and squeezed, sucking him dry.

My legs felt weak. He wobbled back, steading himself with a hand on a shelf. Pulling off the condom, he wrapped it in a paper napkin from one of the shelves.

He helped me straighten my clothes and tame my hair before he scooped me up and sank down on the table with me in his lap.

"You're so hot," he whispered in my ear.

I wrapped my arms around his neck. "You make me feel beautiful. Powerful."

"You can use your power on me anytime, gorgeous."

I caressed his mouth with mine. "We should probably get out of here."

I picked up my ripped panties off the floor. His eyes were hot as he watched me stuff them in his back pocket, choosing to go commando.

He pulled me close. "I don't want to let you go. Come home with me."

The clean scent of his shirt smelled faintly of my perfume. "Evan," I said softly, taking off my glasses. I rubbed them clean with my shirt. "My life is ... complicated. I need to keep things simple. No strings. No complications."

He hesitated slightly, and I held my breath as anxiety washed over me. What if I hurt his feelings? Had I taken advantage of him?

When he smiled and said, "Simple works for me," I swear I heard bluebirds sing. A tidal wave of relief swept me up.

He shoved his hands into his jeans. "What do you want to do now?"

"I guess I should go home," I said, but indecision rang clearly in my voice. How did two people actually keep things simple?

"Do you want to hang out?"

Sorta? Maybe ... yes. My inner voice wasn't making this easy.

No strings meant Evan and I should not hang out, but no matter how hard I tried, I couldn't inject enthusiasm into my tone. "I have test papers to grade and need to get groceries."

"You like dogs, right? You could come over and meet my pup."

He wasn't giving up. Why wasn't he just a normal guy? Love 'em and leave 'em?

"I have a fireplace and popcorn."

I love popcorn, and fireplaces were my weakness on cold winter days... "Are you trying to charm me, Evan Shurden?"

"Is it working?"

"Maybe," I said on the fence.

I'd spent my entire life pleasing others. Mom insisted I take dance lessons, etiquette and acting classes, and gymnastics. She signed me up for debutante balls and charity luncheons and guilted me into attending.

At school, the principal encouraged me to go to Parent Teacher Association meetings and attend curriculum committees, so I did. Name it, I have the membership card.

I'd spent my life treading water, always over my head, never unable to swim in my own direction. Maybe it was time to set aside the pile of *Should Dos* and explore the things I wanted.

Like Evan.

Tempted to explore this sexy, charming man, I decided to throw caution to the wind. It was a school holiday, and I should enjoy it.

Chapter 7
Evan

I unlocked the door to my house with Val squeezed up next to me. She drove her car over, but as soon as she parked, she was on me like glue, and I loved it.

Fumbling for the lock, I tried to calculate how many pairs of dirty socks and boxers I'd left around. Stepping inside, Val followed me into the small foyer.

Cocoa rushed out of the bedroom. Her nails scrabbled on the scarred wooden floors as she raced to us.

"Hey, sweet puppers. How cute are you?" Val dropped to her knees inside the door, giving pets and crooning baby talk, while Cocoa's tail wagged hard enough to wiggle her frame.

Swooning with happiness, the dog's rapturous moans almost embarrassed me. Val rubbed her brown and white belly.

Leaving Cocoa to distract Val, I made a beeline for the socks and shoes I'd left by the couch. Like a human vacuum cleaner, I snatched everything up and stuffed the large pile into the coat closet and slid the door shut.

"Smooth."

"Better than making you step over the mess."

Val smirked at me as she gave Cocoa a final pat and stood. My little pup rolled to her feet, following us into the living room.

Taking in the architecture and the floor-plan, she said, "Your place is fantastic. I wish I'd bought it instead of renting."

"She needs work. I probably need an under-construction sign on the door like Egglectic."

"It has character."

"She's got that alright. The hardwood floor needs refinished. The kitchen needs new counters and still has the original 1950s appliances."

Her eyes lit up. "Vintage."

Fine for her to say, but living with an oven that scorched frozen pizza, and a fridge that barely kept my beer cool? That was another thing entirely.

I winced. "The bathrooms are tiled green to match the bathtub and toilet."

"Oh, dear God." She giggled. "At least it isn't pink."

I nodded in agreement. "I'm surprised how much I'm enjoying bringing her into the modern age."

She walked over to the small fireplace mantle, studying the birds I'd carved. She focused on the Oyster Catcher with his orange bill and legs.

"Did you make these?"

"I did. My dad is a contractor. He uses reclaimed wood in his work. I steal pieces that call to me."

She ran an index finger along the arch of its back. "You're talented."

My cheeks heated at the compliment. "Thanks."

"I draw sometimes, but I've never tried sculpture."

"Your rat caricatures were great."

She laughed. "Yeah. I'm pretty sure that's out of my skill set."

She moved toward the tan leather sofa that sat in front of the fireplace and sat. "Tell me what you've changed so far."

I joined her, Cocoa wedging herself between us. "I painted last summer before I moved in and put in a hot water heater."

Val giggled, covering her mouth with her hand. "I'm sorry. I have a friend from high school who tells her kids that mommy and daddy needed to check the water heater, every time they—"

"Bend over the barrel?" I laughed.

She nodded. "But they have to have sex in the garage, and I imagine there are quite a few hazards."

I wiggled my eyebrows. "I hear the spin cycle is good, though."

She snorted. "So, what are your plans for the place?"

I leaned back and rested my ankle on my knee, watching her pet my dog. "Redo the entire kitchen ... granite countertops, new cabinets, and appliances. My college roommate visited in February. He promised to help me knock out a wall upstairs to make the main bedroom bigger. And of course, the bathrooms..." In my experience, most women hated listening to construction talk. "I don't want to bore you."

Her lips parted slightly as she scratched Cocoa's ears. "My Uncle Fazio made his living as a carpenter. I used to hang out with him in the summers when I wasn't at Gran's. I loved watching the houses he worked on come back to life."

"My dad owns a carpentry and rehab business in Asheville. My siblings and I all worked there in the summer, and I ran the place for a while after he had a heart attack. He wanted me to stay, but it wasn't my dream."

"Is teaching?" Her head tilted toward me as she listened. Her delicate neck exposed with her hair pulled back. Her green glasses perched on her nose emphasized her smart and sexy vibe.

The urge to lean forward and kiss her was strong, but I answered her question instead. "For now, anyway. Teaching kids how to work with tools to fix and create, it's important. Especially now with cell phones and social media."

She nodded, her eyes twinkling. "Working with your hands is both relaxing and rewarding."

My thoughts screeched to a halt. Sexual innuendos? Was she flirting? How do I balance no-strings sex and flirting?

Before I could over-think it, she stood. "Show me around."

I laughed awkwardly. "We're in the living room."

"Nice." She drifted around, studying the windows, the crown molding, and the tan and gold curtains my mom had made.

I followed her into the kitchen.

"It's a mid-century time capsule. I love that huge stainless-steel sink."

"It's the only thing I'm keeping."

Seeing my space through her eyes delighted me. Her excitement at my real wood cabinets whetted my appetite for her.

"It is a big space, room for an island or bar, and you need granite counters."

"You know your stuff, gorgeous."

I led her into the mudroom, where she admired my new Maytag washer and dryer. She turned, catching me slack jawed while I pictured her enjoying the spin cycle.

Reading my mind, she tsked, "Naughty boy," and wandered out to investigate the dining room.

The antique cherry table gleamed, rich and satiny, but the chairs around it were yard sale chic, mismatched and worse for wear. I wondered if she'd let me take her there. Her hair splayed out over the wood and her legs spread wide…

"And what's upstairs?"

I coughed. This tour was killing me. "Main bedroom, guest bedroom, office, bath."

She took the stairs two at a time. I couldn't wait to see her in my bedroom. On her back. With a wickedly satisfied smile.

First door on the right was the guest room. Boxes and renovation supplies were stacked on the floor.

She winced. "Hideous wallpaper."

I barked out a laugh. "You don't enjoy stained and faded Hunting Party in Pursuit of Fox?"

She backed out, closing the door. "Not at all."

I grinned. "Me neither."

Down the hallway, she peeked into the bathroom. "Do you keep your eyes closed the whole time you're in here?"

I leaned against the doorframe. "I leave the light off and shower in the dark."

She spun around, palms on my chest, her laughter like a tinkling bell. The husky notes were a sweet aphrodisiac, thickening my cock.

I pulled her close to meet her lips. Her body molded to mine, soft and warm. Savoring the taste of her lips and tongue, I nibbled at her lips. Her hands tangled in my hair, and I slid mine down to cup her butt.

She broke off the kiss, holding my face in her palms. "Can I see your room?"

Cocoa raced ahead of us.

The sun was streaming in through the navy curtains. On one wall, a large painting of the Blue Ridge Mountains hung over my king-sized bed. A mirror on the opposite wall reflected the red and gold trees shrouded in mist against the blue and black of the hills.

"I stripped the old, faded rose wallpaper in here right after I bought the house and painted the walls."

She stared at the painting, absorbing its beauty. "Is that your home?"

I nodded. "My mom's an artist. She mostly works in textiles and quilts. She painted this when I was a baby. It's the view from our back door."

"I love it."

Val trailed her fingers over the quilt on my bed. A red and gold fan pattern. "Did your mom make this quilt?"

"*Elisi*, my grandmother. I mentioned her to you at the carnival. She turns ninety during Spring Break."

Another bird carving, this time a red-tailed hawk, sat on a small table by the bed.

"You are full of surprises, Evan." She fiddled with the sleeves of her sweater, pushing them up to her elbows, exposing her delicate wrists and forearms.

Intimacy turned to fury when I saw the fingermark bruises.

"Who hurt you, Val?" My words came out in a dangerous growl. I watched her eyes wide before she yanked the sweater sleeves down.

"It's nothing."

"It's not. Bruises like that come from anger and violence."

She spoke quickly, her eyes cast down. "It was a misunderstanding with an old friend of the family. I bruise easily. It doesn't even hurt."

I took her hand, lifting her wrist to my lips and kissing each mark gently. When my mouth touched the inside of her wrist, brushing the sensitive skin, she let out a raspy breath.

Pulling her close, I kissed her gently, wanting to erase the hurt she'd experienced. I had no intention of going further. My only wish was to provide comfort.

We stood a long time, hugging in the sunshine. The rays turning giving her hair golden highlights.

She eased back, her eyes searching mine for something. "You're a good man."

"Most days I try to be."

She nodded, filling her hands with my hair. "I want to see you naked."

"Only if I can see the rest of what you've got hiding under there."

Her nails scored over my shoulders and down my biceps. "Deal. Take off your clothes."

She released me, and I stripped off my flannel, letting her see what she'd only felt at the restaurant.

Her eyes widened at the sight of my six-pack. Her surprised face ignited a fire in my belly. I reached for her, needing to clasp her tight.

But she shook her head and stepped out of my reach. "You're not naked."

Without taking my eyes off her, I sat on the edge of the bed. Untying the laces of my sneakers, I kicked them off and stood. Unzipping my jeans, I slid them down with my boxers, kicking them off.

Val grinned, fanning herself like a Southern bell. "Well, I do declare, Mr. Shurden. Someone ought to carve a statue of you."

Her pulse hammered at the base of her throat. I wanted to bury my mouth there. To taste the saltiness of her skin and breathe in the cinnamon and vanilla deliciousness of her.

She stepped close, brushing fingers and then lips over the ink on my chest. The tattoo of the eagle in flight spread across my torso and wrapped around my upper left arm. "The artist did a gorgeous job."

Nodding, I captured her knuckles, kissing them. I dipped my head toward her neck, tracing my tongue and teeth across her collarbone.

Her fingers traced the curve of my butt, leaving a trail of heat in her wake. "Do you like it rough?"

I'd dreamed of Val for a long time, imagining she enjoyed romance and sweet caresses. I'd take the initiative, pleasuring her until she moaned with passion, squirming under my hands. Never once did I picture this scenario.

"Am I gonna need a safe word?"

Her tan face blushed deeper red. "No."

I pinched a pert nipple through the fabric of her sweater and raised an eyebrow. "You sure? I always thought eggplant would be a good safe word."

Without a word, she swatted my butt. Reacting, I picked her up and threw her over my shoulder.

"Evan!" she shrieked.

Dropping her on the bed, I watched her bounce. Cocoa, thinking it was a game, jumped onto the bed, lapping her exposed skin. Val squirmed, laughing.

"Come on, Cocoa. Want a chewie?" I called. She leaped off the bed with a bark. I grabbed a rawhide from the jar on my dresser and tossed it into the hallway and the fluffball streaked after it, and I kicked the door shut.

In two strides, I returned to the bed. Pulling Val's red sweater up over her head, I flicked the front closure of her bra open, peeling the satin away from her breasts.

Pretty budded nipples begged me to pleasure them. After a teasing flick of my fingers, I followed with my lips, sucking the nub into my mouth.

She arched up, back bowing off the bed. I trailed kisses up her sternum. Nibbling along the edge of her chin.

Her eyes grew hazy, and I lifted the glasses from her nose.

Tugging her boots off, I massaged her feet, kissing my way up her calves to her knees. Gripping the waistband of her Navy skirt, I peeled it down legs that went on forever.

It was my turn to gasp in a shuddering breath and stare at her beautiful breasts, soft belly, and the mound of sweet pussy.

Her husky voice coaxed, "Evan, please."

Spreading her legs wide, I swirled my tongue along the apex of her thighs. My tongue and mouth consumed her, drinking her in. The heady scent of her arousal drawing me in.

She moaned, and my balls tightened at the sound of her pleasure. Her moans of arousal became my goal, my existence. Her legs shifted as she squirmed under my lips. Flicking her clit, I slid my fingers into her wet heat until her hips and legs strained.

She clutched at the quilt, balling up her fists in the fabric. "Evan..." she moaned, writhing on the bed, but I held her hips still, pushing them back down to the mattress.

"Tell me what you want, gorgeous."

"I..." she panted. Her head thrashed on the bed.

My fingers slid deeper into her core. My other hand found her clit, keeping her on the edge, but not letting her go over.

"I need more." Her body arched, tight, hot, ready to come. Somehow, her fingers found my cock. Her tight fist almost blew me away.

"Careful," I whispered.

She shook her head. "I want you inside me."

I shifted up, reaching for the condoms I kept in the small drawer by the bed.

Taking it from me, my siren ripped open the package. Her hand stroked as she rolled the rubber down my throbbing shaft.

Pushing me back against the pillows, my long legs stretched out as she straddled my hips.

The wet heat of her engulfed me as she took me inside her one slow inch at a time. Her muscles clenched tight as she moved. Finally seated, she paused. I met her heavy-lidded stare, savoring her.

And then her body rocked against me. She rode me hard, thrusting her hips, plunging down on me over and over.

I relished her gasps and moans of pleasure as captured her breasts. Shifting forward to suckle them, a tremor traversed her body.

She pulled my hair, her teeth nipping at my flesh. The pain sent a jolt of pleasure straight to my balls. My cock bulged harder as she drove us harder.

"You're so tight, I can't take it." I growled, spinning out of control.

I reached, finding her clit and the rhythm she needed. Her muscles clamped down, making my eyes cross and my toes curl.

Her hips thrust forward; her eyes closed. A beam from the sun captured her in its light. Loose tendrils of hair streamed down her back and around her shoulders as the spasms inside her grew, washing over her, and I followed her over the edge.

My heels dug into the mattress. I lost all sense of time and space. Her body surrounded mine as I tumbled into the storm.

We drifted together. I soothed her soft skin with its sweet and salty perfume. I rolled with her, tucking her into my body. Our legs tangling as she cuddled into me.

"I've forgotten all my words," I whispered.

"Mmm, mind-blowing?"

"Yes, that," I nodded, holding her closer still.

Cocoa nosed the door open, jumping onto the bed. She settled her furry body next to Val's naked hip, closing her eyes with a sigh.

I sank deeper into the mattress. Val played with the hairs on my chest, rubbing across my muscles.

"You're incredible," I said, finding my words at last. "*Uwoduhi.* So beautiful."

"Cherokee, right?"

"Yeah." I brushed a soft kiss across her mouth. "I'm glad you chose to come over."

Val's brown eyes sparkled. "I bet you say that to all the girls."

"Hell, no. Cocoa and I are very exclusive."

Cocoa yawned loudly and flipped over onto her back. Val reached back to pat the dog. "Well, that's good to know."

Somewhere on the floor, I heard my phone beep. Ignoring it, I pulled Val closer. Nuzzling her neck, she giggled when I tickled her.

My phone beeped again. And then again.

"Do you need to get that?" Val asked, shifting away from me. She placed her glasses on her nose.

I rolled onto my back, pulled the condom off, and threw it in the trash can by the bed. "It's probably my mom sending me pictures of the dogs."

"Sure," she said, but her tone was wary. Once again, I wondered who had hurt her. I wanted to wipe that hesitant, worried look off her face.

When the notification sounded again, I gave in. Striding naked around the bed, I dug my phone out of my jeans. Sitting on the edge of the bed, I opened my messages.

2:33 PM

Yona: Hey.

2:34 PM

Yona: Thanks for the money.

2:34 PM

Yona: The kids send their love.

2:36 PM

Yona: Call me when you have a chance.

"Everything good?" Val sat up.

"Yeah, it's fine." Tossing my phone down on the bed without responding, I turned to hug her, relishing how her breasts molded against my chest. How would she react if I told her I never wanted to let her go?

A new text came in and then another. Val eased back and gesturing toward my phone. Face up, the screen showed a picture of Yona and a preview of the texts.

2:40 PM

Yona: The heater's broke. Who's the guy we use?

2:43 PM

Yona: Love you. ♥ 💋

Val stiffened. Her shoulders tensed, and she gathered the sheet around her.

I jumped, scooping up my phone, I turned it off, placing it the screen down on the little table.

I cursed myself. I didn't need to check in the mirror to know that I wore a guilty frown.

Val apologized. "I shouldn't have read your messages."

She wouldn't understand. Part of the reason I'd taken the job in Marchfield was to put space between Yona and me. While Yona's dependence on me eased my guilt, everyone in Asheville assumed I would step into Noah's shoes.

"Yona's my best friend's widow. They have two girls. Noah died last June in a car accident, and I've been helping them out."

She quietly listened. "It sounds as if you and Yona are close."

"I've known her since fifth grade."

The distrust on her face was plain. "She loves you."

"She relies on me. She's like family."

I was fucking this up, but I didn't know what to say. My relationship with Yona was complicated.

Her lips twisted. "I don't send kiss emojis to my family."

"Val, It's not like that. She's just being funny."

"I know I said no strings, but I'm not into cheating."

Her cold, flinty tone and pale face hit me like a punch. She stood, grabbing her clothes off the floor. She yanked her sweater over her head without putting on her bra.

"Val, come on. Let's talk about this." Feeling vulnerable and in need of some armor, I grabbed my jeans and pulled them on.

She stepped into her skirt and began searching for her shoes. "There's nothing left to say."

I should've silenced my phone. None of this would've happened. "Please, Val—"

Her angry eyes flayed me open. "Do you tell her you love her?"

"I tell the girls I love them, and sure, I've said it to Yona on occasion, but it..."

"Yeah, I get it. It doesn't mean anything." Shoes on, she stood. "I'm going to cut my losses and run."

"Wait, Val. Stay," I said, reaching for her. She evaded me, spinning away. I dug my hands into my pockets.

"Why?"

I don't know. We'd agreed to keep feelings out of this, but I couldn't let her leave believing the worst about me.

"I'm fucking this up and you're jumping to conclusions. If you'd just listen—"

She charged at me to pound her tight fists against my chest. "Stop telling me what to do, Evan."

Taking a step back, I sat on the edge of the bed.

She threw her hands up in frustration and paced away from me. Spinning back around, she said, "You don't understand my point of view. In the last two days, my father canceled my credit cards and locked me out of an investment account my Gran set up for me. He and my mother are using it as leverage to get me to marry the man who left those bruises on my arm. So, you'll have to pardon me if I'm a little over listening to people tell me what to do."

Her eyes welled with tears; the emotion reflected in them unbearable to watch. My instincts screamed to protect her, to stand between her and all those who hurt her. I ached to hug her, to smooth back her hair, kiss her temple, and promise to help her anyway I could.

"You can trust me."

A tear slid down her cheek, and she wiped it away with her fist. "I can't trust you. I don't even know you."

"Then get to know me. Find out if I'm worth it. Don't write me off because of one text."

Crossing her arms over her chest, she said, "We agreed this was no strings. You don't need to prove anything, Evan, and neither do I."

Head high, she marched out of my bedroom with Cocoa on her heels. I followed as far as the living room, but Val let herself out.

Leaving me to watch her drive away from the front window.

Chapter 8
Val

Bright and early Tuesday, I camped out by Audrey's classroom with two hot chocolates and a pink and white box of pastries from Pat's. Only a minute passed before I heard the tap of her boots coming down the hallway. She did a little dance when she saw me.

"What's in the box?" She unlocked her classroom door and switched on a little lamp at her small group table.

"Your favorite." Following her, I shut the door behind us. Placing the pastries and the drinks on the table.

"It's a chocolate croissant morning? What happened?" Audrey opened the lid. Drizzled with chocolate and topped with a strawberry, the pastries smelled delicious.

Sitting in a student chair, I asked, "Good news or bad news first?"

A mouth full of chocolate didn't stop her from saying, "Girl, always lead with the positive news."

Taking a big bite of a second croissant, I savored the smooth, dark chocolate filling before saying, "After everyone left the restaurant, Evan and I did it in a closet."

Her green eyes widened. "Your closet? What about all your shoes?"

"Not my closet." I snorted. "The big one at the Egglectic."

Audrey gazed blankly at me, her nose wrinkling in confusion.

I wiggled my eyebrows and fed her another clue. "The one in the party room."

"A supply closet?"

I nodded. "It's big. And there was a table."

"Just to be clear," Audrey paused, speaking each word carefully. "You had sex with Evan on a work surface in a supply closet. Spill the tea."

"He's gorgeous, Aud, with muscles for miles and all that tan skin. He let me lead, and it made me feel feminine and powerful."

For a while anyway.

Audrey squirmed in her chair. "It's hot when big, muscled guys let the woman set the pace, right?"

Hell yeah, it was.

"The chemistry between us was smoking hot."

She wrinkled her nose playfully. "Like when the science club mixed hydrochloric acid and ammonia together, and we thought the school was burning down?"

I grinned. "Hotter."

She fanned herself with chocolatey fingers. "And his baguette?"

"Long, hot, and buttered."

"Impressive." She giggled. "And the No Pants Dance?"

"The man knows how to use his hands. I thought I might die of pleasure. He bent me over the table and took me from behind. It was so hot."

"Bravo!" she applauded while laughing.

I joined her for a moment before sobering. "After, he invited me back to his house.

She pounded excitedly on the table. "You had a two-fer!"

I snickered. "Possibly a three-fer."

"Three-fer? No such word," Audrey said like she knew everything. "Three orgasms are a thruple."

"A thruple?" My shoulders shook with laughter. "Isn't that sex with three people?"

She grabbed a dictionary off a nearby shelf and flipped it open to a random page. "It's a multiple meaning word. Thruple: Plural Noun. Three orgasms in one night. There's a picture of your face by it."

I reached for the book. "Show me."

She snapped the book closed and put it back on the shelf. "Take my word for it."

Grinning from ear to ear, I said, "You're terrible." But then I sobered quickly. Talking to Audrey always helped me feel better, but now I had to tell her how everything went to hell.

I'd spent the remainder of Monday brooding. I hadn't asked Evan if he was involved with anyone. No, I'd just thrown myself at him, thinking the no strings clause would be enough.

If only I'd ended the encounter in the closet and gone home, I wouldn't feel like a home wrecker. I wouldn't know about Yona at all, but that didn't absolve me of all guilt.

I took a sip of my drink, bracing myself.

Audrey gestured to my frown. "I take it we're at the bad news?"

I swept the crumbs off the table and lobbed the trash into the can by the door. "After the Triple-O, Evan got some texts from a woman."

Thunderstruck, she stuttered, "Wait? What?"

I was such a fool that it hurt to think about. "She texted him a bunch of times. I saw the last one. She said I love you."

Her outrage comforted me. She waved a fist at me. "Did you key his car?"

Audrey was my ride or die. She'd be first in line to destroy anyone who hurt me.

Her eyes glinted evilly. "I'm going to send all my troublemakers to him today for time-out with a list of ideas for how to annoy him."

I smiled weakly at her idle threat. "We both agreed to no-strings."

"There's no-strings and then there's common decency, Val."

"He said Yona was his friend."

She crossed her arms over her chest. "You don't say I love you to your friends."

"I'd felt the same way in the moment, but last night I remembered I tell you that I love you."

"That's different."

"He's known her since fifth grade, and she's his best friend's widow."

Audrey threw her hands up. "You're making it hard for me to stay angry with him."

"I'm angrier at myself. I never asked him if he was seeing anyone before I jumped him."

"He should have told you."

Sighing, I admitted, "I'm not sure I gave him a chance."

Reaching out to touch my hand, she said, "I wish you'd called me."

"I texted you when I got home, but you didn't respond."

Audrey blushed. "Oz and I were pole dancing."

"Did you get a three-fer?"

"My picture is next to yours in the dictionary."

It felt good to laugh with her. "I'm happy for you, Aud. You deserve all the happiness in the world."

"You do, too. I hate that you're upset."

But I wasn't angry anymore. Sometime last evening, I'd come up with a plan. My parents and Logan wanted to control me, but what if I took control?

Mom had given me a kernel of an idea. If I had a serious boyfriend, they'd back off. Maybe if I could convince someone to pretend to be my boyfriend.

And who better to ask than Evan? After yesterday, he wouldn't be tempted to sleep with him again, and he owed me one.

At two in the morning, it'd seemed like a bullet proof plan. I'd get some breathing room from Mom and Dad and stick it to Logan. In return, I'd go with him to his Gran's birthday party and save him from all the single ladies.

But I wanted to run it past Audrey first.

"I have an idea. It may be totally crazy, though."

Audrey leaned back in the chair. "Lay it on me."

"I'm going to ask Evan to be my pretend boyfriend until after Spring Break."

Audrey's eyes narrowed. "Why?"

An excellent question. In the cold light of the school's fluorescent fixtures, it seemed less logical.

I patted my pants pockets, searching for the scrap of paper I'd jotted my notes on. "I made a list of reasons."

Pulling out the paper, I scanned the list. "First, my parents want me to marry and have babies. If I'm in a relationship, they'll be less likely to throw Logan at me."

"Won't they nag you to marry Evan?"

"Yes, but I'd have more control because Evan would be on my side."

Audrey nodded, then sipped her hot chocolate. "So far, I think it's insane, but go on."

Glancing down, I read the next item. "Second, now that I know Evan is in a relationship, it takes the sex issue off the table."

Audrey's brow furrowed. "I'm not sure..."

"Third, if Evan doesn't want to help me, I'll threaten to tell Yona everything and break her heart."

Her mouth dropped open. "You wouldn't!"

"You're right." I shrugged. "But Evan doesn't know that."

"You would blackmail him?"

I shook my head. "Not blackmail, a favor. Then he's off the hook."

"Any other brilliant reasons on your list?"

"There are three more bullet points, but I can't read my handwriting."

Audrey sighed. "The potential for catastrophic failure is high. Your plan is riddled with loopholes."

"It'll work," I said with more bravado than I felt. Spelling it out for Audrey had emphasized the cracks in my plan, but I'd superglue it all together.

"You need to consider some things. Why not cut financial and social ties with your parents?"

"It wouldn't make a difference. Mom and Dad are more tenacious than Pitbulls. Besides, there's something going on that I don't understand. A fake boyfriend will confuse them while I figure out what they're up to."

"I guess." She thought for a moment and then said, "You don't know Evan very well. Are you sure you want to spend time with him in order to pull it off?"

I waved that concern away. "Only a few hours, tops."

"Third, what if the chemistry is still there?"

"He might make me horny, but I'll never trust him again."

"You'd be in close proximity though."

"This isn't a romance novel." I scoffed.

"They're tropes for a reason. Fake dating, close proximity. You play with chemistry then—BAM! You're in love."

"Shit happens, too. Listen, I'm a stressed-out, overworked teacher. Tryouts for *Villains Incorporated* start tomorrow. Chemical reactions require energy, and I have none."

"Why not get on the Marchfield Hearts app and find a real boyfriend?"

"Boyfriends are too much work. You pretend their socks don't stink and their jokes are funny. And don't get me started on sports! All those men run around trying to find the ball while wearing cups to protect the other balls they love so much."

Audrey groaned. "Oz wants me to go fishing with him. Why? He doesn't get pedicures with me."

"Exactly. I don't have time for stuff like that. I only need Evan to..."

She snorted. "Fill your cream donut?"

"You're so immature."

She shrugged, laughing. "Give you some regular hot beef injections?"

"Stop, I'm not kidding. Evan will charm my parents. They'll love him. And the best part is, it's already working. I talked to Mom this morning, and they already want to meet Evan."

"You already told your mom?" Audrey barked. "Isn't that jumping the gun?"

I brushed off her doubts and questions with a wave of my hand. Evan would do it. This plan would work.

"What if he says no?"

"I told them I'm busy next weekend. So, if Evan won't do it, I'll have two weeks to find someone else."

Her mouth dropped open. She put both hands on her cheeks.

I rolled my eyes. "Stop making the Macaulay Culkin *Home Alone* face."

"I can't help it. This is like watching a bungled robbery in slow motion, and I can't turn away."

I ignored her snarky tone. "I should've found a fake boyfriend years ago. Mom wanted to know all about him."

"How'd she take that he's a teacher?"

"Well..." Mom would never accept Evan if she thought he was an underpaid educator.

Audrey pushed. "You didn't tell her?'"

"I told her he owned a carpentry and renovation business."

"Val!" Audrey exclaimed. "How do you think the real Evan, middle school teacher, will take this?"

I shrugged. "He'll be fine. He used to work for his dad's business and knows the ins and outs."

"Not only are you going to ask him to lie about your relationship, but also about his job and life."

Audrey's frown made me a little queasy. When I'd invented this story, I hadn't considered how Evan would feel. I only saw the benefits to me.

"And what will you do when they want you to marry him?"

I shrugged. "I'll lead them along for a while, then I'll fake break up with him."

"A foolproof plan. One hundred percent success rate."

I refused to hear her sarcasm. She wasn't telling me anything I didn't already know. It was a crazy plan, but what choice did I have?

"It'll work. I know it."

Audrey opened her mouth, but the bell ringing interrupted her. The sound of students entering the building filtered through the closed door.

I jumped up. "Gotta go. I'll text you later."

***

I spent the rest of the morning with my eighth-graders who couldn't name the president or the three branches of government at the beginning of the year. Today we delved into political parties.

When lunch rolled around, I raced to the copy machine to print off interest forms for tomorrow's tryouts. I'd been the Drama Coach for the last four years, and it was time to pick a new group of students.

As a teen, I loved acting. I performed in every show in high school. I even took a job at an after-school improv program, working with elementary students doing improvisation. Those little ones were hilarious and heartbreaking, silly and serious. I loved them.

I'd considered studying drama in college, but my parents disapproved. In the end, I majored in historical restoration and political science. But I took education classes on the sly. After all, what is teaching, but acting on a classroom stage?

Taking the stack of papers off the copier and my lunch, I raced out of the room. I needed to post the papers in front of the auditorium before I ate.

At the end of the hall, a set of closed fire doors opened into the main atrium of the school. I barreled through, skidding across the waxed floor.

And crashed into something warm and hard.

Stumbling back, I teetered on my boot heels and lost my grip on the forms. The papers flew up into the air as strong hands reached steadied me.

The touch sent electrical currents of sensation through me. My nipples hardened in reaction. Heat gathered in my center.

Tilting my head back past broad, muscular pecs and up to a chiseled jaw covered in dark stubble. My startled eyes met a chestnut brown pair.

The same eyes I'd watched darken into a rich chocolate, hazy with erotic pleasure.

A shower of white interest forms rained down on us.

"You sure know how to make an entrance." Evan smiled.

I breathed in his masculine scent, reminding me of cedar forests in the mountains. And trysts in closets.

I glanced down at where he continued to hold me, the warmth of his palms burning through my dress.

He released me, and I stepped away. "I apologize for running into you."

Kneeling, I gathered the papers into a stack.

Evan bent to pick up a stray page. "Are you the drama coach?"

Straightening the stack, I stood. "Yes."

"I used to make sets and run tech for performances in my high school."

He handed me the paper. His fingers brushed over the sensitive skin on the back of my hand, triggering a montage of sexy memories from yesterday. I forced myself to focus on what he was saying,

"I'm sorry about how things ended yesterday." His face was tired and sad.

Taking a deep breath, I said, "There's actually something I'd like to talk to you about."

"Okay." He paused, obviously surprised. "Do you want to meet Friday after school?"

"Sure," I agreed, glancing down at my watch. There were ten minutes before the next class started. "I need to run. I'll text you."

Hurrying across the main hallway, I passed the band room. A loud, slightly off-tune version of *Walking on Sunshine* emanated from within.

Outside the auditorium, I put the stack of forms on the ticket booth's counter. When students arrived at tryouts, they'd fill out the sheet, allowing me time to get organized.

On my way back, I caught sight of Evan walking toward his classroom in the elective wing. Tall and athletic with his black hair tied up in a man bun, he was sex on a stick. I drooled over his wide shoulders, narrow waist, tight butt, and long legs.

Even at a distance, I wanted to knock boots with him.

What should I do about that?

Chapter 9
Evan

After school, I met Oz and Keith for b-ball. They were both excellent athletes. Oz attacked like a berserker, moving the ball fast and furious, all while shouting curses as well as encouragement. Keith was formidable and sneaky. He scored without the rest of us seeing it coming. We'd traded off for an hour, playing one-on-one until we were exhausted.

"Fuck me," Oz groaned. He walked off the court to the bleachers and sat. "I need water."

Clapping him on the shoulder, Keith handed him a bottle. "Evan was on fire today."

"He's a menace. I should have had that last shot." Oz waved his empty bottle in my direction.

I sat down. "You're too slow, old man."

"I'm three years older than you, moron," Oz groused.

Keith and Oz began discussing a young man they'd both taught, tossing out ideas to entice him to attend school and do his assignments.

Relaxing back against the bleachers, I drank deeply from my own water. I'd need this time to assess my body and de-stress. Teaching demanded so much brain power that I needed to shove it aside for an hour or two.

But I couldn't suppress when I'd called Yona after Val stormed out. She'd cried over the phone, making me feel both helpless and frustrated. She missed Noah and was struggling to raise the girls alone. I listened and commiserated.

After I hung up, I knew getting involved with Val was a mistake. I'd committed to Yona and her girls and Marchfield Middle. Anxiety crept through my chest at the thought of stretching myself beyond those limits. The no-strings clause had saved my ass.

"Earth to Evan," Keith joked.

"You want to get some dinner?" Oz set down his phone. "Audrey says she and Rachel can meet us at Pie Palace in half an hour."

"Sure," I agreed, happy that they'd invited me. I usually went home to write lesson plans or grade work, but today I wanted companionship. "I need to grab my stuff and change."

Keith stood. "We'll meet you in the foyer in twenty."

I jogged out of the gym into the deserted main hallway. Turning left, I approached the auditorium doors as they opened, and a dark-haired form rushed out, right in my path.

Screeching to a halt, I hoped she'd see me, but she was like a magnet, drawn straight to me.

I wanted to laugh as she bounced off my chest again. Her wide eyes flashed to mine.

"Are you stalking me?"

"It's my dastardly plan. I hide in plain sight and wait for you to walk into me."

She snorted. "I believe it."

"I figured Oz, Keith and I were the last ones here."

"I held auditions for *Villains Incorporated* today. Why are the three of you still here?"

"We shoot hoops on Wednesdays."

I realized my hands still rested on her shoulders. Hers held my hips. If I shuffled my feet, we could imitate middle-schoolers slow dancing.

Easing back a little, my eyes traveled up her body. She wore brown boots and an emerald dress that ended at her knees and flared across her hips. A gold necklace knotted at her throat, and her hair knotted on top of her head.

She leaned toward me. Her breath mingled with mine; our lips close to touching. I imagined myself kissing those rosy-red lips.

Remembering my earlier reservations, I cleared my throat and stepped away, putting three feet between us. "About Friday. I can't meet you because I've decided to go home for the weekend."

Saying it aloud, I realized a trip to Asheville would do me good. I could check in on my parents and Yona.

She blinked. "Oh, I wanted to apologize. I overreacted at your house."

I shook my head. "I handled it wrong. Helping Yona is my responsibility, but she's not my girlfriend."

She nodded. "Thank you for explaining, and I'm sorry you lost your friend."

"Noah's loss is still raw, but we're healing."

"He must have been a great person."

I nodded. Noah had been a great guy with so much to live for. It hurt knowing how much he'd miss.

Val fell silent, biting her lip. Her forehead wrinkled in thought. I'd seen it in my own mirror. She was battling her inner demons, and, God help me, I wanted to join the fight.

"Everything okay?"

She straightened my shoulders. "Would you consider helping me with something?"

Keep it light, Shurden. I forced myself to not react. Don't lay your honor at her feet.

I winked at her. "I enjoy a good proposition."

"It's complicated. I told you about my parents and the issues I'm having with them."

Unable to stop myself, I stared at her wrist, the bruises hidden under the sleeve of her dress. My voice sounded gruff when I said, "I remember."

Her throat moved as she swallowed hard. "I wondered if you might help me."

What was she suggesting? "I don't understand."

"I hoped ... I mean..."

I lifted her hand, gently folding it inside my own. "Spit it out, Gorgeous."

She took a deep breath, her eyes on our hands. "Would you pretend to be my boyfriend?"

I let go of her fingers, dropping my hand to my side.

She charged on. "It would just be for a few weeks. I promise not to take too much of your time."

Warning sirens and red flags engaged. Of all the favors I thought she'd ask; I'd never imagined this. Not only did lying give me hives, but I also lived as free of drama as possible. Not to mention that I vowed to stay away from her.

"I don't know...."

"We'd only have to see my parents once or twice. Just enough to stop them from nagging me to marry Logan."

The protective warrior awakened inside me, but I tried to keep a lid on it. Val was beautiful and kind, but this was a level of crazy I wasn't ready for.

Her voice rose, and she spoke faster. "I know it sounds nuts, and I wouldn't ask except something feels strange with my parents. I mean, they've been difficult and annoying for a while now, but I need to know what's going on."

I tried to remember why I shouldn't agree to help. It was hard to think over the drums of war. Images of Yona, Jacy, and Fala filtered through my mind. I had enough on my hands keeping them safe. Could I handle more?

"Val..."

The creases around her eyes deepened with defeat. Something in my heart twisted hard at her misery.

Someone coughed. A loud, irritated voice distracted me. "There you are, Valentine."

I spun around. A man in a gray pinstripe three-piece suit stalked toward us. Right away, I knew this guy couldn't be a teacher. We tended to wear easy-to-wash clothes, like khakis and button-down shirts. This guy wore a silk shirt. Maybe he worked in the administration downtown.

His brash voice echoed through the empty school. "I texted you an hour ago to be ready at six."

Not administration then. A date?

Val's face clouded. Fury and something else ... fear?

She marched forward. "How did you get in the building?"

"The man at the front desk. This visitor's badge is ruining the weave of the Armani."

He shot a hand out at me. "Logan Stephenson."

This was the asshat who had bruised Val. I left his hand hanging. The top of his head reached my shoulder. I moved closer, forcing Logan to tilt his head up. Thin and wiry, his hair slicked back with thick pomade. He smelled expensive, like roses and amber.

He took a cautious step back, dropping his hand to his side.

I said, "I'm Evan Shurden."

He said, "Ahh, you're the construction magnate."

I glanced at Val. "Uh, I'm not..."

"Aurora told my mother your company is very prosperous. I couldn't find it on Google though. You should work on your SEOs."

"Shut up, Logan." Val hissed the words, her brown eyes narrowed.

I couldn't follow this conversation. Aurora? Wasn't she a Disney princess?

Logan offered me his card. "My father's always searching for companies to sponsor the Richmond SuperSonics."

My mouth fell open. His father owned the SuperSonics? I wasn't that into football, but they were one of the top five teams in the NFL.

Val's angry voice cut through the mental haze. "Logan, why are you here?"

"If you picked up your phone, you'd know I made reservations for dinner."

That sounded like my cue. I should get my stuff and let Val manage the asshat. I took a step back as Val's eyes flashed. Her hands formed fists on her hips.

"So, you can leave me to pay the bill and find my way home? You owe me three hundred dollars."

He sneered at her. "Do you want me to apologize?"

The hostile anger in his tone told me he wouldn't. The protector in me bristled. I couldn't walk away.

"I'm done talking to you," Val hissed. The sound of her voice echoing off the empty walls of the school.

Logan adjusted the cuffs of his shirt. "Valentine, stop behaving like a child." He reached out to grab her wrist, but she spun away from him.

I lunged toward him but was too far away to stop him. Logan reached out again, catching her upper arm.

I saw red. "Let go of her," I growled.

"I'm a family friend of the Bellinis and have known Valentine since birth. Her parents have given me their blessing, and I will with Valentine alone..."

"I don't give a shit. Let her go."

Logan tilted his head up to meet my eyes. I knew what he saw in them- fiery death. Maiming. Dismemberment.

He loosened his grip, and Val yanked her arm away, stepping out of reach. "If you'd listen, Valentine, you'd know..."

She shook her head, fury staining her cheeks pink. "I don't care."

"She's asked you multiple times. You need to go."

Logan backed away. His face was purple, his eyes cold with rage. "You'll regret this."

She needed a restraining order and a bodyguard to keep this guy away.

Or a fake boyfriend...

I stood up to my full height. Anger puffed out my chest, and my voice was as sharp as ice. "Is that a threat?"

In the distance, I heard a door open. Oz and Keith walked into the main hall and headed toward us.

"Evan, you ready?" Keith called.

Oz saw the disdain on my face and approached warily. His eyes flashed from me to Val, then settled on Logan.

"Everything okay?"

Val said, "Yes." At the same time I bit out, "No."

Oz's eyes narrowed. "The custodians want everyone out, so they can turn on the alarm."

Keith read the name off his ID sticker. "Mr. Stephenson. May I escort you to the exit?"

Logan turned to Keith, snarling, "I can find my way out."

Keith fell into step next to him, anyway. "That's a nice suit. If you don't mind, who's your tailor?"

"Aldman's of Richmond." Logan answered as they walked away, his snide tone indicating that Keith couldn't afford them.

"Do they hand piece suits or just tailor them?" Keith continued as if he was deaf as they shepherded Logan down the hallway.

Val reached for the fist I still held clenched. "I'm so sorry that happened."

I stepped back, breaking contact with her, forcing myself to relax and uncurl my fingers. My emotions clashed, rage faded into confusion and simmering anger.

Val had used me. She lied to her mother before she'd even spoken to me. Even though I would have gone down swinging to protect her a moment ago, I hated her manipulation.

"That's what rich, entrepreneur boyfriends do, right? Protect their lady?"

She paled at the joke.

"I was awake all night telling myself this plan would never work. I knew it was too much to ask, but I need help. There's something strange going on, and I'm not sure who to turn to."

My gut flip-flopped. The outrage inside me dissolved into sympathy.

She rubbed her hand over her upper arm where the asshat had grabbed her, and I stepped closer.

Brown eyes swimming in tears met mine. "I'm so sorry, Evan."

She needed a confidant, someone objective to help her route out a problem with her family. It was the exact same job I performed for Yona. Watching out for her and stepping in when needed.

She wiped her eyes with the back of her hand. "I'll tell Mom it didn't work out. She'll believe it. No one in my family thinks I can find a boyfriend, anyway."

I wrestled with the hero in me. If I agreed to help her, I'd get tangled up in her lies. And what if at the end I liked being her boyfriend? I'd spent months mooning over her from afar. What if I fell in love with her?

As much as I wanted to sign on the dotted line, how would I protect my heart?

She sighed, stepping away from me. "I'll let you go. Oz and Keith are waiting."

She turned toward her classroom and walked away from me. With each step she took, my heart sped up. If I let her walk away in her time of need, would I be able to live with myself?

What if she ended up hurt because I didn't play a part in the masquerade? Would her family force her to marry Logan? Could I live with myself if that happened?

It was temporary. I could step into an alter-ego and pretend to be the man Val wanted. I'd build a wall around my heart that even she couldn't scale. Even as my head warned me to stop and think it through, but my heart demanded I step forward and shield her.

My running shoes squeaked on the floor as I jogged after her. "Wait, Val..."

I stopped beside her. "You hungry? We're going to Pie Palace for dinner. Audrey and Rachel are meeting us."

Her voice wobbled with concealed emotions. "I–I appreciate the invitation, but I should go home.

"Okay," I nodded. "If, you're sure."

But she didn't walk away. I waited. I'd never push, but I would give her time to think.

Finally, she said, "Do you really want me to go?"

I answered her question with one of my own. "That idiot is a prick. Why do your parents want you to marry him?"

She hung her head. "They say they want grandchildren, but I know there's more to it."

My interest piqued. A mystery. A missing motive to root out. My heart and mind aligned. I should help her.

"I'll do it."

She stared, her mouth dropping open. "What?"

"I'll be your fake boyfriend."

Her face brightened and her mouth curved. "Thank you! I promise you won't regret it, Evan."

"I do have some conditions, though."

"Anything," she nodded, her face serious.

"I don't want to lie to our friends."

She sighed. "We'd never be able to fool Audrey, anyway. This is just for my parents."

"We need a clear exit strategy."

Her head tilted to the side while she thought. "Once we get to the root of things, you can break up with me."

I nodded, even though her words made me a little sad.

"Last condition. You owe me a favor."

Chapter 10
Evan

An hour later, Val and I crowded around a table with our friends, wolfing down pizza at Pie Palace.

I watched Val devour a slice of their Utopian, an all-veggie pizza. Apparently, the encounter with Logan hadn't affected her appetite, even though it left me with a brick in my gut.

Had I really agreed to be her fake boyfriend after I'd convinced myself to let her go?

Right now, I had four texts from Yona on my phone about the ongoing water leak issue, and I'd just signed up for more?

I was in over my head, but I kept treading water. I could teach, placate Yona, and keep Val out of trouble.

Of course, I could.

I took a bite of the Caveman pizza on my plate. Deliciously loaded with pepperoni, salami, bacon, ham, and ground beef, despite being a heart attack waiting to happen.

Oz had acted like he hadn't seen Audrey in three days, grabbing her close and kissing her long enough to make Keith groan and throw a napkin at them.

Rachel seemed to light up when Keith sat next to her. Now that she had a semester under her belt, she looked less like a deer in the headlights.

Keith whispered something in her ear. Rachel blushed and swatted him on the shoulder. She reminded me of my sister, Gennie, and I wondered if anyone told her about Keith's reputation.

"This is the first time since September that I've been out on a school night." She smiled around the table, but especially at Keith. "Thanks for inviting me."

Her blue eyes met Keith's as he lifted his glass, and he sloshed beer on himself. I bit back a smile at his flustered expression, relaxing for the first time in an hour.

"Oh, no!" Rachel patted his stomach with a paper napkin, waving to the server to bring more.

Keith blushed and stammered. "By tomorrow, everyone in town will be talking about how I peed my pants." I'd never seen him lose his cool with a woman before.

Val joked, "I've wanted to throw a drink at Keith plenty of times."

Audrey chuckled. "Remember when you gave my beer to the new P.E. teacher at happy hour last year? I almost dumped another over your head."

Keith put his napkin on the table. "You and Oz wouldn't have fallen in love if I hadn't."

Oz squeezed Audrey's hand. "And now we're getting married."

"How did you guys meet?" Rachel said.

"I'll tell you tomorrow." Audrey threw her bestie a glance. "There are other things to discuss tonight."

Val stiffened. "There really aren't."

"Who was that guy at school?" Oz asked.

"Evan was ready to pile drive him," Keith added.

Val bit her lip. "He's not important."

"He's a douche." I shrugged, trying to underplay my anger. I wasn't a violent man, but I would pound Logan into the ground if he touched Val again.

"He is," Val agreed, and then tried to change the subject. "How about those Knicks?"

Oz and Keith cracked up. "When have you ever cared about basketball?"

"I watch," she said, dismissing the men with a shrug.

The give and take banter among friends reminded me of Noah. My heart twisted with a twinge of grief as I remembered clowning around with him and teasing him about his growing love for Yona.

Rachel asked Val, "Is he your ex?"

Swallowing and then taking a sip of water, Val paused before answering. "It's much more Gothic horror than that. My parents insist that I marry him."

Keith tilted his head back, laughing, but he sobered when he saw my glare. I turned to Val and asked, "Why?"

She sighed bitterly. "I'm a spinster with no children."

"Is this a Jane Austen novel?" Oz asked, and the women gaped at him.

"Whoa, hold up," Audrey burst out. "What do you know about Jane Austen?"

Oz shifted in his seat. "Bobby and I read *Pride and Prejudice* in Afghanistan. It wasn't bad, but I liked the version with the zombies better."

Leaning over, Audrey gave him a loud kiss. "We'll talk later. Keep going, Val."

"Logan has one line," Val said. She deepened her voice, imitating the asshat. "Valentine, we must talk. Our parents expect you to fall in line immediately. Come to your senses and marry me."

The others chuckled, but nothing was funny about that idiot. He was dangerous, and I needed Val to see it. "You need to take out a restraining order on him."

Val's eyes widened. "I - I'm not sure-"

"It's a good idea." Audrey nodded. "What if he caught you alone in the parking lot or at your house?"

She hesitated, her face pale. "I'm not sure. Logan's annoying, but—"

Annoying? More like abusive.

"He put his hands on you. Bruised you."

Val's face paled. Her hand trembled as she reached for her glass. "I'll think about it."

I took her other hand in mine, twining her cold fingers with my warm ones. She needed to face reality, but I hated upsetting her.

"Let's change the subject." Keith took the last piece of pizza from the tray. "How long until Spring Break, y'all?"

The conversation turned back to school and the upcoming holiday. Val shoved her last bite of pizza around her plate, deep in thought. When her cell rang, she moved to a nearby alcove to take the call.

"I bet that's her mom." Audrey shushed us, trying to hear Val's conversation.

"Why are we listening?" Keith whispered.

"We want to be supportive." Audrey hissed.

Oz muttered, "It feels intrusive, Red."

Unable to sit still, I walked over to her. Despite all the resolutions I'd made to keep my emotions out of this situation, the defender in me overruled them one-by-one.

Val glanced up, reaching out and took my hand. Her fingers squeezed hard.

"Mom, I'm fine. That's ridiculous. Logan is misconstruing what happened." She listened, biting her lip as her mother spoke.

"What? No!" she yelped, panic on her face. "No, no, no, no. You don't need to do that."

I could hear a stern female voice reply through the speaker, but couldn't make out the words. After a lengthy pause, Val responded to her mom despondently, "Okay. I'll see you then."

Slipping her phone into her pocket, she rolled her neck from side to side as if to loosen the tension. "This is an absolute disaster."

"Want me to take you home?" I hoped she'd let me bundle her up and bodyguard her.

"No." She glanced toward her friends, who turned away quickly. Following her back to the table, I scowled at their curious expressions.

Val said, "That was Mom. Guess who's coming to dinner?"

Audrey gasped. "They've never visited before."

"Logan fed them some bullshit about Evan, and they believe I'm in danger."

Rachel cocked her head to one side. "They believe Logan's story over yours?"

Her hands flew up. "She didn't give me a chance to tell my side."

My warm fingers wrapped around her cold ones. "They can't force you to marry him."

"My dad tried to cut off my money and cards. What will he do next?" She snorted. "It's pathetic. He co-signed when I opened them, but I paid all the bills. I never thought to take him off."

Oz scowled. "Have you checked all of your accounts?"

She nodded and pulled her hand from mine. "Evan, I know I asked you to help, but I understand if you don't want to get involved."

She was offering me an opportunity to back out of our deal, but I couldn't let her struggle through all this alone. She needed a partner, and she'd picked me.

I reached out my hand. "I stand by our agreement, Val." She hissed out a relieved breath and shook it.

"What did you ask him to do?" Keith asked. "I'll help you bury the body."

"Same," Oz said with a growl.

A smile blossomed on Val's face. "Thank you, but there's no need. I asked Evan to pretend to be my boyfriend, so I could get to the route of the issue."

Four pairs of eyes shot to me, and I met them all in turn, trying not to squirm under the scrutiny.

"Reversed *Pretty Woman*. I like it." Rachel nodded.

"I thought we'd have more time to figure out the details. I'm not sure we can pull it off before Friday."

I'd known I'd have to meet her parents, but it didn't stop the anxiety from creeping into my gut. I was a terrible liar. Could I pull this off?

"That gives you a day and some to prepare." Audrey grabbed a pen from her bag and a napkin.

Val slouched in her chair. "I thought we'd have more time. This isn't going to work."

Tapping the pen to her cheek, Audrey said, "Let's start with the meet cute. What's a good story?"

"What's wrong with the truth?" I asked. "I rescued her from falling at the Winter Carnival."

Val's lips lifted. "And I punched him in the nose as a thank you."

Everyone chuckled, but I watched the smile drain off her face. She released my hand and groaned. "I wish I hadn't lied to Mom about your job."

"It's okay. Telling her I owned a contracting business is close to the truth. I ran Dad's company for years after his heart attack, so I know enough to fake it."

Val's fingers tightened on mine, gratitude shining from her eyes. I fell into those cinnamon pools, staring back into them.

Audrey coughed, and I jerked my gaze to her. "You'll need to act like a couple by Friday, so let's play a game. We'll all write down everything we know about you both on a napkin in two minutes. Then we'll call them out. It will be fun, and you'll remember the details."

A game. The quintessential teacher strategy for reviewing before a test. Research suggested gamifying education was highly effective, so it could work for Val and me. I swiped at the itch of reluctance on the back of my neck.

"I'll keep score and time you guys," Rachel volunteered.

Audrey passed around pens she borrowed from the waitress. "Make two columns, one for Val and one for Evan. Write in either column, just write everything you can think of about them. Rachel will read them and award points as she sees fit."

"Got it." Keith clicked his pen open.

"Is everybody ready?" Rachel asked. "Okay, go!"

Two minutes to write everything I knew about Val? Did I have enough space?

VAL
Best friend: Audrey
Favorite movie: Princess Bride.
Favorite color: green
Favorite treat: chocolate croissant with hazelnut latte
Birthmark shaped like New Jersey
Upper right cusped—crooked
Scar on her right forearm
Scent: orange and lilies

I added a couple of things to my side that Val didn't know.

EVAN
Can play "Smells like Teen Spirit" on the guitar
Loves horror musicals—"Phantom of the Paradise"

"Time!" Rachel called out, and I tossed my pen down.

"Oh my, you're a naughty lot." Rachel grinned. "This one says Evan can take it to the hole."

The table erupted in laughter.

"That's basketball slang." Keith explained. "It means he's good at getting the ball into the basket."

Rachel lifted her eyebrow, her smile gone. "No mansplaining needed, Darling."

"Back away slowly, Keith," Oz suggested.

"Better yet, apologize." Audrey dared him.

Rubbing the back of his neck, Keith said, "I'm sorry, Rachel."

"Accepted. Moving on, this one says Val is great at hands-on learning."

"True." Val snickered.

An image of her face while she fondled my balls streaked through my mind even as Audrey raised her hand.

"I wrote that. Those puzzles you make for the students and the Jenga reviews are genius."

"You also said Val loves donuts with sprinkles." Rachel giggled. "Pina Coladas and getting caught in the rain."

Keith moaned. "That song is in my head now,"

"You're welcome." Audrey smirked.

Rachel picked up another list. "This one says Val was on the swim team."

My eyebrows rose. "Me too. The 100-meter breaststroke was my best time," I said. "You?"

"Of course, it was breaststroke." Her face glowed with humor. "I won the 200-meter Butterfly."

"Our first commonality." Audrey clapped. "Keep going, Rachel."

"Val was on the debate team."

Surprised, I laughed. "I was on the affirmative team in junior and senior year."

Val squealed. "Me too."

Rachel picked up the next list. "Evan's favorite color is pink."

"Wrong," I said.

"What's wrong with pink?" Val asked.

"It's not UNC blue."

Oz gave me a high five.

"His favorite song is *We Are the Champions*." Rachel continued reading.

"Good try, but also wrong."

"What is it then?" Val asked.

"*I Kissed a Girl* by Katy Perry. It's the only song I know all the words to."

Everyone cracked up.

Finally, Val said, "That song rocks."

Rachel transitioned another napkin. "This one is very detailed. Is your favorite color green, Val?"

"Yes."

"Is your perfume something with orange and lilies?"

She thought for a second. "Yeah. *Garden Daze* has those scents in it."

"Do you have a birthmark shaped like New Jersey?"

I tried not to squirm. When I wrote this list, it sounded funny and light in my head. Now I began to feel like a stalker.

She laughed. "Nope."

"Yes, you do." Audrey insisted. "I've seen it when you wear your bikini at the beach."

I began to dream of summer. Val in a bright red bikini made of strings and minuscule scraps of fabric lay on a towel in the warm sand.

Rachel turned her attention to the next item. "Evan, can you play Smells Like Teen Spirit?"

"Sure can." I nodded.

"I declare this one as the winner." Rachel pushed mine to the center of the table, where Val snatched it up. She waved it at me.

"You like *Phantom of the Paradise*?

"It's a horror rock parody of *Phantom of the Opera*. What's not to like?"

Her lips pursed. "I've never met anyone who's ever heard of this movie."

Audrey laughed. "You've made me watch it three times."

Val studied me. Her glasses framed her squinting brown eyes, and I felt like the proverbial bug under the microscope.

"Is this your list?"

"Yup." I tried for a casual tone, but it came out serious.

"How do you know this much about me when I know nothing about you?"

Watching her face, I waited as the realization showed there. I could see it in her eyes as she put two and two together. She knew I liked her.

Swallowing hard, I somehow managed a casual tone. "Gorgeous, I pay attention."

Chapter 11
Val

By Thursday evening, I was ready to jump out of my skin. I'd spent a long day teaching about state and local governments. Then topped the day off with a read-through of the play with my new thespians. They were a squirrelly bunch, but they had potential.

I wanted a shower, comfortable clothes, and an early night, but my bread always falls on the buttered side.

This was why I stood in the cold outside the school building, shining my phone's flashlight down at a flat tire.

"Damn it," I groaned, leaning against the side of my car. My teeth chattered as the wind blew, reminding me it was only mid-March. My cherry-red dress was pretty, but too thin to provide warmth. Since I'd left my coat in my classroom, I would be a popsicle soon.

Getting in the driver's seat, I idled the engine. Could drive the three miles home on the wheel's rim? I decided to text Audrey instead.

6:35 PM
Me: Hey, I have a flat. Can U get me?

I waited for her response, my stomach churning. Anxiety had ridden me hard all day. Paul Revere shouted a new warning inside my head, repeating: *Your parents are coming! Your parents are coming!*

I'd barely slept and came to school disorganized and tired. My students scented my stress like wolves and circled, testing me for weaknesses sniping and picking at me.. By second block, my head pounded, and I wished I'd called in sick.

Of course, I'd never do that. Writing out substitute plans was a thousand times harder than suffering through the school day.

My phone buzzed, and I saw a return text from Audrey.

6:38 PM
Audrey: Oh no, I'm with Oz in Wreyport.

6:38 PM
Audrey: We're making a registry list at LifeStyled.

The words on the screen blurred with my tears. I knew they planned to complete the register today, but I still wanted to flail my fists on the steering wheel.

6:39 PM
Me: No worries. I'll try Bobby.

I hadn't even opened my contacts before Audrey texted me back.

6:40 PM
Audrey: She and Mel are closing on their new house tonight.

I considered throwing away my phone against the pavement in frustration.

6:40 PM
Audrey: Call Evan.

Despite the warmth of my running car, a shiver run down my spine as I debated my options. Of course, Evan would come to my rescue, but I hated him to see me as a damsel in distress.

Again.

I could deal with the situation on my own. With determination, I stepped from the car and rummaged through the trunk for the heavy tire wrench I'd seen people use on TV. With the aid of my phone's flashlight, I attached the open end of the wrench to the bolt. I was Rosie the Riveter, ready to take on the world.

"Lefty loosey," I muttered, grabbing the bar with both hands.

I strained my muscles and grunted. Nothing happened. The bolt didn't even move a little or protest under pressure. Trying again, I pulled down on the long handle, leaned back on my heels, and used my body weight.

My right heel twisted, flinging me off balance. I let go of the wrench, wheeling my arms like a cartoon character attempting to avoid falling on the asphalt.

As if sensing I might be successful, the wrench jumped off the bolt and fell.

On my toe.

Howling in pain, my phone flew into the air and scraped across the ground. Losing my own battle with gravity, the rough surface of the pavement bite into my knees and hands.

"Fuck! Shit! Damn!" I yanked off my shoe and grabbing the toe that throbbed painfully. My knees and palms smarted, and I let out a short scream of rage.

Cold and bleeding, I limped over to my phone, typed into Google with my thumbs.

Ted's Towing Service popped up on the cracked display. Placing the call, the dispatcher warned me the wait was two or more hours.

Fuck.

Leaving my dignity on the pavement, I hobbled over to warm up behind the wheel. Resting my head back against the cold seat, I heard my phone notification chime.

6:51 PM
Audrey: Did you call him?

6:52 PM
Me: I called Ted's Towing.

6:52 PM
Audrey: What's the ETA?

I didn't want to text her back, knowing she wouldn't like the answer.

6:55 PM
Me: I'm texting Evan now.

Finding his contact information, stared at the selfie he'd taken with my phone when we'd traded numbers last night. Pursing his lips like he was kissing the camera, his eyes crossed. He looked ridiculous.

He'd dared me to add a picture to the contact in his phone, so I'd attached one with my tongue out.

6:56 PM
Me: Hi, Evan. It's Val.

I waited.

My phone screen went dark. The stars in the indigo sky twinkled. The Big Dipper's ancient light glowed down on me.

Refreshing the screen, I stared at my message, willing him to answer. The phone went dark again. I'd wait five more minutes before calling the garage in the next town over.

7:00 PM
Evan: Hey, Gorgeous. What's up?

7:01 PM
Me: I'm stuck at school with a flat.

7:03 PM
Evan: I'm at the gym. I can be there in five.

7:04 PM
Me: Thank you so much.

Relief swept through me. Five minutes was nothing. I might even kiss him when he arrived to show my gratitude.

Ignoring my stiff, aching hands, I fumbled in my purse for lipstick. I flipped on the interior lights and applied a layer of Habanero Red. The reflection in the visor mirror mocked me. When had I ever put on lipstick to get my tire changed?

I wiped the color off with a tissue and stuffed everything back in my purse as headlights cut through the darkness.

He pulled into the space opposite mine, his headlights blinding me. I heard the truck's door open.

"Val? You okay?"

"I'm fine," I called as I got out of the car, every muscle screaming.

"Your dress is torn." His eyes assessed me from head to toe. "Is that blood on your legs?"

I shrugged, not knowing what to say.

"Where's your shoe?"

I glanced around the dark lot. "It's around here somewhere."

Evan rocked back on his heels; his face unreadable. "Why don't you find it, while I change your tire?" His voice was soft and slow, as if he spoke to a dangerous beast.

Or a crazy social studies teacher on the edge.

"We're going to have to call someone. Those bolts are stuck."

He crouched in front of the tired, fitting the blasted wrench on the nut.

"It's not going to move. It's stuck," I reiterated as he flexed his very impressive biceps, turning the wrench as if sliding through butter.

"I think I can manage it."

"I loosened that one," I muttered.

Evan had my tire off and was grabbing the spare out of the back before I could blink.

"Wanna get your shoe? I'm almost done."

My knees smarted with every bend and extension. Picking up the broken heel, I took the other one off and threw them both in the backseat.

"You're good to go." Evan dusted his hands across his thighs.

I reached out to shake his hand. "Thanks, so much. I don't know what I would have done if you hadn't been available."

His palm touched mine, and I winced.

"Did you hurt yourself?" he asked, squinting at the ragged scratches.

I pulled my hand away. "It's nothing. I scraped them when I fell."

He tucked his hands in the front pockets of his jeans. "How did you fall?"

"Trying to change the tire. My shoe broke." None of that would make any sense to him. Anticipating an argument, or at least a chastisement, I braced myself.

Evan stood quietly for a moment. "Someone should look at those wounds. Clean them."

He wasn't going to scold me for being silly enough to think I could change the flat? Or roll his eyes? The tension drained out of me, leaving me cold and exhausted.

"I'll do it when I get home."

"Mind if I come, too?"

Despite my vows to think of him as a friend, thoughts of him naked, holding me, loving me with his tongue and hands as his cock drove into me. My eyes trailed up his chest to his face and met his eyes. "I should go home alone. I'll be fine."

"What time are your parents arriving tomorrow?"

"Around four."

"We should rehearse our story."

Logically, I agreed. But I also wasn't sure if he and I should be alone together. I could spout off endlessly about keeping things platonic, but could I follow through?

"I want to, but..."

I leaned closer to him, welcoming his heat. My body reacted to his on a visceral level.

"An hour. You can quiz me while I clean the gravel from your scrapes."

"An hour," I repeated like a parrot, barely restraining myself from snuggling up to him.

"I'll be out of your hair by eight-thirty."

Two minutes later, his were headlights in my rearview mirror as I led him to my apartment. My raw hands stung against the steering wheel, and I welcomed the pain. It was a wonderful distraction from the hormonal disco happening inside my body.

When I parked in front of my place, Evan pulled into the space next to me.

I let us into the darkened living room. Switching on the light, I glanced around the neat space. The rusty red and gold curtains against the cream walls. My sofa and chairs, inherited from my Gran, were luxurious brown leather.

The kitchen branched off the living room. Large enough to hold a small table and chairs, and filled with appliances, gadgets, and all sorts of things people had given me. I loved to cook, but during the school year, I ate mostly from the microwave and the air fryer.

Evan closed the door behind himself. "Nice place."

"I like it."

"I like the colors. And your art." He nodded toward a giant framed print of Georgia O'Keeffe Canna Red and Orange.

"Of course, you do." I rolled my eyes.

"Hey, you put it on your wall."

"It was a gift from my Aunt Daisy. She thought the colors went well with the furniture. She has no idea of the symbolism. At least, I don't think so."

"I'm picturing a dotty aunt around a hundred years old. Never had sex in her life, let alone masturbated."

"Don't talk about her like that." I scolded. "She's only ninety-two."

He chuckled, pretending to search my apartment. "What other dirty art do you have stashed around your apartment?"

"Wouldn't you like to know?" I countered.

"I promised I'd be out of your hair in an hour, so I'm on the clock. Where's your first aid kit?"

I started down the short hallway to my bedroom, gesturing toward the door on the right. "In the hall bathroom. Do you mind if I put on pajamas first? I'm freezing."

He winked at me. "What kind of pajamas?"

"The unsexy flannel kind."

"If you must."

I listened to him opening drawers and cabinets, searching for the bandages and antibacterial ointment as I picked out pajamas. Choosing a set Audrey had given me for Christmas, I smiled at the hedgehogs dancing across the flannel.

Great for comfort. Zero for sex appeal. Perfect for keeping things platonic between Evan and me.

Barefoot, I padded into the master bathroom.

"Do you mind if I take a quick shower?" I called down the hallway toward the living room.

"Take your time." He called back.

I quickly removed my contacts and clothes and jumped in. The hot water stung my palms and knees, so I hurried even faster.

After drying off, I put on panties and my flannel armor. Placing my glasses on my nose, I felt a hundred times better. I brushed my damp hair back out of my face and walked out to the living room.

Evan's eyes traveled over me. "Where were your glasses earlier?"

"I wore my contacts today."

"I like the glasses. They're sexy."

I snorted. "Said no one ever."

"I mean it." He smiled. "Have a seat, and I'll dress your wounds."

I sat on the couch. "I can do it."

"Nope. You grill me with questions, and I'll clean you up. That was the deal."

Seated across from me on the coffee table, he rested my right leg on his lap and rolled my flannel pants up. Small pulses of electricity trailed from his fingers as they skimmed along the skin of my calf. I shivered.

"Still cold?"

"No." I sighed, closing my eyes until tweezers pulled at a gash. "Ow!"

"You have gravel in this one. Ask me a question. It'll keep your mind off what I'm doing."

While he played the game of Operation on my knee, I stared at the ceiling. My mind sought out relevant questions. "Who was your best friend in school?"

"That would be Tommy Einstein. Ironically, he wasn't the smartest kid in class, but he was hilarious. Noah, Tommy, and I got in trouble together."

I sucked in a breath between my teeth as he poured antiseptic over the cut. "What kind of trouble?"

Blowing gently on my wound, he eased the pain and sent sparks of electricity across my skin.

"Once, the three of us stole my dad's truck and drove it to Boone and back, trying to find a convenience store to sell us beer."

"How old were you?"

"Thirteen. Luckily, we didn't drive off the side of a mountain."

"Did you get caught?"

"Dad was waiting for us when we got back. We had to do yard work every day for a month."

He wrapped my scrapes with gauze. "How about you? Who was your best friend growing up?"

"Natalie Howard and I were inseparable from first grade through high school."

"Did y'all ever get in trouble?"

"I would sleep over at her house because her parents slept like the dead. We'd sneak out and go to parties."

"Did you ever get caught?"

"Nope."

He put my leg down and picked up the other, whistling between his teeth. "These are deeper."

Grimacing, I said, "I landed on that side."

Evan picked up the tweezers and started cleaning. "Keep asking questions."

I fixated on the dark hair of his man bun held in place by a simple leather cord, fighting the temptation to reach out and unravel it. A sharp sting emanated from my knee. I bit my lip and fisted my hands, wincing at the pain. "Who was your best and worst teacher?"

"Mr. Rayburn taught tenth-grade Geometry and coached the baseball team. He had this rule about getting detention if you were late, and I was tardy often. I served my share of detentions, but I kinda liked it. He talked to me and listened to what I had to say."

"I love that," I said even as I gritted my teeth when the tweezers poked a sore spot.

"And Ms. Thatcher, ninth grade English. She had black hair all twirled up on her head in a bun and scary reading glasses perched on the tip of her nose. She enjoyed embarrassing the failing students in front of the whole class. We hated her and made her life miserable. She quit after that year."

"She didn't like kids or understand them."

He nodded. "Almost finished picking out the dirt."

"What's the first concert you ever went to?"

"Mom and Dad took me to see The B52s, the GoGos, and the Psychedelic Furs when I was three. Mom says I boogied my butt off during the whole show."

I imagined Evan in tiny toddler jeans and a band t-shirt dancing to *Love Shack*. The image was so clear, it made my heart ache. "I saw My Chemical Romance my junior year."

His fingers lingered on the underside of my knee as he wrapped the bandage. "You were an Emo kid?"

"No. I went with friends. I'm a music chameleon."

"What?"

"I love any music around me, no matter what it is. I once saw Billy Ray Cyrus and Linkin Park, two concerts, one weekend."

"Which did you like best?"

"People watching was the best at both. Billy Ray's fans were in their fifties and threw their panties on the stage. Everyone wore black and heavy eyeliner at Linkin Park."

He smoothed my pants leg down, then took my left hand. Red scabs dotted my palm, hot and angry-looking. "When's your birthday?"

"April 17th. I'm an Aries which makes me confident, bold, honest, and competitive. What about you?

"February 16th. I don't know what that makes me."

"Hmmm, Pisces. Creative, compassionate, and spiritual. I wanted to be the horoscope writer for the newspaper as a kid. I imagined myself with a crystal ball, generating prophecies every day."

"You had big ambitions. Psychic and clown."

I'd never known anyone who listened to me and remembered what I said. Evan concentrated on me, and it was sexy as hell.

He dabbed my hand with antiseptic, and I jerked back. "That stings."

His breath whispered across my skin as he blew away the sting. His eyes collided with mine. Deep, dark pools I wanted to explore. Too soon, he focused his attention back on my hand, wrapping it in gauze.

"Where did you learn to do that?"

He eased back a little, switching to my right hand. "Mom always blew away my hurt."

"It helps."

I sat quietly while he finished bandaging my hand, his head tipped over my hand. The line of his neck called to me, begging me to drag my mouth along its sinewy length. Maybe staying platonic wasn't absolutely necessary?

"How do you know all those things about me? My favorite color and cookie?"

"I told you; I pay attention. The color wasn't hard to guess. You wear green at least twice a week, and you purchased two boxes of chocolate chip cookies from the technology fundraiser in October."

I could feel the blush creep over my cheeks. "What about the birthmark?"

He smiled. The flash of teeth made my heart beat faster. "Did you hit your head, gorgeous? I've seen you naked."

"I remember."

I couldn't catch my breath. My nipples grew pebble hard, aching for his touch. I wanted to strip naked for him.

His hand curved around my neck, and he eased closer, his legs wide, trapping mine. His earthy, woodsy aroma enticed my senses.

I inched closer forward, relishing the heat radiating off him. Reaching up, I cupped his face with my gauze-wrapped palms. I kissed his dimple, the short stubble of his beard rough against my lips.

My tongue brushed across the seam of his mouth, seeking entrance. Wild electricity crackled between us when he deepened the kiss.

His strong arms lifted me to his lap. I straddled his hips and pressed my core against his hard cock. The sting of pain replaced by pleasure.

Calloused fingers edged under the hem of my pajama top, pushing up the flannel to reveal my bare breasts. He tested their weight, then lifted one to meet his mouth. I leaned back, arching toward him as he sucked the peak deep into his mouth.

Moaning, I rocked my hips against him, wanting him inside me.

As if from a great distance, I heard a knock in the vicinity of my door.

"Valentine."

Was he calling my name? Why did he sound so far away?

Lifting his head, Evan's breath was hot against my neck. "Did you hear something?"

Another louder knock pounded on the door. "Valentine. It's your mother."

Shit.

I leaped off his lap, scanning the floor for my pajama top. I threw it over my head.

"Wait." He reached for my top.

"Stop." I hissed at him, batting his hands away.

"It's inside out." He laughed softly.

I whipped it off again like a star in *Girls Gone Wild*, turning it right side out.

Why was Mom here? Now? Couldn't she have waited, I don't know, twenty more minutes?

"Valentine, open the door." Mom hammered on the door.

Groaning, I put my pajama shirt right-side out. "Brace yourself. They're here early."

He sat on the sofa, covering up his hard-on with a pillow while I went to meet the firing squad.

Chapter 12
Val

"Hey, ladies." I squeezed into the teacher's dining area and pulled a chair between Audrey and Rachel.

More like a bomb shelter than a teacher's lounge, the flickering fluorescent lights, smell of old tuna sandwiches, and stale fries meant no teachers ever ate here, preferring to eat outside in good weather or in their rooms. That made it perfect for an uninterrupted bestie debrief.

I wiped down the dusty table with antibacterial wipes. "Thanks for meeting me during your planning time."

"We had to hear the rest of the story. You left off with Evan cleaned and bandaged your scrapes." Rachel sighed as if it were the most romantic thing she'd ever heard.

Audrey crossed her arms over her chest. "I can't believe you wore the hedgehog pajamas after all the grief you gave me last year about my Llama Reading Pajamas last year."

I sat down next to her. "I already apologized this morning, Aud. Who knew flannel PJ's weren't the modern-day chastity belt?"

Rachel's blue eyes sparkled. "Where did you buy these pajamas? They're hunky men magnets, and I need some."

"I'll hook you up," Audrey promised, then turned to me. "Finish the story."

I stalled. "Where was I?"

"Your parents interrupted—"

Audrey cut Rachel off. "They cock-blocked you."

I snickered. "I'd chosen to throw caution to the wind. Endorphins were a go. I was on Evan's lap and primed for release when there was a knock on the door. So, there I am, grinding against a hard cock, my boob is in Evan's mouth, and my mother is beating on the door and yelling, 'Valentine, open up.'"

Audrey gaped at me. "Well, shit."

"Exactly. I leaped to my feet and threw on my top inside out."

"Uh oh." Rachel's face lit up with humor.

"Evan tried to take it off to fix it, but I slapped his hand. We spent fifteen seconds having a slap fight before it dawned on me that he wasn't trying to take it off, but put it on correctly."

Both my friends dissolved into laughter. Thinking back on it, the situation was pretty hilarious. In the moment, though, I'd been frantic.

"What did you do?" Rachel grabbed the folded paper towels out of the dispenser on the table to dab at her eyes.

"I stripped off my top, flashing Evan before putting it back on the right way. Meanwhile, he's sitting there with a huge boner."

Rachel groaned. "How will I look him in the eye later today?"

Patting her hand, Audrey snarked, "Just stare over his shoulder."

"I can't. He's too tall."

I threw up my hands. "I could stop the story there and ask you for some fashion help."

"Absolutely not," Rachel protested. "I have to hear the rest."

"Well, Evan's sitting on the sofa with a pillow over his lap, and I went to open the door. Mom waltzed in, 'Surprise. We're early. I was dying to go to that sweet little art gallery in downtown Marchfield but didn't think we'd have time after dinner tomorrow.'"

"Did she see Evan?" Rachel asked.

"He's kinda hard to miss. Apparently, Mom has the same shrinking effect on Evan's boners as she does on my soul."

Audrey's shoulders shook. "Your mom does have a shriveling personality."

"Mom was pleased to meet him. She patted his knee and asked for his life story. Evan was the proverbial deer in the headlights."

"I think Aurora had a similar effect on me when I first met her."

I'd invited Audrey to my parents' house as my plus one for mandatory parties. The first time, Mom insisted Audrey change out of her black cocktail dress into one of her designer gowns. Audrey hadn't known whether to be insulted or honored.

Rachel gasped. "Wait, is your mom named after Sleeping Beauty?"

"She's acts like a princess." I didn't know if Gran and Gramp had planned it, but Mom turned out spoiled and entitled.

"Finish the story," Audrey insisted, "Before classes start again."

"In the middle of Mom grilling Evan over where he went to school and what his siblings do for a living, Dad comes in. He and Leo were outside smoking cigars."

"Who's Leo?" Rachel asked. With her chin propped on her hands. With her wavy dirty blonde hair and big blue eyes, she looked younger than twenty-nine.

"Their driver," I explained. "Mom and Dad never drive themselves."

In all honesty, Mom was a high-functioning alcoholic. I'd known it since high school when she'd run her car off the road on her way home from her book club.

She'd checked into rehab to avoid jail time, and Dad hired Leo before she'd returned from the program, enabling her to continue drinking.

I continued, "Dad walked in and clapped Evan on his shoulder hard enough I heard the thump across the room."

"Poor, Evan. Did they run circles around him?"

"Nope. He oozed charm. They ooh-ed and aah-ed over how he'd rescued me and then patched me up. Mom fluttered her eyelashes at him so much, I thought she would try to take Evan home with her, and I could see

Dad sizing him up. I bet he asks Evan to invest in some scheme tonight. Finally, they left went the hotel."

Rachel pressed her fingers to her lips. "What did Evan say about them?"

"He just said, 'Well, they're a lot' and went home. And now I'm wondering if other thirty-year-olds get cock-blocked by their parents."

Audrey coughed and raised her hand. "Yup."

My voice rose several octaves. "Really? And you didn't tell me"

"It was at Christmas. You were away."

"What happened?" I demanded.

"Short version, Oz and I were having naked time under the Christmas tree. Oz went down to Christmas Town and was so naughty Santa crossed him off his list. All of a sudden, he stops. I'm like, 'Oz, baby, please.' But then we heard a car door slam outside. He wanted to check the window, but I was so close, clinging to him like moss."

Rachel sighed. "I wish I had a boyfriend."

I patted her hand while nodding to Audrey to continue.

"There's a ruckus outside. People talking. I recognized Jason and Brandon's voices. It's my family, so I jumped, accidentally kicked Oz in the head, shouting 'Where're my pants?' Oz tossed me my jeans. I pulled them up commando style, not even thinking about the purple panties he'd peeled off me ten minutes before."

"Oh my gosh." Rachel squealed. "What happened?"

"My brothers each hauled in a pile of presents. Mom and Dad brought more. I'd just pulled on a sweater to hide my nipples when a decoration catches Jason's eye, and he nudges Brandon. Jason says, 'Interesting ornament, sis, but are you sure you want to hang it next to the baby Jesus?'"

Laughing so hard, I can't see straight, I gasped, "Your panties?"

"Oh, yeah. My purple and lace panties were on the damn tree. And Oz just smiled and said, 'It's my gift to the newborn king.'"

The three of us cracked up.

Wiping my eyes on another brown paper towel, I said, "How about you, Rachel?"

"Nothing as hilarious as your stories, but my dad walked in on me once when I was masturbating. I covered up fast, and he was oblivious. Ironically, he reminded me to return any water bottles to the kitchen and clean them with the bottlebrush."

Was it possible to bust a gut from cackling so hard? My stomach tightened, and I massaged my aching cheeks.

"I feel a thousand times better."

Rachel snorted. "I no longer feel bad that I don't have a boyfriend."

I glanced at the clock on the wall over the door, shocked to see we only had five minutes before the next class.

"My parents are picking me up for an early dinner after school before driving home to Richmond. I need your opinion on outfits." I pulled out my phone to show them pictures. "I brought them all to school with accessories and shoes. What do you think?"

"Oooh." Rachel gasped. "They're so pretty."

"I like the red one. It's a power color." Audrey said, then took my phone to see at the options more closely. "But the gold is the jam. Sexy, strong, and symbolic."

"I agree," Rachel said.

"Gold it is." I hugged them both before we hurried to our classrooms.

After my last class, I changed into the gold dress in the tiny faculty washroom. The soft, silky material slid over my hips, stopping above my knees. The deep 'V' showed off a hint of cleavage and highlighted my necklace. A present from my parents when I turned sixteen. The diamond pendant sparkled.

I freshened my make-up, slid on my matching INEZ peep-toe heels, and fastened them around my ankles.

Standing in front of the mirror, I felt strong and beautiful, ready to take on the world.

My phone chimed as I folded my school clothes and put them in a bag.

4:36 PM
Mom: We're here.

4:37 PM
Dad: Don't keep us waiting.

4:38 PM
Me: I'll be right there. I just need to sign out.

I took a deep breath and exhaled. Evan was meeting us at the restaurant. With Evan's help, I'd discover the truth.

And the truth would set me free.

Chapter 13
Evan

Despite the early dinner reservation time, my stomach growled on my way to meet Val and her parents at Violet's, the in-house restaurant in the remodeled Frian Hotel. I'd never eaten here because the vibes weren't for my crowd. They could have hung a sign saying older couples or marriage proposals only.

I passed my keys to the valet attendant, slightly embarrassed about having my truck parked amongst expensive luxury cars. Then walked up the red-carpeted stairs to the lobby.

Straightening the sleeves of my sports coat, I wondered if I should have worn my suit, but in the lobby, people wore everything from shorts to tuxedos.

Easing past an older lady dripping in more jewels than Megan Thee Stallion, I squeezed through the lobby. An enormous flower arrangement of white lilies gave off an overwhelmingly sweet aroma.

Should I have brought flowers as a gift?

A lady in a rose-colored ball gown rushed by with a poodle dyed Pepto pink from head to tail. A man in a salmon-pink tux stood waiting by the window for them. She kissed his cheek, and they disappeared into the bar.

Feeling more and more like I fell down the rabbit hole, I continued toward Violet's at the end of the corridor.

As predicted, only older couples sat at tables by the windows, and I hoped no one expected me to propose tonight.

I saw Val right away, and my breath caught. Her gold dress sparkled and shimmered in the candlelight. Her sun-kissed back was bare. As she turned, I could see the scoop in the front that dipped low into her cleavage. She radiated beauty, but it was her inner glow attracted me the most.

Matt Bellini wore a red and blue plaid vest over a blue long-sleeve shirt with a tie knotted at his thick neck. He drank from a pint glass as he checked out the waitress's butt.

Val's mother, Aurora, was a pinched-faced, petite woman. Her orange and green dress which showed off her tanned skin and slim frame, but her shoulders hunched. She drank white wine from a large glass, and the bottle rested on ice beside the table.

Val and her parents sat in tense silence as the hostess led me to the table.

Val stood with a smile. "Evan, you remember my parents." She tucked her hand around my elbow, molding herself to my side.

I stood straighter as Matt rose and extended his hand. "Nice to see you again."

Matt gripped my hand, clasping hard and turning my wrist down in a power move. I could have stopped him, but I played the good boyfriend card and let him win.

Moving around the table, I took Aurora's hand. "Mrs. Bellini, you and Val could be sisters."

Aurora nodded, searching my face and finally giving me a tight smile. "Do call me Aurora."

I was barely seated when Matt spoke. "I knew a Greg Shurdan in Yale. Any relation?"

I shook my head.

"That was Gregory Shrordan, dear. I don't believe we know any Shurdans." Despite the streaks of silver in her dark hair, Aurora could have passed for forty, if not for the deep grooves around her mouth, which deepened with every frown.

Val whispered in my ear. "My parents always search for social connections. Ignore them."

Matt finished his drink and gestured for the waitress to bring two more.

"My family is from North Carolina, but I do have an uncle who went to Harvard," I said with a small smile.

"Oh?" Aurora brightened. "Where in North Carolina?"

"The western part of the state in the mountains, close to Asheville."

"The Biltmore Estate is in Asheville. Such a shame they opened the house to the public."

I smiled as charmingly as possible. "Cornelia Vanderbilt's decision to open the house to tours during the Great Depression saved both the house and the town." No one grew up in the area without knowing about the history of one of the largest mansions in America.

"A great tax write-off, too." Matt burped.

The waitress brought the pints, and Matt gestured for me to take one.

An awkward silence descended over the table as I sipped the bitter lager. Being an only child must be rough for Val. My siblings bickered and teased so much dinner was never this quiet.

Trying to fill the gap, I turned to Val. "How was your day?"

She slipped her hand from mine to gesture with excitement. "My classes discussed checks and balances and why we need that system. The kids got it."

"You should be proud. It's a tough concept."

She nodded. "One of my kids compared it to having your parents looking over your shoulder, ready to ground you if you stepped out of line."

Aurora finished off her red wine. "Be a dear and pour me another glass." She gestured toward the bottle next to me.

I took the bottle out of the ice and refilled her glass. Aurora ogled my upper body as I reached across the table to pour.

I felt a bit like a deer caught in the sights of a cougar. Family dinner took on a whole new meaning.

She took a long sip and said, "Valentine, you're wasting your potential as a public-school teacher."

The disdain in Aurora's voice spoke volume.

Val sighed. "I disagree."

"Education needs qualified professionals with kindness and patience." I intervened. "Your daughter is an excellent teacher. The parents and students love her."

Matt's steely eyes scoured over me. "Are you ready to settle down and marry, Evan? Have kids?"

I paused. "Um..."

"Don't start on him, Dad," Val said.

Matt took Aurora's left hand. The diamond on her finger gleamed as big as a grape. The prisms it created in the candlelight could blind someone. "Marriage is a blessing."

The Bellini's opulent wealth made me uneasy. The strength of my parents' marriage was based on mutual respect and caring.

Matt's words interrupted my thoughts. "We want you settled before it's too late."

Val glared at her father. "Too late for what?"

"You're thirty. Time's ticking."

Val clenched her hands, her knuckles white. "You just met Evan, and you're already harassing him."

Matt shrugged. "Being direct saves time."

Val turned to me with desperation in her eyes. "I'm sorry about this. How was your day?"

Without thinking, I answered, "The boys were full of themselves, showboating for the girls."

Matt and Aurora squinted at me. Under the table, Val's hand squeezed my thigh.

Fuck. I'm supposed to be a contractor, not a teacher.

I cleared my throat and continued, "I keep reminding the men of proper workplace etiquette. No whistling and catcalling. We could be sued."

Matt relaxed back in his seat. "Employees are a challenge."

Hearing my father's voice in my head, I said, "It's impossible to build a house without a team, though."

"I'd love to see your operation sometime. I'm always looking for new investment opportunities."

I was an ant under a magnifying glass. My cheeks burned as I glanced at Val. She opened her mouth to speak, but Aurora beat her to the punch.

"How did you two meet?"

Val's gaze flew to mine. Thank God for the review games.

"At a fundraiser for the school." My voice rose an octave as I lied. Pretty soon I'd be doing a Michael Jackson impersonation. "I, uh, donated five thousand toward a home remodel to the silent auction and wanted to check the bids."

"We kept outbidding each other on an item, and we met after I won." Val picked up her water, gulping it down.

"What did you win?" Aurora asked. She smiled, but it didn't quite make it to her eyes.

Val sucked water into her windpipe, coughing and gasping for breath.

Patting Val on the back, I said, "She stole a year's gym membership out from under me."

Aurora snickered. "You must be joking. Valentine would never exercise."

Val straightened. "I bought it for a friend's birthday."

"For Audrey?" She snorted. "I doubt that. She's as allergic to exercise as you are."

"For your information, Audrey and I went to a studio class the other week."

Seizing on this seemingly innocent topic of conversation, I pressed her for more details. "Oh? Where?"

"It's a small woman-owned business called Polar Vortex. It's an all-women's gym. We took a ... strength and balance class."

"Isn't that a—" Val kicked me under the table. I guess pole dancing wasn't on the list of approved topics of conversation.

Aurora's gazed bounced back and forth from Val to me. Her hazel eyes sharpened with hawk-like accuracy. "Why would you bid on a women's gym membership, Evan?"

She had me there. I searched for a believable response while sweat pooled at the base of my spine. "I enjoy competitive bidding."

Snickering, Matt said, "You drove up the price on that membership, so Val would get hot and bothered." He lifted his beer. "Evan, I like your style."

He liked my style? The one where I enjoyed pissing off women?

Matt reached into his breast pocket and pulled out a business card. "Call me if you want to take your business to the next level."

Taking the card, I read, "Hedge Funds, huh?"

He finished off his drink, setting his glass down with a thump. "Now, I know what you're thinking."

That unregulated hedge fund scheming led to the latest real estate market crash?

Matt continued before I could respond. "You want to know how you can get in on it."

Val groaned. "Dad, stop."

"How much capital do you have floating around? Put up a hundred thousand, and I can guarantee a two hundred and fifty percent return over the next three years. How's that sound?"

Impossible? Hard to believe? Incredibly unlikely?

I kept my voice neutral. "That sounds interesting, sir."

"Call me, Matt, please." He puffed up, smiling like a shark anticipating a fresh kill.

I took a sip of my mostly full beer. There was no way I'd give Matt any money, even pretend money.

"I invest most of my capital back into my own company and its workers. Sad as it makes me, I can't take you up on your generous offer."

Matt's eyes narrowed, his face sour.

"We should order," Val suggested.

The waitress appeared and recited the specials. After ordering the fresh Cobia with asparagus and rice pilaf, I glanced at my watch.

Five thirty? Were we stuck in a time loop?

An hour later, my head was ready to explode. My face and neck were tight from smiling. I'd pushed the food around the plate, my appetite destroyed by inane chit-chat.

We'd discussed garden clubs, the latest stock market crash, and their choice of political candidate.

Aurora shared a summary of her latest book club novel, *Wanted for Pleasure*, including the sex scenes.

I'd caught the ladies at the adjacent table listening to the description of the Earl of Mountbatten's bulging manflesh and his paramour's glistening honey pot. They'd blushed like virgins, tittering behind their hands even though they had to be in their eighties.

As the waitress cleared the plates, Matt switched to bourbon. Aurora finished the bottle of wine.

"How are they getting home?" I whispered to Val.

"Chauffeur." She mouthed back.

Who had a chauffeur these days? Was I in *Downton Abbey*?

Matt belched again, covering his mouth afterward. "Before we wrap up, how serious are you about my girl?"

Val closed her eyes, shaking her head in silent exasperation.

I fiddled with my tie. The picture of an awkward boyfriend. "Very serious."

"What do you find appealing about her?"

Shocked, I stared at him. Was he intentionally being an asshole?

Val needed a protector, a fucking hero, to rescue her from this farce. I needed to get my head in the game and do my job.

"She's optimistic and finds the bright side on the worst day, and she's kind and compassionate. When she works with students, she lights up. We have a lot in common."

Aurora cupping her hands over her mouth and whisper-shouting to Matt. "He's hooked."

Matt leaned toward her. "Logan's a better match."

"We're both here." Val's cheeks burned with embarrassment.

"Sometimes you have to hear the truth," Matt snapped.

Imagining myself tipping over the table and lunging for Matt. I even heard the satisfying crunch of my fist breaking his nose. I'd whisk Val away before the police came, and we'd run away to the Maldives.

Instead, I counted to ten, reigning in my anger. "I've met Logan. Val deserves better."

"If you love Valentine, Evan," Aurora began. "You should propose, and we can have you married by May."

"Why, Mom?" Val's voice rose with frustration. "Tell me what's really going on."

Aurora's eyes met Matt's, his frown making her turn away. Matt shook his head. Val was right. There was something going on between them.

Matt folded his arms. "It's simple. You're getting older, and we want grandchildren."

"I know there's more." Val's eyes spit fire at her father. Why weren't you demanding grandkids a year ago? Why did you try to take my money?"

Aurora took the lead. "A teacher's salary is not sustainable for your lifestyle. You need a man to take care of you."

"I've taken care of myself for years, Mom."

Matt scoffed. "You've dipped into your grandmother's trust more than once."

"Who cares? There's enough money to live on for the rest of my life in that trust. I can splurge now and then."

"It's irresponsible. I've told your mother we should take legal action to become guardians to protect the trust from your recklessness."

Val's bitter laugh rang out, drawing the attention of the other diners. "Good luck! It's all in my name. Admit it. You want to invest it in a pie in the sky scheme."

Aurora's face grew pale. She reached blindly for Matt's arm. Her fingers white against his blue shirt.

Matt's face reddened, and he drained another glass of beer.

Val's fingers tightened on my leg. "I'm right, aren't I? You and Logan want the money Gran gave me. Well, it's my money and I refuse to give it to you."

"Hush, Valentine," Matt growled. "It's not polite to talk money over dinner."

Val snorted in disbelief. "I think we're done here."

Picking up her tiny gold purse, Val stood like Aphrodite rising in a sea of golden foam. She reached her hand toward me. "Are you ready to go?"

I'd heard women radiated beauty when they were furious, but I'd never witnessed it until now. Val glided like a goddess through the tables. The glow of her skin, heightened by the gold shimmers of her dress, drew every eye.

Stopping to get Val's coat, I texted the valet. She stood silently beside me, her sculpted expression giving no indication of the rage that seethed inside.

When my truck arrived, Val yanked open the door and disappeared inside before I could help her. The door slammed shut in my face.

The valet gave me an expression of sympathy as I tipped him and slipped behind the wheel.

Driving away from the hotel, I glanced at her. "Where can I take you?"

"Home." she snapped as I pulled out of the lot.

I'd only driven a mile before due turned in her seat and glared at me.

Not sure what was coming, I waited. It didn't take long.

"Why did you say that stuff?" She growled like an angry tiger.

Thinking back, I couldn't remember anything I'd said to elicit this response. "I need context."

"'Val's so optimistic and great at her job. Everyone loves her.'" Her mocking impersonation hurt a little. "Why would you say that?"

Since when is it bad to compliment someone?

I shrugged. "It's true."

Teeth bared; she pounded her fist on the armrest. "You don't know anything about me."

That didn't seem fair. I'd spent time getting to know her. Both physically and emotionally. "I thought we were friends."

Waving her fists, she yelled. "But they think you're in love with me!"

I like to think of myself as a calm, rational person, but this illogical attack was getting under my skin. My hands tightened on the steering wheel. "Wasn't that the point? I'm your fake boyfriend."

"Yes." She pounded her fist on the door again. "No, I don't know, Evan!"

Frustrated, I lashed out. "You're blowing this out of proportion."

Val's body twisted toward me, and I wished I'd stayed silent. "How dare you!"

"What the hell does that mean?"

"Don't yell at me!"

"I'm not yelling," I said through clenched teeth.

She lifted her face to the roof and screamed in fury.

Turning into a grocery store parking lot, I parked near the back, so I didn't run my truck off the road.

She had every right to be angry, but taking it out on me seemed fruitless. I was already on her side.

Beside me, Val vibrated with anger. In the glow of a streetlight, I could see her left eye twitching. Her leg jerked up and down as she tapped her foot with her arms clasped tightly over her chest.

"Are you okay?"

"No." Folding over, she put her arms over her head. Her shoulders shook with sobs.

Eventually, her body stilled, and the tension drained out of her. I wanted to rub her back, soothe her, but I knew better than to touch her without permission.

"What can I do?" I asked, ready to slay dragons for her.

She sat up and wiped tears from her cheeks. "I'm fine. Please, just take me home."

Five minutes later, I parked in front of her apartment. She stared out the window, not moving.

Opening my door, I walked around to her side. "Come on, I'll walk you to your door."

She slid out, walking like a ghost beside me, her face damp and pale.

At the door, she turned to me. "I'm so sorry. I made a terrible mistake dragging you into this."

"We'll figure it out."

It struck me that every time she let me off the hook, instead of running, I promised to help.

Just a few days ago, I'd convinced myself that between Yona and school, I was too busy to get involved. My plate overflowed, and my sanity was regularly tested.

Now that I'd seen the level of crazy Val dealt with, did I really want to get in deeper? And how exactly could I help her with her money problems and parent issues?

My family joked that I have a Superman Complex, but it was a condition I struggled with. As a kid, I rescued wild animals. In school, I stood up to bullies. I got in fights defending a girl's honor. I couldn't help myself.

When Dad was sick, my family relied on me to change my plans and help with the business. The pressure of holding it all together required a heroic effort.

And when I finally thought it was my turn to live my life, Noah died. I pledged myself to help Yona, Jacy, and Fala.

And now I was doing it again.

Val's voice startled me. "I appreciate everything, Evan. But this is my problem. I'll figure it out on my own."

As much as I wanted to fight it or dismiss it. I was a Superman. Rescuing people was inherent inside me. Something I had to do.

But I hesitated too long.

Val slipped inside before I could find the words to bind myself to her and closed the door behind her.

Chapter 14
Evan

After school, I changed into sweats and running shoes, planning to head to Firehouse Gym and lift weights. The whole day had been one long fuck up after another, and I needed to blow off some steam before going home.

My classes focused on career planning, architectural design, safety, tools, and machine use. That's right, I showed eleven to thirteen-year-olds how to safely use saws and power drills. Most people think I'm crazy. Aside from the headaches I get from listening to thirty students hammer, I loved it.

Today was a whole other jar of nails though. Tossing my school clothes into a duffel, I stuffed my laptop into my backpack along with a stack of papers to grade.

The seventh-grade class just completed mockups for bat houses, which would be hung in the trees around the school. They'd researched local bat species and designed houses which would appeal to them. We'd produce the best two designs, so I had to study the plans tonight before making my learning goals for tomorrow.

Jogging into the main hallway, I caught sight of Val. She was with Audrey and Rachel, walking toward the exit together. All three were beautiful women, but my eyes zeroed in on Val. Her long ponytail swayed back and forth across her upper back, and I followed it like an arrow down to her curves.

We hadn't spoken since dinner from hell, but she haunted me. The quirky, sexy woman, who didn't want strings had wrapped them around my heart, anyway. I thought about her all the time: in bed, in the shower, while drinking coffee, or eating lunch.

I missed her. I'd considered calling her but hadn't known how to bridge the gap. Seizing the opportunity to catch her before she left, I started to call out, but Bobby, Oz, and Keith appeared out of a side hall and intercepted me.

"Hey," Oz called out. "You leaving?"

"Today was stressful, so I'm squeezing in a workout," I said.

Bobby nodded. "The unannounced fire drill as the kids came in riled up everyone."

"And then the Wi-Fi crashed," Oz sighed. "Half of my lesson depended on internet access."

"Marnie's teen living class tripped a circuit breaker by setting all the ovens to broil," I added. "I didn't have power for most of the day."

I eased past them, hoping to catch Val in the parking lot. "I'll catch you guys later."

I didn't get far. Keith said, "She's busy tonight."

I stopped. Was I that obvious? "Who?"

"Rachel, Audrey, and Val are cooking dinner," Oz said. "They told me not to come home before six."

"Wanna join us?" Bobby asked. She opened the door, holding it for the guys.

"Sure," I said, changing gears and following them into the deserted gym. I set my bag on the bleachers and stretched my tense muscles.

Bobby and Keith began a game of HORSE, challenging each other to shoot from different angles. Their trash talk was as outrageous.

"That's some weak sauce, Bobby," Keith teased. "All water, no meat."

"Save your trash talk for someone who cares." Bobby grunted as she hooked the basketball toward the net. It rolled around the rim and went in. "You couldn't make that basket into the ocean if you were standing on the beach."

"Ignore the idiots," Oz said.

"They're hilarious." I chuckled, stretching my hamstrings.

He sat on the floor to stretch his legs, pausing to study me. "You know, Audrey and Val have no secrets."

"Must be awkward for your sex life."

Oz barked out a laugh. "I've got mad skills. Nothing to be self-conscious about."

"Did Audrey mention that Val froze me out?"

"It was a topic of conversation." Oz jogged in place.

"Any conclusions?" I asked.

"My take is Val's a firecracker, and her parents drive her insane. You got caught in the crosshairs."

Pretty accurate.

Bobby and Keith concluded their game and joined us, grabbing water and guzzling it down.

"What are you two whispering about?" Bobby sat on the bleachers near us.

"If I were to guess," Keith capped his bottle and set it on the stands. "I'd say they're talking about women."

"The blind leading the blind." Bobby arched her brow. "Val's been pissy lately. How'd you fuck up, Evan?"

I grabbed the ball off the floor and hurled it toward the hoop.

"I didn't fuck up," I said as it swished through the net.

Keith whistled and retrieved the ball. He passed it to Oz. "Val's story differs."

Pivoting, Oz looked for an opening, but I blocked the shot. In possession, I turned and tossed it toward the goal. It bounced off the rim with a clank.

"What did she say?"

"I heard from Rachel that the fake relationship was a bust." Keith sunk the ball.

Recovering it, Bobby asked, "The parents hated you?"

"They drank like fish and asked a ton of questions. Her dad tried to get me to invest in his hedge funds and informed me he liked Logan better."

Keith made a layup. "They still want her to marry that pompous jerk?"

Since I'd had time to visualize the bigger picture, my gut warned that Val's parents were up to something. Her dad especially came off as selfish and greedy. I couldn't tell if her mom was complicit or just wrapped up in her own miserable reality.

"Val's known Logan since birth. He's the son of her parents' best friends." I recovered the ball and passed it to Bobby.

She passed to Oz. "I'm sure someone could say the same about Jeffrey Dahmer."

"Val's father is more like Bernie Madoff." Oz missed the basket and jogged after the ball.

"Serial killers and swindlers. Dinner sounds like a kick in the nuts." Keith winced.

"Val got steamed, and we walked out. Then she was pissed at me because I was too nice." I stole the ball out of Oz's hands.

He blocked my run on the basket. "Audrey says her parents bought your act too well."

"Huh?" I asked.

"Your act was too perfect. They think you're rich and in love," He continued, sinking a free throw. "Now, you're another horse in the race, and her mom is pressuring Val to choose."

Anger spiked through me. How could two adults be so blind to the kind, caring daughter they raised? All they saw was a pawn to use for their own needs.

But what could I do? Val pushed me away, determined to handle it on her own, and maybe that was for the best. I certainly had enough of my own shit to deal with.

We transitioned into a two-on-two game. Playing hard, I suspected we all tried to outrun our own concerns. Though we kept the ball moving, Keith and I were no match for Oz and Bobby. When the score reached thirty to twelve, I lay down on the court. My heart pounded from the constant turnovers.

Bobby crowed, "Y'all better hit the showers 'cuz your game stinks." Despite the trash talk, she sat down next to me, breathing hard.

"Damn, y'all brought game today." Keith panted.

Oz wiped sweat off his brow with the edge of his shirt. "Keith, your game is like one of your texts to an ex-girlfriend—hopeless, pitiful, and blocked."

I sat up. "Ouch. Anyone wanna grab a beer at Barrel before going home? I'll buy."

"I can't," Bobby said. "I have to go help Mel. We're painting the living room tonight."

"Why not wait until Spring Break?" Keith asked.

"Because we're painting the rest of the house, then."

"When's the big move?" Keith slipped sweats over his shorts.

"We've booked the truck for the last Saturday of Spring Break. I've procrastinated, so Mel's riding my ass."

"Rain check then," I said, picking up my stuff.

Bobby nodded. "Any time after next week."

Wow, the first week of April had snuck up on me. "That's right! School's out next week." The idea of a whole week off filled me with joy.

"How could you forget? I've had a countdown going since the Winter Carnival." Keith smiled. "Break can't come soon enough."

"You're traveling?" I asked.

"Hell, yeah. I'm going home to visit my family in Louisiana and get drunk with my high school friends."

Oz said, "You're getting too old for that crap."

"Speak for yourself, Grandpa." Keith slapped Oz on the back. "What are you doing? Hanging out at home, having sex morning, noon, and night?"

"Sounds pretty good," I nodded.

"Sometimes you make an old dog like me jealous," Keith agreed.

"Damn right, I do," Oz laughed.

Bobby asked, "What about you, Evan? Any big plans?"

"It's my *Elisi's* ninetieth birthday. I'm going home for the party."

"Val said something about going with you."

I shook my head. "We haven't spoken in a week, so I bet that doesn't happen."

Bobby clapped a hand on my shoulder. "Take the bull by the horns, man."

What the hell did that mean?

"Val was very explicit before she shut her door in my face. She didn't need my help."

Oz rolled his eyes. "Figure it out. All I know is when Val's unhappy, it makes Audrey mad as hell."

"I don't even know what happened."

Keith laughed. "No man ever does. Women are insane."

Bobby punched Keith on the arm. "Women are enchanting and mysterious."

Keith rubbed his arm, snickering. "That's what I meant."

"Don't listen to this idiot. You need to validate her feelings," Bobby said.

"Like for parking?" Keith snickered.

Bobby glared at him. "This is why you aren't in a relationship."

"I could be if I wanted to be."

"Doubtful."

Thinking back, I'd tried to listen and understand Val's reactions, but she'd thrown it all in my face. I'd played the role just as she'd coached me, but it wasn't good enough.

People expected me to jump in and save them. Yona and my students depended on me. Even my parents relied on me, but Val had told me to back off.

"She didn't want me to fix her problems?" I asked.

Bobby snorted. "Men always want to fix shit. Val's a grown woman, capable of solving her problems. You just need to listen."

Driving home in my truck, Bobby's words rang in my ears.

Yona asked for my advice. Her grief was so huge it incapacitated her at times, and she couldn't more forward without assistance.

Despite all her problems, Val didn't need a hero to sweep her off her feet. She was strong. What if Bobby was right, and she'd rather have a sounding board?

Using hands-free calling, I rang her number. When she didn't pick up right away, I prepared to leave a message.

"Hello?" Val sounded breathless, like she'd run to answer the call. Music played in the background, and I could hear women singing along.

"Hey."

"Hi."

Her voice was strained, as if she were unsure if she wanted to speak with me. Doubt crept in. I should invent an excuse and hang up.

I heard Audrey's voice in the background. "It's about time he called."

Flowers by Miley Cyrus reached the chorus, and I could hear Rachel singing along.

"I'm cooking dinner at Audrey's," she said apologetically.

"Yeah? What's on the menu?"

"My Gran's Sunday sauce and fresh pasta."

My stomach growled at the thought of rich meat marinara over homemade pasta. "You're busy. I'll call you later."

"Invite him over!" Rachel yelled over the music.

I heard a muffled conversation which ended with Val asking, "Do you want to come over for dinner?"

"I'm drooling at the thought of Sunday sauce. Thank you for the invitation, but I'm ripe from shooting hoops, and I have to grade some projects for tomorrow."

"Okay," she said.

The music switched to Beyoncé's *Irreplaceable*, and the silence grew between us on the phone. Awkwardly, I said, "The kids designed bat houses."

"Fat?" she asked, confused. "The sauce is pretty rich."

"Bats," I yelled.

"Bats? Why would I cook bats?"

I smothered a laugh. "I'll let you get back to the fun. I'll talk to you later."

"Wait!" I heard rustling as she walked a little farther away. "Can you hear me?"

"Sure can."

"I wanted to apologize for Friday."

"That's not necessary. You warned me."

"My parents..."

"Don't apologize for things outside your control."

The seconds ticked by.

I heard Audrey say, "Talk to him."

Then Rachel muttered, "He's not a mind reader."

Val cleared her throat. "If not my parents, then I should apologize for my reaction to them. They pluck my every nerve, and I took my frustration out on you. I'm very sorry."

I eased to a stop in my driveway and parked. "It happens. Parents are the bane of every child's existence."

"Mine ruin everybody's good time."

Her soft sigh connected with the ache in my chest. Her sorrow leached across the phone lines.

"Did I make it worse?"

She paused again. I heard laughter and pots clanking.

Audrey called, "My hands ache from kneading these dough balls."

"Val told us to keep going until our arms were like limp noodles," Rachel whined.

I couldn't help laughing. "Are you having pasta al fornication over there?"

Val stifled a chuckle. "No."

"Cunni-linguine?"

"Ew, stop," she demanded, even as the lightness of her voice returned.

"Okay, I won't suggest penne-tration."

"Oh my God, Evan. You were a perfect gentleman the other night, but your puns stink."

"No one's perfect."

"Well, I've never had a man pay such close much attention to me."

"Those guys were idiots," Audrey called.

I agreed. What other kinds of assholes had she dated? "If the men you dated didn't want to learn everything there is to know about you, they're fools."

"My dad, too," she continued. "He doesn't see me or my mom as long as we show up for parties or client dinners."

Audrey called out. "I'm done kneading the balls."

I snickered. "Is Oz home already?"

"Ignore her," Val said.

"I'm trying."

Val snorted. "I thought I knew the boundaries of our relationship. No strings, and fun times, right? On Friday night, you knew the right answers. Having you by my side felt perfect, and for a minute, I forgot it was all a lie. It freaked me out."

Her words eased the sore spots around my heart and hope bloomed in the tiny cracks. It sounded like she might like me a little.

What if I told her how much I like her?

Instead, I joked. "So, you're saying I need to rein it in?"

"Yeah," she said, then laughed. I savored the sound.

"I'll practice being a terrible date. How about I burp, show up late, and forget your birthday? Will that make us okay?"

I imagined the smile on her face. "Sounds great."

I sighed in relief.

"Y'all made up yet?" Audrey yelled. "I'm hungry."

Val shushed her friend. Then asked, "What time are you picking me up on Sunday?"

"Uh, what?"

"What time do we leave for Asheville?"

My heart stuttered. I assumed she would bail out of the trip. "You still want to go?"

"You suffered through dinner and my crazy reaction. And I still owe you that favor."

I rubbed the back of my neck, not sure what to say. Of course, I wanted her to come, but could I handle being close to her for that long without my feelings taking over?

"I figured you wouldn't..."

Her soft voice filtered down through the phone line. "I want to go."

Part of me wanted to pump my fist in the air while another cautioned I tread carefully.

"I'd planned to leave early. Is eight, okay?"

"Sure. How many days am I packing for?"

"Her birthday is Tuesday, and so is the party. I told my mom I'd leave Wednesday."

"Easy enough. One last question. What kind of party is it? How should I dress?"

This question was beyond me.

"Wear what you want."

Audrey shouted, "Give her specifics, or she'll bring her whole closet."

"Do you have us on speakerphone?"

"Audrey is fluent in my body language."

"Uh, okay. I'm wearing dress slacks, a button-up shirt and a tie. Does that help?"

"No sports coat or suit?"

"No."

"Sneakers or dress shoes?"

"Is this a quiz, Gorgeous?"

"I need to know."

"Ahh, Dress shoes?"

"Okay, I can work with that. I'll see you tomorrow at school, and I'll bring you leftovers. Good luck with the bat houses."

I sat in my truck for as the darkness grew around me. For the first time in days, the world felt back on its axis, and yet it spun faster around me.

I was grateful I'd spoken to Val, but now we were off on another tangent. She wasn't my girlfriend, but she was coming home to meet my family. They'd have expectations because I'd never brought a woman home with me.

But more importantly, how would I hide my growing feelings from Val?

Chapter 15
Val

Sunday morning, I zipped my suitcase closed as the doorbell rang. I slipped on my rose Clark's loafers that I'd paired with distressed jeans and a lightweight green sweater.

I glanced in the mirror for the twentieth time. I looked fine, but the nerves plaguing me on the inside didn't show on the outside. I'd been up for hours, unable to sleep from worrying.

A five-hour ride in the car, followed by entire days with Evan's family? I wasn't ready, but I owed him.

Of course, I could tell him I'd come down with a cold. One white lie, and I could cuddle in bed, watch movies, teach myself how to knit, or work on my art. The possibilities were endless.

Stiffening my spine, I clasped the handle of my rolling suitcase, grabbed the garment bag, and hurried to the front door.

"Hi," I said, taking in Evan's long frame in jeans and a gray fisherman's sweater.

The cables and knots in the fabric emphasized the strength of his muscles, and I itched to trace the stitching and across the warm skin underneath. A tightness grew in the pit of my belly and between my legs. I said I wanted a platonic friendship, and here I was drooling over him.

Should I ask if he'd be up for a Spring Break fling?

Evan cleared his throat. "Good to see you, too."

Heat flooded my face as my gaze jerked away from the zipper of his jeans. "Uh, sorry. I'm running behind."

His eyes sparkled with humor. "There's always time for you to check me out."

Struggling to find my balance, I noticed the time. "Oops. You wanted to leave at eight. It's ten after."

His lips quirked. "Are you always like this in the morning?"

Horny? No, that's all because of you. "Late?" I choked out instead.

Leading him into my apartment, I stepped back, giving myself space. This man was the banana to my cream pie. The eggplant in my lasagna.

I needed a distraction,

I hurried into the kitchen to fill my water bottle. "Waking up is my nemesis. I have four alarms set."

He leaned against the door jamb, his smoky eyes watching me.

Awkwardness washed over me. I let out a high-pitched giggle. "Crazy, right?"

He cocked his head to one side. "Methodical, not crazy. It works for you."

"Great answer." I mimed checking off an item on a clipboard. "You passed."

His slow grin transformed his face, lighting up his eyes. "I get excellent performance reports."

A small dimple appeared below his left cheek. My insides melted. Shaking off the desire to tackle him to the ground, I said, "I'm ready."

"Is this another test?" His deep voice rumbled low in his chest and a fire lit in his eyes.

We really needed to get in the car, or I would jump him and screw all regrets.

Pasting a bright smile on my face, I replied, "Nope. Ready to leave.

Tossing my garment bag over his shoulder, he lifted my suitcase with a grunt. "What's in this?"

I followed him out of my house and locked the door. "My clothes, flannel jammies, three possible dresses, and—matching shoes."

"Three?"

"Be careful," she scowled, lifting her pretend clipboard. "This is another test."

He shrugged. "I thought you'd have more."

Stowing my suitcase behind the passenger seat, he hung the garment bag on the hook over the door.

Cocoa couldn't contain her joy. I patted her head, and her tail wagged with doggie delight. "I didn't want to crowd the sweet lady."

In the truck, Cocoa scrambled over the armrest, landing on my lap. Her soft body vibrated with joy.

"I hope you don't mind riding with her. My mom would cry if I didn't bring her home for a visit."

Evan reached around me to pick her up, but I shooed him away. "I love dogs. I've wanted to get a pet forever, but my apartment has stupid rules.

"Cocoa, mind your manners."

Her soulful brown eyes promised she'd be good. Tucking in her short legs, she lay her head on my knee.

Evan shut the passenger door. He came around the front and slid behind the wheel.

"Are you going to let me drive your truck?" I asked innocently, even though it was another test. Men and their trucks were weird and letting me drive would mess up all his settings, mirrors, and whatnot.

Evan shrugged. "Sure, if you want."

"You don't want to ask if I can handle it?"

"Can you?"

"Of course. It's a pickup, not a helicopter."

"Okay." He jingled the keys. "You want the first or second shift?"

"Second."

"Sure thing, Gorgeous." He started the engine, pulled out of the parking lot, and headed for Route 58.

Settling back into the comfortable seat, I watched the bare trees fly by. Spring break arrived early this year, only a few days into April.

Puffy white clouds raced across the sunny blue sky despite the chilly temperature. Cocoa licked me before falling asleep while I stroked her back.

Evan gestured toward the speakers. "Do you have a genre preference?"

"Music chameleon, remember? What do you like?"

"I've got some eighties and nineties stuff on Spotify, mostly rock."

"That's fine," I said. "Quick question: Do you name your playlists?"

"What do you mean?"

"This guy I dated a while back had one called 'Proud and You Know It.'"

"What? Was he gay?"

"No, but he sympathized with the movement."

"Why did you break up with him?"

I scowled at his profile. "How do you know I broke up with him? He could've broken my heart."

He sent me a doubtful glance.

"Okay, you're right. I broke up with him because he had dresses in his closet."

"He was a Drag Queen."

"Nope." I shook my head. "Married."

"Fuck." Despite the curse, his voice resonated with sympathy.

"I spilled wine on my blouse during dinner, and he offered me one of his wife's."

"What a piece of trash."

"I couldn't agree more."

He reached over and took my hand, bringing it over to rest on his leg.

I wanted to run my hand across the soft denim of his jeans. It was a struggle, but I kept my hand still. "So, do you?"

"Do I what?"

"Name your playlists?"

He shrugged and gestured to his phone, so I took it out of the cubby. Clicking on the app, I found his favorites.

I giggled, "One's called Fuck Off."

"For the drive home after a shitty day."

I nodded. Every teacher needed scream-o-songs for those days. "What about G?"

"For use in the classroom. No curse words or sexy overtones."

"G-Rated. Love it. How about Play These if you Want to Get Fired?"

"Self-explanatory."

"Okayy." I scrolled further down. "Ooh, I like this one: Highway Stuff. Is this Road Trip music?"

"Play it and see."

"What if it's your sexy playlist?"

"Why would I call it Highway Stuff?"

"Perhaps you're camouflaging it."

"From who?"

"I dunno, Evan. Yourself?

He waggled his eyebrows. "If I had a sexy one, I'd call it Beats for the Sheets."

"Ermagod." I snorted so hard Cocoa woke, licking my face and making me laugh harder.

By the time I recovered, the dog had abandoned me for the backseat. Evan merged onto the Interstate as Steppenwolf's *Born to be Wild* blasted through the speakers.

I shifted in my seat. "How much longer?"

"What, are you eight?" His deep, easy-going chuckle caused my heart to leap, expanding in my chest.

"It's a legitimate question."

He rolled his eyes. "Four hours and forty-five minutes."

"I'm going to have to pee before we get there."

He switched lanes to pass a car. "No problem. Just let me know."

"I might get hungry, too."

"I have snacks, but we can stop somewhere."

"I'll probably fall asleep."

"Do you snore?"

"No." I swatted his arm. "It's a habit from childhood. Mom loves to tell people how much I cried as a baby and hated naps. Nothing worked except putting me in a car. To this day, the hum and the movement of the car knocks me out."

"If you fall asleep, I'll pull over and draw a penis on your forehead."

"Then I'll meet your parents with hairy testicles on my forehead. And your Gran. I'd never wash it off, and everyone would see how you branded me.

He pinched his nose and rubbed his forehead. "You win."

"It wasn't a contest."

"Name your prize anyway."

I snuggled back into the seat, closing my eyes. "Tell me about your family."

"Mom is registered with the Cherokee Nation. She works in an indigenous art gallery called *Tocoa*, which means beauty. She oversees designing and running the shows. You know the wine and cheese nights where people talk nonsense about the meaning of art?"

"Sounds fun."

"She thinks so. You already know that my dad is a contractor. He builds houses and renovates historic structures. Shurdan and Sons is busy year-round."

"He wanted you to work with him."

"Felix, Gennie, and I worked there every summer. I came back after I graduated from college and worked there full time. I didn't mind it, but I wanted to try something different."

Her face said she totally understood. "You'd rather teach kids how to use tools and build things for themselves."

He smiled. "Yeah."

"What about your siblings?"

"My little sister, Gennie, is an opinionated feminist. She loves telling Felix and me that men need to wake up and admit women rule the world."

I'd always wanted a sister. Someone to talk to and tease. "She sounds fun. What does she do for a living?"

"She's a stay-at-home mom."

"My younger brother, Felix, works for the National Park Service. They move him around every year or so, but right now he's working close to home in the Smoky Mountains."

"Evan, Felix, and Gennie ... alphabetical order? Your mom should've been a librarian."

"My *Elisi* worked as a librarian before she retired. Wait till you see her. She's got the whole bun and the reading glasses style. And the stare. She can silence a room with a single scowl."

His voice sounded further and further away. My body grew heavy, and I snuggled back into the seat. Slipping into sleep, I dreamed of a large library filled with colorful books. Evan stamped library cards and checked out books while I gave him a blow job under the desk.

***

The feeling of deceleration woke me, and I peeked into the visor mirror to make sure he hadn't followed through and drawn on my forehead. All clean. I glanced at the clock, shocked to see we only had an hour left.

He exited the highway and parked in front of a rest area. I shivered in the chilly air as we walked Cocoa and took turns in the restrooms.

Back in the warm cab, he pulled out sliced apples and almond butter, dark chocolate, and red grapes from a small cooler. Munching, I settled into the driver's seat. Adjusting all the mirrors, the steering wheel, and the seat, I finally sent Evan a toothy grin.

"Ready?"

He winked, "Any time."

Before backing out, I connected my phone to his Bluetooth and cranked up my Hear Me Roar playlist. Prime for singing along.

Traveling west on Route 40, we sang along to tunes by Green Day, Madonna, and Abba. He sang well, slipping into falsetto to hit the high notes and crack me up.

As promised, he knew all the words to *I Kissed a Girl* by Katy Perry.

"What's the story there?" I asked.

"Summer camp talent show. Three of us dressed in drag and sang the whole song, complete with rocking dance moves."

"Did you win?" I smiled, trying to picture a young Evan in a dress.

"Second place. A pop-locking hip-hop routine stole first."

The hazy blue mountains in the distance grew closer with every mile. They were a welcome sight. One I had missed.

Evan bobbed his head and sang *Sweet Caroline* with Neil Diamond and me. The sun touched his dark hair with highlights of gold and made his skin glow.

A little hitch stuck in my chest. A squeeze around my heart. And lifted my hand off the wheel to rub my hand across it.

No! No, no, no, no, no,

Catching feelings for this man would end in disaster. We worked together. My family was falling apart. It would be too easy for one or both of us to get hurt.

Better to focus on the facts. This trip was quid pro quo. Paying it forward. Returning a favor. Just two friends, meeting his parents and attending his Gran's party.

I repeated the list in my head. I needed to make flashcards and study them in my spare time.

When he reached the chorus, belting out the words, my resolve melted. He was too cute, too flawless.

"You're the first man to sing along with me."

"Bum-Bum-Bum." He rocked the chorus. "What?"

I lowered the volume on the stereo. "None of my dates ever sing along. They get bored and check their phones."

"You have terrible taste in men."

Without thinking, I blurted out. "What about you?" Way to make a fool out of myself and mess this all up.

I felt his eyes studying me while I drove. "I'm exempt. Fake dates don't count, right?"

Something in his voice called to me. I didn't dare glance at him. Here in this warm bubble with his pup sleeping on the back seat ... was his heart melting, too?

I wished I could see his eyes, but I kept mine trained out the windshield. The winding road climbed up into the mountains. Pine trees crowded at the sides of the road. Little patches of snow glistened in shady places tucked under the branches.

"Our exit's coming up in two miles."

"Great," I said with false cheer. Nerves bundled in my belly. "Am I going to meet Yona?"

A beat of silence passed before he said, "She's got a list of things a mile long for me to fix. She and the girls will be at the party, too."

My mind played across the mixer board of emotions, trying to guess his tone. Was he embarrassed that I'd asked? Did he dread the two of us meeting? I couldn't tell.

"That's cool, Evan." Despite my casual response, I felt my anxiety rising. I sucked in a deep breath and let it out.

He reached over and touched my fingers on the steering wheel. "Everyone will love you."

I forced a smile. "What did you tell your parents about me?"

"Nothing. Only that I was bringing a date for the party."

"Ah, so not a surprise, but not a full debrief."

"At the time, I didn't know if you were coming, so I thought it would be better if it didn't work out. On the bright side, I didn't tell them you were a ballerina or a garbage inspector."

I winced. "Touché."

He smiled. "I couldn't resist teasing you."

I exited toward Asheville, and Evan directed me to turn up a gravel road that twisted up a mountainside.

"Almost there," he said. I could hear the excitement in his voice. He obviously adored his family and wanted to see them. A twang of jealousy thrummed in my heart.

He pointed to a long driveway leading up to the side of a large house. I pulled in next to an SUV.

Two stories high, the log house blended into the mountain and forest behind it. A porch stretched across the front, and I knew the view from the rockers would be epic. The house had a prime view of a valley and the tree-covered mountains that soared toward the sky around us.

Cocoa barked as I killed the engine. Butterflies danced inside me.

The front door opened. A short woman with Evan's black hair and coloring stepped out to join a red-headed man with Evan's smile and height. They waved.

"That's Mom and Dad," Evan said, shrugging on his jacket. Cocoa barked again, her tail whapping against the passenger door.

Frozen in the seat, my instincts begged me to drive back down the mountain and find a hotel.

Cold air whooshed in as Evan got out. Cocoa scampered over to the couple. Both lavished the dog with attention and treats. My parents would complain about getting dog hair on their clothes.

Evan came around to my side of the car. "Ready, Gorgeous?"

His calm, reassuring tone soothed my frazzled nerve endings. "Are you sure you want to do this? Lie to your family?"

"It's not a lie for me. I like you. I have for a while, and I'm glad you're here."

I shook my head, trying to process his words. "Wait! What?" My heart pounded, trying to beat right out of my chest. He liked me? He'd tossed those three words out with ease. Part of me wanted to say them back, but my throat closed, and I choked. The words stuck hard.

He lifted his arm to wave as his voice lifted to shout to his parents. "We'll be right there."

"Come on, Val, it's cold out here."

His impatience ignited a small fire in my belly, stilling the butterflies. How dare he say he liked me when I couldn't question him or debate his authenticity? I couldn't run away either. Not without stealing his truck and embarrassing myself.

Out of options, I unbuckled the seatbelt and grabbed my coat from the back seat.

Evan held out his hand, and I slipped mine into his. Twining our fingers together, he led me toward the house.

Chapter 16
Val

Putting one foot in front of the other, I followed Evan across the slate pathway toward his house.

Made of thick aged and weathered logs, the oversized cabin stretched up two stories. Bright lights shone from the windows, and a cheery wreath of pinecones and flowers decorated the front door.

I slid my hand across the backs of the rockers and Adirondacks on the porch. Two porch swings hung at each end. No matter the cold, I couldn't wait to try them out.

Evan hugged his parents, and they fawned over him before he introduced me.

"Look at you," his mom fussed. "You're too thin. And your hair is so long."

"Stop, Mom." He rolled his eyes. "You're embarrassing me."

"Should I make an appointment at the barber for you while you're here?"

Evan swung his arm around her shoulders and turned her toward me.

"Mom, Dad, this is Val Bellini."

His mom's brown eyes sparkled with curiosity. Her hair, twisted into a thick braid, touched the curve of her back. She pulled me into a hug. I breathed in the scent of cinnamon and peaches. "I'm Deyani, and this is Chris. It's so nice to meet you."

Chris shook my hand. He was tall and lean. Dressed in a cozy flannel shirt and worn jeans. "Honey, let Val come inside. It's cold out here."

Deyani stepped back. "Of course, come in. We have a fire going."

Polished wood gleamed on the floors and walls. Thick beams supported the second floor and framed the enormous river-rock fireplace. The exposed chimney ran up to the second story.

A cheerful fire crackled in front of a plush, rust-red sofa and matching set of easy chairs, which beckoned me to curl up. Thick, woven rugs littered the floor, and windows stretched wide to bring the mountains and sky inside.

Giving them time to catch up, I wandered over the large floor-to-ceiling windows that framed the mountains still dusted with snow. The stark beauty of the surroundings reminded me of my childhood home.

I'd spent much of my time alone when I wasn't at Gran's, reading or exploring nature. At school, I could be funny and popular, but I never had a best friend. No one slept over at my house or sat up all night texting me.

As an adult, I was much the same. Always friendly and approachable, but I was also reserved. I treasured my friendship with Audrey, but was never quite sure why she picked me out of the crowd.

The few relationships I'd had always ended before I really felt anything. I enjoyed going out, but my emotions had never been engaged, which is why they never lasted.

And now Evan wanted more than a friendly, no-obligation hook-up, and I didn't know how to react. I could make a joke to hide my embarrassment, but my inner loner would rather stare out the window at the lonely winter landscape.

Deyani walked up next to me. "Is everything all right, Val?

Could she see my emotions written on my face? Homesickness engulfed me, but I knew those days were gone. My Gran was gone, Audrey was engaged, and I needed to woman up on my own.

I smiled, letting the emotional mask drop down over my face. "I'm fine, just a bit tired."

Deyani studied my face for a moment and then guided me away from the window. "How was your drive?"

Evan entered through the front door with my luggage. "She slept through most of it."

"Did you bore her with your school talk?" Deyani asked.

Chris chuckled. "He never stops talking about the kids."

"Neither do I." I grinned. This conversation felt so much safer.

"You're a teacher, too?" Chris asked. He took my coat as Evan took my luggage through a door, clomping down the stairs out of sight.

"I teach Civics at the same school as Evan."

Chris walked over and took Deyani's hand. "I thought Evan and I would work together, but teaching is his calling."

Deyani nodded. "I just wish he hadn't moved so far away."

Talking about school helped me feel more balanced. "He is a wonderful teacher. The students love him."

"Well, he loves Marchfield. After meeting you, I can see why. Come, sit down."

Chris and Deyani sat in the easy chairs in front of the fire, leaving me to perch on the sofa. I heard Evan on the stairs before he entered the room.

"Your feet are so loud," Deyani said. "They're shouting at us."

Evan bent and kissed her cheek before coming to sit next to me. "Sorry, Mom."

Bowls of crackers, chips, cheese, and dips were set out on a large coffee table. My stomach growled, reminding me we'd only had snacks for lunch.

Cocoa woofed at the front door flew open and two little girls came running inside. "*Nisi! Nisi!* We're here." The girls were tiny versions of Deyani. Their round faces filled with excitement and delight.

I relaxed, slipping into the background, watching their interactions. The children were adorable and well-loved.

Deyani spread her arms wide to gather the two children in. "Hello, my precious ones."

Evan rose to help a woman carry a large suitcase and a box of toys into the house. She wore a sweater with a traditional black and white Native American diamond design on it. Even though she was taller than Deyani, the resemblance was striking.

Behind her, a blonde Norse God closed the front door and dropped another suitcase by the door. He was tall, muscular, and looked like he'd been ripped off the cover of a romance novel.

I gaped at his beauty, and when he smiled, I swore I heard angels sing.

I rose to meet them, Evan sidling up beside me. "That's Gennie's husband, Kurt."

Blinking, I looked away from Kurt. "I feel like I stared into the sun."

Evan teased, "He's from Sweden. His beauty is unfair to regular men."

Across the room, the girls played with Deyani's braids and chattered like magpies. Chris knelt and opened his arms. "Hey, now. No hugs for *Eduda?*" The little girls dashed to their grandfather for hugs and tickles.

"The little one in pink is Inola. She just turned three and the bigger one is Ama. She's almost eight."

"Thanks," I said, filing the names away.

Evan pulled me forward for introductions. "This is my bratty little sister, Gennie, and her husband."

Gennie hugged me. "Hi."

"Val says you're hurting her eyes, Kurt. Put on a hat or something," Evan suggested.

I pinched him. "If Kurt wants to dazzle me with his radiance, you stay out of it."

Kurt laughed, and I blinked. Not the deep, robust sound of a glowing god, but the he-hawing bray of a donkey erupted from his mouth.

Gennie winked at me. "Kinda takes it down a notch, doesn't it?"

The two little girls launched themselves at Evan. He gathered them close. "Hey, brats. How's it going?"

Ama gave him a stern glare from her perch on his hip. "We aren't brats."

Evan smiled. "Are you sure?"

"We're good girls. The elf told Santa, and we got presents."

"Well, then, I must be wrong. Are you butterflies instead?"

Inola wiggled to be let down. "I'm a puppy. Woof."

Evan lowered them to the floor and crouched down. "I like puppies. You know why?"

Both girls shook their heads.

"They like to chase." Evan woofed and began to chase the shrieking children around the room. Cocoa barked and trotted after them, tail wagging.

"It's always a circus," Gennie said as Kurt joined the fun, chasing his daughters. "Ama and Inola think the sunrise and sets on Evan."

"Come sit down, Gennie," Deyani called. "You must be exhausted."

Together, we walked over to join her in front of the fire. Settling onto the sofa, I said, "I love your sweater."

"It's Jamie Okuma. She's a genius with fashion."

"The design's so pretty."

"She calls it the parfleche pattern. It's named after traditional tribal rawhide bags."

We chatted a bit about shoes and fashion until the game of chase wound down, and Evan joined us. Ama climbed up into his lap and Inola plopped between Gennie and me on the sofa. Scooching close, she ran her fingers across the beaded bracelet at my wrist. Before long, she was in my lap, touching my earrings and necklace.

Gennie relaxed back into the chair with a sigh. "Is Felix here yet?"

"Not yet," Chris said. "He had some loose ends to tie up before making the drive."

Inola's warmth seeped into me as the conversation ebbed and flowed around us. We whispered together, sharing little stories about puppies as she twirled my bracelet.

Inhaling the sweet smell of her hair, I felt a pang wishing for my own baby. My eyes lifted to Evan, sitting next to me from where he and Ama made faces at one another.

He'd be a great father.

Gah, give me a little girl and a warm fire and my hormones flew out of control! Stuffing all thoughts of babies back into the depths of my mind, I focused on the conversation.

Before long, the front door banged open. A large man with flowing black hair entered. He had a backpack slung over his shoulder and wore dirty jeans and a white t-shirt. Two sleeves of tattoos ran down his arms. I could make out a wolf, howling at the moon, among a series of ceremonial patterns and designs.

Deyani rushed over to hug the man, then drew him toward the rest of us. "Val, this is my second child, Felix."

"Hi, Felix." I waved to him from under Inola, who sprawled over me, sound asleep.

"Welcome, Val." What was it with the men in this family? Felix could probably lure the animals in the forest to him, just by speaking in that low, soft voice.

Soon, everyone gathered around the fire with more snacks spread over the coffee table. They chatted about family things, birthdays, and holidays.

Conversing with my parents never left me warm and fuzzy. I remembered holidays with my Gran when things were good. Dad stopped working long enough to pay attention to me. Gran and Mom would cook together, and I'd listen to them chat. Things changed after Gran died and we moved to Richmond.

Deyani excused herself around seven to make dinner. I passed Inola to Kurt and went to see if I could help.

"How do you feel about fry bread? I don't make it often, but the kids love it."

"Is it like pancakes? Or Naan?"

"More like Naan. I've already mixed it up and patted out the rounds, but it needs to be pan-fried."

"It's like the Frittelle Gran taught me to make." I melted the shortening in a large cast iron pan.

Deyani threw in a kernel of corn. "Don't start until it pops."

Deyani moved around me, preparing the rest of the meal. "How long have you and Evan been together?"

I reminded myself to answer honestly as much as possible. "A month or so."

The kernel swelled and puffed out, flying out of the pan and over my shoulder. I picked it off the floor and tossed it in the bin before placing two dough rounds into the pan. The disks swelled in the heat, browning fast. I flipped them, waiting until both sides were golden.

"Here's the platter. Cover them with the towel so they'll stay warm," Deyani instructed.

I added more dough to the pan. "Has Evan told you anything about me?"

Deyani shook her head. "Not much. Evan always plays his cards close to his chest. He told me he'd met a teacher who was beautiful in body and spirit, and I can see he's right."

I blushed, flipping the bread over.

She continued, "He has a big heart and a penchant for helping people."

"I have first-hand experience with that. He saved me at the Winter Carnival."

"I'd love to hear what happened."

As I told Deyani the tale, it dawned on me how often Evan had saved me. He'd deflected Logan, fixed my flat tire, and landed a hand with my parents. He was Superman to my Lois Lane, always leaping in to protect me.

I needed to stay focused on reality. I was only here because Evan had needed a favor, a date for a party. I'd go home and never see these people again.

Deyani's chuckle brought me out of my thoughts. "You're lucky he was there to catch you."

"Yeah," I muttered and continued frying bread.

Deyani bustled to the table and back, carrying bowls of sauces, meats, vegetables, and sides. I added the heaping platter of bread on the table as she called everyone to eat.

Felix said a prayer of thanks. Then chaos erupted as everyone talked at once, excited to dig in.

The happy, loud family overwhelmed me. Was it a week or so ago that I was whisper-arguing with my parents in Violet's?

Evan nudged me. He held a plate of meat in a spicy red sauce. "It's venison. If you don't want to eat Bambi, you should skip it."

I'd eaten fish eggs on crackers in ballrooms, blood sausage in my uncle Vino's Italian chalet, and fatback on a trip to Charleston, South Carolina. I could handle game. "I'm trying everything."

Loading my plate full of squash, beans, fry bread, turkey, and boar, I watched Evan pile the food onto the fry bread, squeezing it in half like a fat tortilla.

Making my own, I bit into the food. Spicy and flavorful, it was like nothing I'd eaten before. When I cleaned my plate, Chris laughed.

"I like this one, Evan."

"I can't remember. Who was the last girl he dated that we all met?" Gennie teased.

"It must have been before my time," Kurt added.

Evan blushed. "I brought—"

"Yona doesn't count," Gennie interrupted.

My eyes bounced between Gennie and Evan as the food in my stomach hardened into a brick. How often had Yona been invited for dinner? Had his parents expected he would marry her someday? Evan assured me they were friends, not lovers, but that didn't mean no one had hopes of that changing.

And even if their feelings grew into something else, it didn't have anything to do with me. I wasn't Evan's girlfriend, and I never would be. Sitting here in the middle of this family proved it. We were too different.

"Oh, leave him be," Deyani scolded.

Evan cleared his throat. "It's okay. Mom. The answer is none." His eyes swept over mine. "I've never invited a woman home for dinner."

"Until now," Gennie fanned her face and sighed dramatically.

Felix caught my eye. "I hear you're directing a play."

I could've kissed Felix for changing the subject.

"It's a middle school play, full of hormonal teenagers. My job is more lion taming than directing, but we'll be able to pull it together before opening night in May."

"Evan was in several plays in high school." Chris patted his son on the back.

"I made sets and worked the lights."

"It's a team effort," I said. "Drama requires more than actors. It needs sets, costumes, and lights."

I met Evan's eyes, and he smiled.

Chris nodded. "Were you ever in any plays in high school?"

"Almost all of them."

"Really? Any great parts?" Gennie asked.

"Oh, I was never a leading lady. I excelled as the comic relief."

Chris smiled. "I bet your parents were very proud."

Dad was always too busy. I understood that he never had time for anything except work.

But Mom always promised to come to every show, and then would miss them all. Her excuses ranged from last-minute committee work to migraine headaches. The rollercoaster of hoping she would attend turned into disappointment when she didn't and hurt a hundred times more than Dad's disinterest.

I felt a little tug on my jeans and smiled into Inola's brown eyes.

"Up?"

She scrambled onto my lap, leaning her weight against my chest. Sitting among these people who loved each other, I felt a tug in my heart.

My parents threw men at me, but family dinners and small children seemed more effective.

When everyone finished eating, Chris cleared the table. The other men followed suit. I could hear them loading the dishwasher and scrubbing pots and pans while trash-talking and egging each other on.

Deyani slipped into the kitchen, returning with berry crisp and vanilla ice cream. Chris brought out bowls and spoons, and soon we were in a food utopia again. The sweet berries mixed with the soft, buttery topping and melted ice cream, and sent my taste buds soaring.

My legs were falling asleep when Kurt picked Inola up off my lap. "We usually don't let them stay up so late, but tonight was a special occasion." The little girl yawned, triggering my own.

"Are you tired, *Oginalii*?" Deyani asked me.

Whatever she'd called me was an endearment, and it cracked the wall I'd constructed around my heart.

"Getting up early, driving six hours, and eating such a wonderful meal wore me out."

Deyani hugged me. "Take her down and show her your bedroom, Evan."

Evan's eyes widened. "My room?"

"The guest room is set up for Ama and Inola. Besides, I remember what it's like to be young and in love."

Gennie passed through with plastic cups of water for the girls. "You didn't let Kurt and me sleep together until we married."

"We had an empty guest room then." Deyani shrugged.

Gennie grumbled, "It's because he's a boy, right? That's so unfair."

Feeling like I was watching a tennis match, I tried to referee. "I'd be happy to sleep on the couch."

"Oh no, Val. Gennie's being silly." Deyani cocked her head to one side and crossed her arms over her chest, daring her children to argue.

Giving in, Evan took my arm in his and led me to the stairs leading to the lower level. "This way, my lady."

He opened his bedroom door. "Are you okay with this, Val?"

Part of me wanted to protest. To go back upstairs and insist on sleeping on the couch or going to a hotel. Keeping things simple between us would be next to impossible if he and I shared a room.

On the other hand, I didn't want to cause a scene. His family welcomed me in and made me feel at home, and I didn't want to ruin it. Evan and I were mature adults. He knew I didn't return his feelings, and he was okay with it. We could share a bed.

A large handmade queen bed, covered in a blue and yellow quilt, took up most of the space. A matching chest of drawers sat in the corner. A fat glass lamp, filled with stones and shells, sat on the night table, and two bookcases under the window lured me in with books, trophies, and other treasures from his youth.

"They kept all this stuff?" My bedroom at home had been converted into my mom's office as soon as I moved out.

"Yeah, it's a shrine to my childhood." He opened another door. "But it has a private bathroom."

I peeked in at the gleaming sink and shower. "You're so lucky. I didn't get an en suite bathroom until I moved into my apartment."

"It's a funny story. When I was a kid, I was a huge slob. Gennie refused to share a bathroom with me, so when we moved here, I got this room, and she and Felix shared the other. Mom showed me how to clean it, and never set foot in it again until I went to college. She says she hired three women to help her fumigate, sanitize, and smudge sage it to get rid of the *asigna*."

"I'm guessing *asigna* means demons."

"Excellent use of context clues."

A yawn swallowed my giggle. "I'm tired."

"I spend the night on the sofa upstairs." He offered.

"We're adults, Evan. We can sleep here without having sex."

He shrugged; cheeks stained with pink.

I touched the soft quilt. Not sure why I didn't want him to sleep on the couch, I just knew I didn't want him to go.

Taking a deep breath, I said, "What side do you want?"

He blinked and stood, shoving his hands in his pockets, but not before I saw his erection. "Doesn't matter."

"Is my suitcase in here?"

He gestured to the closet.

I bent to unzip my suitcase and rummaged around for my pajamas. Evan let out a long, raspy breath, and I tilted my head over my shoulder. "Is it okay if I use the bathroom first?"

He jumped toward the hall door. "It's all yours. I'm going up to hang with Felix. I'll be down soon. Don't wait up if you're tired."

The door slammed hard behind him. Sinking down on the bed, my mind flew from one possibility to the next. Was he embarrassed to sleep with me? Did he think I'd attack him?

Or was it Yona? Despite all the evidence to the contrary, I couldn't help wondering if he hadn't told me something. Maybe he even hid it from himself.

Another crack opened in the facade I'd pasted over my feelings, but I feared examining it. If I let those feelings out, I'd get hurt. Destroyed.

I couldn't risk it.

Chapter 17
Evan

When I woke up at six the next morning, my mouth tasted terrible, and I had a headache. But those issues were nothing compared to my throbbing boner.

Val's warm length pressed against my side, her hand rested on my thigh, inches from my balls. She smelled of vanilla and cinnamon, both innocent and spicy.

I cracked one eye open as she breathed in a small, sighing snore. The sheet was shoved down, exposing miles of silky skin. Her pajamas, black skin-tight tank, and shorts melded to my bare chest, and her leg draped over mine, her foot tucked between mine.

I took a deep breath, trying to ignore the erection that tented the sweatpants that rode low on my hips.

From inside my childhood bedroom, I could hear the chatter of the girls and my parents from other parts of the house. No matter how I wanted to wake Val and have my way with her, this wasn't the time or place.

I closed my eyes, trying to relax, but the dull throb at my temples ached. Felix, my freaking little brother, had drunk me under the table last night.

At the time, it'd seemed better than lying awake next to Val, trying to keep my hands off her. But after drinking a half dozen beers, I still couldn't fall asleep on the couch in front of the dying fire.

I returned to my room around one. Easing onto the mattress and hugging the edge as far from Val as possible, I planned to stay in the Friend Zone.

I'd finally settled and was almost asleep when she swooped in like a heat-seeking missile, cuddling up with a soft sigh. I nudged her over, but in her sleep, she refused to stay on her side. I spent the rest of the night holding her, listening to her sleep sounds, and memorizing the feel of her.

Part of me regretted being honest about wanting more. Her face showed more than she thought, and I'd noticed how she had isolated herself afterward. I didn't want to do anything else that would make her uncomfortable.

Morning light filtered through the curtains, and I considered getting up and leaving Val to sleep. Shifting her over, I tried to slip out from under her.

"Where're you going?" she mumbled. Her hand trailed from one hip to the other, grazing my aching cock.

Biting back a groan, I said, "Gonna get some coffee and ibuprofen."

"What time is it?" Val stretched, yawning. Her arms rose above her head. Her soft breasts pushed up, nipples hard beneath her tank top. Sitting up, she brushed away the hair from her face.

My appetite for her increased. Cursing myself, I smoothed the strands over her shoulders, barely able to get out the words. "It's early. Go back to sleep."

She winked at me, sending a bolt of electricity through me. "I'm awake." Did that mean what I thought? What happened to we're adults and can be mature?

Giving her an out, I said. "My parents and the kids are up."

Propping herself up on her elbow, the sleepy arousal in her eyes weakened my resolve. "So?"

My father laughed in a distant part of the house. I winced. "Thin walls."

"I bet we can be quiet."

The challenge in her voice aroused me even more. Her sultry eyes made me feverish to gather her under me and sink my cock into her wet pussy.

"Val." I growled her name, lifting her body away. "I thought you wanted to keep things platonic."

A flash of something flickered in her eyes. There one moment and gone the next. "What if I changed my mind?"

There were questions I should ask, details and boundaries to discuss. Would this take the fake out of the relationship?

She reached out for me, and I let her pull me back. "Did you sleep in your clothes last night?" She gestured to the sweats, barely covering the evidence of my desire.

I nodded as I allowed myself to explore her body. My mouth collided with hers and our tongues danced together. I clasped her shoulders, angling her for better access to her slender neck.

"I always pictured you sleeping naked." She shifted, straddling my hips. Her long legs bent around my waist as she ground against me.

Coherent thought drained away, and I tugged her close, ravaging her mouth with mine. My rough palms stroked her, skating over her shoulders and down to her butt.

Her supple body grazed my chest, sending heat screaming through me. Delicious scents, spicy and sweet, teased my senses. I teased her breasts through the soft fabric of her tank top.

In one hurried movement, she stripped off the shirt over her head. I sucked in a breath at the sight of her. Honey tan skin peaked in dusky rose. My mouth watered.

Gathering her close, I closed my lips around one nipple, sucking it into my mouth. Her delicious, tangy scent seeped into me, along with a desire to brand her as mine.

Sliding onto her side, she lifted the waistband of my sweats. I held my breath as she explored my length, stroking me until my eyes rolled back in my head. My heels dug into the mattress.

"I'm not going to last," I growled softly, reaching for her, but she eluded me.

Pushing my sweats down, she hummed in the back of her throat. "You'll just have to wait."

Light flashed behind my eyes as her mouth sucked greedily. I set my jaw and dragged my fingers into her hair.

She let go of my cock with a pop. Stretching out along my side, she asked, "Do you want me?"

"Hell, yes, Gorgeous."

She kissed me, eased my shirt up, and tossed it away. She teased along the lines of my tattoo, then down to circle my nipples.

I reached for her shorts, helping her wiggle out of them. The scent of her arousal rose between us, as my fingers found her center, dipping in.

"You're so wet for me."

She gasped. I found her clit and stroked as her hips bucked. Her breathing turned ragged as she squirmed, surging up from the mattress.

"I want you inside me." She demanded, grasping at my arms and shoulders.

Her beauty called me. The angle of her chin as she tossed her head back. The shimmering, wet rose of her pussy. I wanted to take and take.

Finding her clit with my mouth, I drew her into my mouth. Savoring her, I let her reactions guide me. Licking, tasting, and swirling my tongue over her. Filling her with one, two, and then three fingers.

"Evan..." she moaned. "Please."

Shifting, I grabbed a condom out of my travel bag.

She took it from me, ripping it open. Her lips parted, her tongue flicking out to lick them as she stared at me. Her obvious desire amped mine to almost painful proportions.

She grasped me, rolling the condom on. Caging me between her arms, she kissed me until I forgot where I ended, and she began.

"How do you want me, gorgeous?"

Rising, she pushed me back, straddling me once more. Breasts high and her brown hair streaming down her back, she took me inside her in one endless gliding motion.

I gripped her hips, helping her set the pace. Wildness took over as she rode me, destroying my restraint. Racing with her to completion, I reached for her, stroking her clit as she pumped her hips again and again.

The grip of her muscles tightened. Heat pooled at the base of my spine. She clutched at my chest; her head thrown back.

"Come for me," I demanded as her body began to clench around me. Her breathy moans of pleasure drove me. Thrusting up, I followed her over. Pulses of light and sensation shooting through me.

Her body sagged onto my chest as our breathing slowed. I trailed kisses along her neck and shoulder while smoothing my hands over her back. Shifting her over, I pulled off the condom, tossed it in the trash, and tucked her close.

"Your tongue is fucking magical." I growled into her ear.

Val wiggled close. "I can't believe how hard you made me come."

"At your service, Gorgeous."

We lay together, listening to the sounds of the house coming alive. I could stay here with her forever, but I knew someone would come looking for us, eventually. "We should probably get up before they send the girls to get us."

Her lips pursed against my shoulder. "Why did you leave last night?"

A part of me debated lying, but I answered her truthfully. "I knew I wouldn't be able to keep my hands off you if I stayed."

Her lips curved against my chest before she leaned up to kiss me. Shifting away, she sat on the edge of the bed with the sheet wrapped around her. "I worried you might feel guilty or something."

I propped myself up on an elbow. "Guilty? Why?"

She shrugged, never meeting my eye. "Lying to your family or sleeping with me when Yona is close by."

Wrapping my free arm around her, I pulled her back against me. My heart pinched. Val might never love me, but that didn't mean I shouldn't be honest with her.

"I'm not lying. My feelings for you are real, but I understand if you can't return them."

Seconds ticked by in silence before she said, "I don't want to hurt you."

I smiled and kissed her neck. "Life is joy and sadness. Don't worry about me."

There was another lengthy pause. "Yona is a better choice than me."

Why wouldn't she believe me?

"Fucking Yona would be like screwing my sister." I rolled away, stalking into the bathroom. Starting the shower, I stepped in before the water ran hot, dousing my head in the cold water. Automatically going through the motions of washing my hair and body, my temper cooled.

When the glass door opened, Val hugged me from behind. Pressing her cheek against my back, she said, "I'm sorry, Evan. I believe you."

The soft vulnerability in her voice melted my anger. Turning, I took her in my arms, holding her as the water washed over us.

I was bending down to kiss her when a voice called from outside the door. "Uncle Evan?"

I froze for half a second before reaching for the shower door. "Hold on, Inola. I'll be right out."

"Where's Val?" Her little voice was right outside the closed bathroom door.

I tucked a thick towel around my hips and cracked the door open. "I think I saw her go outside."

Inola beamed at me. "Breakfast is ready."

"Tell *Nisi* that we'll be up soon."

"Okay." Inola tittered, then dashed out of the room. I tiptoed into the bedroom and shut the door after her.

In the bathroom, Val finished rinsing off. Stepping from the shower, she wrapped herself in a large towel. "Is the coast clear?"

I nodded, trying to keep my eyes on her face. "We're summoned to breakfast."

"Give me ten minutes, and I'll be ready."

"You sure you don't want to stay here and make love again? I can put a chair under the doorknob and text Felix to run interference."

Val's stomach growled. "As nice as that sounds, I'm starving."

She turned away from me to rummage through her suitcase. Her bottom peeked out from under the towel, and I tried not to swallow my tongue.

"Ten minutes, huh? You wanna race?"

"I'll be ready at nine." Val gathered her clothes.

I dropped the towel, sauntering over to where I'd left my duffel. It wasn't on the floor by the dresser where I'd left it. "Did you move my stuff?"

"Me?" She blinked at me in the mirror as she brushed her hair. "It's right over there where you left it."

"No. It isn't."

"Did it get kicked under the bed?"

"You just want to check out my butt."

"You know it. In fact, wait a second." She took a step toward her purse. "I'll take a picture."

I moved fast, picking her up. I tossed her on the mattress, and she bounced once, giggling while I fished my bag out.

She scrambled up and dashed into the bathroom, hurriedly pulling on jeans and a sweater.

"You're naughty," I said, pulling my own clothes on.

She put her hair up in a quick ponytail, then blew me a kiss. "Don't tell Santa."

***

The whole family went to Pack's Tavern for lunch. Over fried pickles and tipsy collard greens, Val joked with my siblings like she'd known them for years. I could tell Felix and Gennie liked her.

We walked around downtown, Kurt and I following Val and Gennie from one shop to another. She had a keen eye for quality and only bought items that were discounted, or she could haggle the price down.

The kids dragged us into Old Europe Pastries for Hazelnut Napoleons. Val moaned at the taste, the bliss on her face almost orgasmic. I had to walk away before I dragged her into the nearest alley.

Back at the house, I watched her play tag with Inola and Ama in the sunny backyard. The girls screamed with delight as she caught and tickled them.

When a beat-up Dodge Caravan turned into the driveway, I sucked a breath in between my teeth. I saw Val hitched a brow before I turned to greet Yona and the kids.

Mom stepped out of the house as the van parked next to my truck. Jacy and Fala jumped out, running over to hug Mom and me.

"How are you today?" Mom asked.

Fala, the older of the two, frowned. She was fourteen, but her round face made her look younger. "I'm grounded."

Jacy pushed forward. Her thin body and angular face gave her the look of a sprite. "She skipped school."

"You're a tattletale," Fala shrieked, pushing Jacy.

Mom extended her arm around Fala, leading her toward the house. "Let's get a drink and cool off."

Ama ran over. "Jacy, wanna play? Val, Inola, and I are playing princess tag."

At twelve, Jacy was too old to play with the little girls, but she let Ama lead her away.

Yona walked up with a birthday bag in her arms. "Hi, stranger. I heard you were home for the party. I thought I'd bring over my gifts.

I took the bag and hugged Yona, meeting Val's hood eyes over her head. Stepping back, I said, "It's good to see you."

Yona's short, plump body was solid and strong, and her smile was wide. Clad in a long brown sweater over leggings, she looked younger than twenty-nine.

It made me happy to see her so well. It had been a long, hard road for her since Noah's death.

Val left the girls playing and made her way over to us. Was it bad that her frown made me a little happy?

"Yona, this is Val..."

I wasn't sure why I hesitated. After confessing my feelings earlier, it felt strange to call her my girlfriend without Val's permission.

Val scowled at me but gave Yona a smile. "I'm Evan's date for the party."

Yona grinned. "Val, it's so good to meet you. Evan has told me so much about you."

Val's eyes challenged mine. "Has he?"

"I wish I could have brought the girls to the Winter Carnival. And the Tricycle Basketball fundraiser sounds so fun."

Val dragged her eyes away. "We try to have fun when we can."

"I wanted to talk with Evan about something, but now I can get your opinion, too." Yona played with the edge of her sweater nervously. "I'm going back to school."

"That's great," I said enthusiastically.

Val nodded. Her smile was reserved, but real. "What are your plans?"

"I want to be a teacher."

I hugged her. "I think that's wonderful. You love kids."

Letting Yona go, I glanced at Val. Her expression was cautious. My stomach flipped anxiously.

Yona continued excitedly. "I'm hoping to graduate this summer and take you up on your invitation to move to Marchfield."

Chapter 18
Val

Blowing out a long breath, I slumped next to Audrey in the empty auditorium. With only five weeks before *Villains Incorporated* debuted, we'd moved into full tech rehearsals, and it was an exhausting, chaotic mess.

I kicked off my shoes, moaning at how great it felt to just sit down. "Thanks so much for helping me, Aud. I couldn't have set up the tech crew without you directing from the pit."

"Dinner and debrief was all the temptation I required."

"You deserve it after suffering through that mess. Pizza isn't enough to pay you back."

She shook her head. "It wasn't that bad."

"It wasn't good either."

"It'll get there."

I sighed and stood. "You're right. Wanna get out of here?"

Together we shut down the lights and locked up the auditorium, walking out to our cars with heavy bags loaded with work to finish. Audrey unlocked her green Fiat and tossed her schoolwork in the backseat.

"My house or yours?"

I hesitated. I didn't really want to go to my apartment, and Audrey's place was cozy. But she didn't live alone. "What's Oz doing?"

"He's out with Bobby and the guys. Playing poker. Or is it ax throwing? I'm not sure."

"Then let's go to your house."

I let her get a head start, putting in an order for pizza delivery, and taking a minute to decompress before following her.

Audrey and Oz had taken a mini-vacation at the end of Spring Break to Cape Charles. We'd texted, but I hadn't seen her until this morning.

I'd asked her to wait until we were in person before I shared the details of the trip. Yona's visit had thrown a cloud over the rest of my time in Asheville. When Evan brought me home on Wednesday, I'd taken a rain check on his invitation to go out and spent the rest of break doing laundry and puttering.

Pulling into her driveway ten minutes later, I walked up the steps to her porch as Audrey opened the door.

"Pizza's on its way," I said.

"What kind?" She bent to pet her cat as he coiled around her ankles.

"Half you and half me."

"Half pineapple and veggies, and half double cheese?"

"I don't know how we're friends. Fruit does not belong on pizza."

"So, you've told me a hundred times, and yet I still love it."

The large gray and white tabby stalked ahead of us. Tail high, he led the parade to the kitchen, where Audrey fed him while I made a quick salad from the veggies in her fridge.

"Make extra, so I can have it for lunch tomorrow," Audrey called as she disappeared down the hallway to change out of her school clothes.

I took a deep breath and let it out slowly. I missed Audrey and the freedom to hang out with her any time the mood struck.

And yet, anxiety itched under my skin. My bestie often forced me to deal with emotions and situations that I'd rather push onto the back burner. I'd delayed this conversation as long as I could, but tonight would be the reckoning.

Returning in pink and black sweats, she said, "I swear taking my bra off is the best part of the day."

"Stop trying to make me jealous," I snickered. "Don't tell Oz. It might hurt his man-feelings."

"He'd take it as a challenge." She laughed.

I tossed a handful of cherry tomatoes to the top of the salad. Audrey set out forks and napkins, and we went to sit in the living room to wait for the pizza.

Sprawled in an overstuffed chair, Audrey said, "You asked for time, and I've been kind and patient, but start talking, Toots."

I opened my mouth but didn't know how to begin. All my thoughts were tangled up inside a strange bubble of emotion.

Audrey's smile faded. "Was it bad?"

"No." I sighed. "His parents were welcoming and kind. His whole family was incredible."

"Then what's making you frown?"

"He admitted he has feelings."

"Ooh, gimme context." Audrey settled back, ready for a good story, while I perched on the edge of my seat.

"I asked him if he was uncomfortable lying to his parents about us, and he said he wasn't lying. It was real to him."

She pursed her lips. "Not a pledge of undying love, but I see where you're coming from. What did you do?"

"He said he wouldn't push me for more, so I kinda left it there."

"Did he use the L-word?"

"No, but later his sister told me he'd never brought a woman home before. Everyone assumed we were serious."

"What was his family like?"

I searched for the right word. "Different."

She wrinkled her nose. "How? Are they aliens? Cultists? Pimps and hoes?"

I snorted, relaxing a little. "No."

"Then what?"

I rolled my eyes. "A Venn Diagram comparing and contrasting our families would have no overlap. His family is huge. A hundred people were at the party. Every one of them was related to Evan."

She nodded. "You're an only child. It's natural to experience culture shock."

"He must have twenty aunties and fifty cousins. Each with children or grandchildren."

"I'm picturing an overwhelming chaos."

"It was so loud. They all talked at once. And they're huggers." I winced, remembering how I was passed from one person to the next, squeezed and patted, my cheeks pinched until I thought I'd scream. All of them approved and thought I was *the One* for Evan.

"Oh, the humanity." She laughed.

"You don't understand, Aud. Who wants to be touched that much by strangers?"

"Touché."

"And every picture of Evan is candid. There's not a single formal picture hanging in that house. Not one."

Audrey giggled, then slapped a hand over her mouth. "My mind is blown."

She could laugh, but it was a far cry from the mandatory sitting we took every year. The three of us dressed in coordinating outfits, arranged by a professional and smiling stiffly at the camera. The shots always underwent touching up because no real emotion could show.

"They live in this big log cabin in the mountains. It has these huge windows. You could die from taking in the natural beauty of the area. Almost all of their furniture is handmade and designed for comfort."

She nodded, "Makes sense. His dad is a carpenter."

I threw up my hands. "There isn't a comfortable chair in my parent's house."

Sensing I'd finished listing the contrasts, Audrey got to the point. "So, your families are different. Who cares?"

I'd spent days pondering the question Audrey posed and was no closer to answering. It just mattered.

When I shook my head miserably, Audrey changed the subject. "What did his grandmother think of the gift you brought her?"

"She liked the handcrafted bag and the romance novels I'd tucked inside, but she adored the red Uggs. She put them on during the party and danced in them all night."

"You made her day." She smiled.

"I swear, I want to be her when I grow up. Every person there adored her. When she tells a story, her voice, the characters … it's magical. And she has so many grandchildren and great-grandchildren."

My friend's voice grew serious. "Can you see yourself as part of a family with children of your own someday?"

"I do, but not with my parents breathing down my neck, making demands, and choosing men for me."

Audrey nodded as if I'd made a huge, life-changing declaration. "You may not want to hear this, but you should set some boundaries with your parents."

"I tried." A bitter laugh tore out of my throat. "I tell them, and they don't listen."

"Take back control. You cut them off from the money, and that was powerful, but you have to do more."

I tipped my head back, closing my eyes. "How do I stop them from meddling?"

"State your ultimatum and then block their calls. Don't answer their texts. Turn off the music and end this crazy dance."

Inch by inch, I lowered my gaze until I met hers. "What ultimatum could I possibly use to make them back off?"

She smiled with her teeth bared like a shark. "A restraining order preventing them from contacting you or any future grandchildren."

My chuckle edged on hysteria. It was perfect. Use their own demands to shut them and Logan out. At the very least, it would give me some room for other things.

Like whatever this was with Evan.

The doorbell rang, and I seized the opportunity to pause the conversation. Audrey knew me and demanded I be honest with her and myself, so I reveled in the distraction and the chance to think.

Tipping the delivery guy, I carried the box into the kitchen. We put gooey slices of pie on plates beside the salad.

In the fridge, I saw an open bottle of red wine. "Do you want a glass?"

She shook her head. "I need to hydrate. I didn't drink enough water. You go ahead."

I poured myself a glass of wine, and we returned to the living room. I'd wolfed down half a slice before Audrey said, "What are you going to do?"

I shrugged. "I'm going to marinate on boundaries and parents."

"Good. Let me know if I can help." She took a bite of the pizza and groaned.

I took another bite, closing my eyes, savoring the cheesy goodness.

"Tell me more about Evan."

"We're from two different worlds."

"Demi Lovato," she gasped. "*Two Worlds Collide.* Must listen now."

We ate while the song played. I waited until it ended before I said, "I'll admit some people are better together, but Evan and I are on opposite spectrums. Fantastic sex aside..."

"Did you hook up again?" Her smile was so bright, I squinted.

"It's complicated."

"Oh, I bet it was."

"With everyone home for the party, Evan and I had to share a room."

"Oh. My. God. You dirty girl. You had sex with him under his parent's roof, and you didn't even have to sneak around."

"I didn't plan on it. I just woke up and..."

She leaned forward, resting her hands on the coffee table. "Your emotions are involved."

I shook my head, panic welling up. "No. Absolutely not." *But...*

We'd spent the remainder of our nights snuggled together under the blankets. My head tucked up against his chest with his arm around me and our legs tangled together.

In the darkness, I'd felt safe enough to let my worries go. We kissed, touched, and talked. I learned so much about him. His childhood, his love of creating and building, and his favorite books. When he admitted to loving fantasy adventure, I downloaded *A Court of Thorns and Roses* by Sarah J Maas onto his tablet, and he'd started reading it aloud, his deep voice so soothing.

I wanted to stay there forever. Or at least for the entire five book series...

Audrey interrupted my thoughts. "Admit it. He's sexy, funny, and kind. You like him."

"As a friend."

With so many benefits....

"More than that." She insisted. "I've never seen you so twisted up over a guy."

"Aud, stop. I don't like him that way." I didn't want to like him. That was the same thing.

"Look me in the eye and say it."

I shot her a glare. "Why are you so immature?"

She smiled, leaning back in her chair. "Pot and Kettle, Val."

"If I had feelings, which I don't, it would ruin everything."

Audrey reached across the table and squeezed my hand. "Or a new chapter begins."

I shook my head. "I met Yona."

Audrey paused, waiting for me to continue.

"She's petite, cute, with one of those round faces everyone wishes they had. High cheekbones, wide eyes, and long eyelashes."

"Should I hate that? Cause I will if you want me to."

I wrinkled my nose at her. "She said Evan told her about me."

"A-plus to Evan for not keeping secrets."

Internally, I agreed, but I was left unbalanced. Evan hardly ever talked about Yona to me. "She's thinking of making some huge changes in her life."

"What kind of changes?" Audrey sat back in her chair. For the first time, I noticed something about her seemed different. Her face paled. Maybe she was tired.

"She's going back to school to get her teaching certificate."

"Well, the world needs more teachers..."

The teacher shortage had hit every school hard, so I didn't begrudge Yona for wanting to close ranks and help children. I just wanted her to do it somewhere other than my town.

I forced my voice to stay neutral. "She wants to move to Marchfield and teach here."

Audrey threw her hands up in exasperation. "Oh, for heaven's sake. Why?"

"Her parents are gone. Her husband is dead. She considers Evan the only family she has left and wants to be closer to him."

Audrey grabbed her phone and opened her calendar. "I can't go this week, but next weekend I'll drive there and mess her up."

I winked at her. "I appreciate it, but it's not necessary. Evan and I are friends. He and Yona can—"

"He and Yona can what, Val? Get married, work together at Marchfield Middle, have kids of their own?

I raised my hands to my ears. Every word she spoke felt like a sword driven into my heart. I would move, change schools before I watched Evan and Yona settle down.

"Case closed. Whether you admit it or not, you like Evan."

"My life is too complicated. The play is a disaster. There's a stack of papers tall enough to lean like the Eiffel Tower on my desk. And my parents! I don't have time for feelings."

Audrey's shoulders lifted. The tiredness was gone, and her complexion glowed. Was she using a new product? Because I wanted some of that.

"Thou doth protest too much, methinks. Check yourself out in a mirror the next time he's around. You light up from the inside. It started with no strings attached, but you guys have knitted a little love nest."

"Love?" I squeaked. My stomach flipped, and I worried I might lose my pizza. "I don't love Evan."

"Okay." Her disbelieving tone turned the butterflies into boulders. They landed with a thunk in the pit of my belly.

Could Audrey really see it so clearly? Was she right? My mind whirled dizzily at the possibility.

I had to go. "It's getting late. Oz will be home soon, and I have to type up my learning goals."

I put my plate and empty glass in the dishwasher. Stevie sat by his empty bowl, staring at me with round eyes.

"Don't let him brainwash you into feeding him," Audrey said, coming in behind me. Stevie yawned and walked away.

She closed the dishwasher door after adding her plate and glass, following me back toward the sofa. "I need to tell you something before you go."

"You're running for President?"

She snorted.

"You're quitting teaching to become a barista in a seaside bar in Barbados?"

"No, listen—"

"You're leaving Oz and inviting me to travel the world with you?"

"No." She smiled a small, secret smile as her hands moved down over her belly.

Realization hit me like a brick. "Holy shit!"

At the same moment she said, "I'm pregnant."

I launched myself at her, hugging and dancing with her. Spinning until we both had to sit on the floor.

"Way to bury the lead, Freemont. How long have you known?"

She tapped her watch. "Eight hours."

I slapped my hand over my mouth.

"I've been busy, and my period has always been hit or miss. I took a test today when I realized it had been almost two months."

"You're having a baby." I giggled. "Can I be her auntie?"

Two fat tears ran down her cheeks. "That's the dumbest thing you've ever said. You and Stella will be the best aunties."

I reached over to hug her. "And you'll be the best mom."

"I hope so."

"I know, and I'll be here to help. I'll babysit, bring you dinners, and whisk you away for breaks."

"You better." She sniffled.

"And you'll have Oz. He's great dad material."

"If I can get him to pick up his dirty socks and stop leaving the toilet roll empty."

I hugged her again. "I never said he was perfect."

We lay on the floor giggling like fools until Audrey sat up and squeezed my hand hard.

"I need to get married."

Chapter 19
Val

"As your wedding planner slash maid of honor, I suggest we start by defining your vision."

Sitting on the floor in Bobby and Mel's small brick ranch house, I picked up my clipboard and pen and waited for Audrey to speak. The thick blue and ivory oriental rug pulled the cream walls and the leather seating together. Big windows overlooked a shady backyard filled with flowering Forsythia and Narcissus.

Audrey sat in a plump black leather recliner with her feet up. Rachel and Mel trailed into the room with bowls of chips and veggies.

Rachel dropped onto the sofa. "I love your house, Mel."

"Isn't it awesome?" Mel beamed. "I've just started decorating and figuring out where everything goes."

"You've got good Feng Shui." Audrey nodded.

"You don't think it comes off a bit like *The Big Lebowski*?" I grinned wickedly.

Mel glared at me. "If you pee on my rug, Val, I will kill you."

"Uh oh, the guidance counselor is using fighting words," Audrey snickered.

"Are we talking about a movie?" Rachel asked.

"Oh, baby," Mel hugged her. "*The Big Lebowski* was before your time."

"Spell it for me, and I'll stream it this weekend."

While Rachel noted it on her phone, I asked Mel. "What else do you have planned for this place?"

"Wait till you see the art I have to put up. I really wanted a Georgia O'Keeffe like Val's, but I don't have that kind of money."

Audrey snorted. "It's a print."

Mel's face brightened. "Ooh, maybe I'll get one then and hang it over the bed."

"Bobby will love it." Rachel snickered.

Listening to them banter, envy curled itself tightly around my heart. Sitting in this lovely home my friends had made their own left me sad.

Since my conversation with Audrey, I'd avoided examining my feelings too closely. Something told me once I began, the walls I'd built around me would completely collapse, leaving me alone and aching.

Tapping my pen against the clipboard, I cleared the emotion from my throat. "While I'd discuss dirty art all night, we need to figure out these nitty-gritty details."

"You're right." Audrey sat up straighter. "My vision? Well, I want the wedding to be soon."

"In May," Mel confirmed.

"That would be ideal." Audrey chewed on her bottom lip.

"Memorial Day Weekend?" Rachel suggested.

She nodded hesitantly. "That's what Oz and I hoped, but...."

"That's a little under a month away," Rachel said, tapping her finger against her cheek.

"It took me almost a year to plan my service and reception," Mel said. "The little details are the hardest because there's a million of them."

Anxiety inched its way in. Not only did I still have to wrap up the play, but this wedding would be during the craziest time of the school year ... State Testing.

"It's not impossible," I said.

Who was I kidding? It was a Herculean task, but I'd get them married in May one way or another.

"Of course not." Mel agreed. "Tell us colors, themes, vibes, whatever."

"Small. Casual. Pink and Green." Audrey ticked off items on her fingers.

"When you say small, what number are you thinking?" Rachel asked.

"I'm not sure. A hundred?"

I pinched my lips together. "Total?"

"On my side?"

"Oh boy," Rachel and Mel muttered together.

"Okay," I said brightly, crossing out small and writing large. "Cake, food, flowers?"

Audrey nodded. "Yes, please."

"We can order from Pat's this week now that we know the colors," I said, making a note. "And I'll call Share Your Buds for the flowers."

Rachel interrupted. "Do you have your dress?"

"Mom and I ordered one during Spring Break. I called the boutique yesterday, and they said they could get it fitted before Memorial Day."

"Great!" I said. One less thing to worry about. "What about locations? Did you cancel your reservation at The Kinsbrook?"

"Yes. They laughed when I asked if they had openings in May." She lay back in the recliner, rubbing her the slight bulge of her stomach.

As far as I knew, no one suspected she was pregnant. She and Oz told their moms, of course. Everyone else thought relatives from out of the country who could only attend in May had prompted the date change.

"You could have the ceremony on the beach," Rachel suggested. "I have friends who own property on the Chesapeake Bay."

Audrey leaned forward. "Do you think they'd let us rent their house?"

"Maybe..." she trailed off, checking her phone calendar. "Oh drat, they have a Memorial Weekend Bash every year."

"That's okay," I said. "Keep thinking."

We sat for a moment, silently considering venue possibilities.

Suddenly, Mel jumped up. "Let me make a call. My friend, Shan, might be able to help."

Audrey perked up. "Who's Shan?"

"She's a friend from college. She and her husband bought a farm outside of Marchfield a year ago. Last I heard, they were renovating the barn to rent out." She hurried into the kitchen to place the call.

Audrey spoke in a whisper. "Do you think they'll be available?"

Honestly? No.

Plan B, marrying at City Hall and a casual party at a restaurant afterward loomed over us. Barrel was available on the Sunday before Memorial Day. It didn't match Audrey's aesthetic, but she might not have a choice.

"This is so exciting." Rachel did a little dance in her seat. Her hazel eyes twinkled. "Thanks for asking me to be a bridesmaid."

"You're part of the sisterhood now." Audrey smiled.

"Of the Traveling Pants?" I smirked.

Audrey shook her head vigorously. "Sisterhood of Extraordinary Women Educating Reprobates."

I snorted. "That's us.... SEWER."

From the other room, we heard Mel squeal.

"Is she okay?" Rachel asked, a concerned expression on her face.

Audrey and I shrugged. We sat in silence for a moment, trying to hear Mel's side of the conversation.

Rachel broke the silence. "Can I tell you something personal?"

Audrey snorted. "Are you kidding? You know all about our sex lives."

"If you want to blackmail us, though, we aren't worth very much," I joked.

"I don't want this getting around school, you know?"

"Want to pinky swear on it?" I asked, extending my hand.

Curling her pinkie around mine, she asked, "How stupid would I be to get involved with Keith?"

"Wait! You mean Keith?" I snatched my hand away with a gasp. "The special education teacher? That Keith?"

Rachel frowned. "I know he has a reputation with the ladies, but he's also very sweet."

Audrey snorted. "Keith is many things. Smart, hilarious, sexy. But sweet? I don't think so."

"Keith keeps everything casual, and he dates lots of women," I added.

"He thinks I'm too naïve and innocent, and I'm too young for him." Rachel's eyes dropped to her lap; her hands gripped together. "But he gives me all the feels, ya know?"

Audrey and I nodded, neither of us sure what to say.

Rachel gave us a half smile, but the shadows behind her eyes were plain to see. Something had happened, and it wasn't good.

"Do I need to hurt him?" I asked.

Audrey added, "I'll help."

"Thanks for the support." Rachel sighed. "He hasn't done anything wrong."

I cut a glance at Audrey. She seemed worried too.

Before I could speak, another loud squeal interrupted us. Then Mel ran into the room. "Guess who's getting married on Saturday, May 27th!"

"Oh my God, Mel." Audrey jumped out of her chair and hugged her hard. "Are you serious?"

"Shan and her husband finished the renovations early. And since they plan to offer a full-service experience to their clients, they hired a pastry chef and a florist a week ago. Since your wedding is before the grand opening in

June, they're available and happy to do it as their trial run."

Audrey brushed tears of joy from her eyes and threw her arms around me. "I'm getting married."

"I'm so happy for you!"

The four of us gathered for a group hug. The comfort of supportive friends surrounded me, assuring me all things were possible.

When I heard my phone ring, I pulled away from my friends. "Be back."

By the time I found my cell, the call had gone to voicemail. I checked the call log.

Mom.

After my heart-to-heart with Audrey, I agreed that I needed to set boundaries with my parents. I'd put it off though, not sure where or how to draw the lines in the sand.

I almost dropped my phone when it started ringing again. She'd keep calling until I answered.

I should turn off my phone. Go back to my friends. I had a life. I didn't need to jump every time Mom called. My thumb hovered over the red button.

Decline the call.

Hang up.

Send her to voicemail.

My mind picked up the chant, but my fingers disobeyed. A lifetime of guilt overrode my common sense, and I answered on the last ring.

"Hey, Mom. I couldn't find my phone." I chuckled hollowly. Anxious tendrils twisted in my stomach.

Her voice was primed with irritation. "I haven't heard from you in weeks."

I took a deep breath. "I told you I'd be away over Spring Break."

"You didn't call when you returned. I thought you were dead." Her tone declared she was burdened with an ungrateful daughter.

"It's busy at school with the play. I'm sorry I didn't call, but I have great news. Audrey's moved up her wedding date to May 27th."

Her long pause was followed by a deep sigh.

Shit.

"Mom, I have to go…"

"What about your nuptials, Valentine? You have two men on the hook. Reel one in."

Deflecting with a joke, I said, "Fishing metaphors? Are you ill?"

"I am distraught. Make jests. I'm just your mother."

Take charge of the situation. Calmly state your expectations and the consequences. It's like disciplining middle schoolers.

"Mom, I want you and Dad…"

She steamrolled over me. "It's my own fault. We spoiled you by giving you everything, and now you won't even answer the phone."

I snorted at that outright falsehood. She'd conditioned me throughout childhood. If she said jump, and I asked how high.

Until now.

"Are you laughing?"

Her shrill voice pushed my buttons. I forced myself to relax.

"I can't talk now. We'll make a plan soon."

Her voice wavered. "I just want to be sure you're taken care of."

She played me like a flute. Her words pushed new keys, making guilt surge to the surface. I ignored it.

"I'm with Mel, Audrey, and Rachel now. I have to go."

"Who?"

"My friends, Mom."

"Are you a lesbian?"

"Mom, stop," I ordered.

"Marion Kingston's daughter, Lea, is a lesbian. Her partner is having IVF."

Lea and I had gone to camp together the summer after fifth grade. She'd shared her care packages with me.

"I'm not a lesbian, but that's nice about Lea. I'll send her a card. I'm hanging up now."

My finger hovered over the end call button, wishing things were different.

Her voice turned cajoling. "Come to dinner on Saturday."

"I can't."

"At five-thirty."

"I have plans."

"Change them." She barreled over my protests. "And bring Evan."

Before I could protest one more time, she did what I hadn't been able to. She hung up on me.

***

I hugged everyone goodbye and jumped into my car.

My head hurt from the long day, and I planned on heading home and going to bed early. I'd curl up in bed and read that novel that I'd started in August but hadn't been able to complete during the school year.

Instead, I turned out of Mel's neighborhood, intending to turn left toward my apartment, but I turned right. Then right again on Daliah Arch, and left on Cooper Drive, pulling up in front of Evan's house.

Lights glowed from inside, and I saw a basketball game playing on his TV.

Putting my car in park, I urged myself to go home. I could text Evan about dinner on Saturday. There was no need to bother him in person.

But the longer I sat, the more convinced I became that I had to see him. Audrey nailed it on the head. I had feelings for Evan. Crazy, unexplored, incomprehensible feelings. And right now, my biggest wish was to hear his voice.

Cocoa's face appeared in the window, her eyes searching the dark. Her mouth opened, a woof I couldn't hear.

Oh my God, I'm such a stalker.

I turned off the car, putting the key in my purse.

"Please let this be a good idea," I whispered as I headed to the front door.

Cocoa barked several times as I lifted my hand to knock. My heartbeat loud enough to ring in my ears.

I knocked.

The door swung open. My heart paused, a beat of shuddering pain before it raced on.

He wore a Marchfield sweatshirt and gray sweatpants. His bare feet and tousled hair contrasted with his usual neat style. I stared down at his brown toes, wondering why I found them sexy.

Cocoa lunged through his legs. She reared up, licking my hand and whimpering. I patted her head without looking away from Evan. He smiled and the dimple in his cheek made my heart seize again.

"Sorry to stop by without calling." I stumbled over the words.

"You wanna come in?"

I nodded. "I need to ask you something first."

"Okay." He leaned against the doorjamb. Loose, sexy, and impossible to resist.

It would be so easy to kiss him, tangling my hands in his hair and pressing myself against him. I yearned for that.

But I wanted something new. I wanted bare feet and snuggling. A place to rest my head with a person who understood me. I wanted to make promises.

But still I held back, rolling my bottom lip between my teeth, biting down to prevent myself from closing the distance between us.

"What are you doing Saturday night?"

"Where're we going, Gorgeous?" His lashes lowered as he gave me a smoldering stare that lit a fire inside me.

"My mother invited us to dinner. I need to establish rules with them going forward, and I could use backup."

I held my breath. What I asked of him was crazy. Why would he subject himself to torture if he didn't have to?

He shrugged. "Okay."

My breath hissed out. "That's it? Okay?"

"Why not?" He crossed his arms over his chest, his t-shirt stretching over his muscles.

I needed to be crystal clear. "We're walking into the lion's den this time. Are you sure?"

"Did you expect me to say no?"

"I just thought..." I didn't really know what I'd expected, but his easy acceptance threw me a curveball.

"I'd do anything for you, Val. I'm surprised you don't know that."

Reliability and support from a man felt foreign to me. Trust opened new vulnerabilities and chances for getting hurt.

There were only a few people I depended on, and all of them were women.

A cool breeze blew against my back. I shivered.

His warm hand swallowed mine. "Come inside."

He wrapped his arm around my shoulder and ushered me in. Cocoa raced past us, running to her bed. Racing back, she dropped a well-loved stuffed squirrel at my feet. I tossed it, and she scrambled after it.

Evan took my purse and my jacket. I watched him hang them next to his coat on a peg by the door, sparking a tiny bud of longing.

What would it be like to share a space with him? To make a home together?

We'd come home every night, and I'd hang my coat next to his and pet the dog. We'd talk about our day, take turns making dinner, and after we'd do schoolwork or cuddle on the sofa.

And go to bed early.

"Want a drink or anything?" He stood nearby, watching me.

Bittersweet emotion welled up inside me.

My best friend would be married soon...

I needed to cut off my parents...
Soon, I'd be alone...

"May I have a hug?"

Without a word, he moved close, wrapping his arms around me. I burrowed into him, holding him as tears flowed down my cheeks.

He held me as I sobbed, never once pulling away, like he would always be there for me no matter what. I felt safe in his arms.

My tears slowed, and I nuzzled into him. Laying my cheek against his warm shoulder, I breathed in the clean smell of his soap.

Finally, he asked. "You okay?"

I nodded against his chest. "Better now."

I felt him staring at the top of my head. I knew he had questions, but he gave me space. The time to consider my emotions before I said them aloud. The time to deal with the hard things.

Leaning back, he cupped my face with his hand. "Wanna stay? Watch the game?"

Cocoa dropped the stuffed squirrel on my shoe, her eyes imploring me to throw it again.

I slid my hand down his arm to thread my fingers through his. "Yeah. I do."

Chapter 20
Evan

Val's parent's house loomed over us as we parked. The gray monolith reminded me of a castle ruin. Tall, with its severe walls and blank windows staring over the mowed lawn. No trees shaded the porch. The outdoor space sat empty, sad, and lonely, as if no one ever sat outside in the warm evenings.

The muted colors, tasteful yet cold. I couldn't picture Val as a young girl growing up in this mausoleum. She was too alive, too vibrant for this place.

When she'd picked me up for the drive into Richmond, the quiet jazz on the radio reflected her mood. After a quick peck on the cheek and some polite questions, she fell silent.

During the drive, Val retreated further and further into her shell. She didn't sing or laugh. I understood. She was bracing for impact, constructing walls to protect herself, but her silence left me with a sense of dread and anxiety.

When she pulled up in front of a building that could easily house four families, she finally spoke, "Audrey calls it the Gray Palace."

"Pretty accurate."

Her fingers tapped on the steering wheel as she gazed at the house. Her nervous energy filled the car.

Covering her hand with mine, I asked, "You ready to go in?"

"No." She sighed, tilting her head back against the headrest.

"We can stay in here as long as you need."

"I'm being silly. They're my parents. I love them. I want them to be happy."

I forced my shoulders to relax and waited for her to continue.

She drew in a wavering breath. "The worst thing is, it wasn't always like this. I loved shopping with my mom, and sometimes Dad would read with me. They were never the warm, cuddly type, but they've changed. Or I have. I'm so tired of fighting."

Loosening her fingers from the steering wheel, I brought them to my lips. "I'm right beside you."

She gave me a small nod before withdrawing her hand from mine. After a brief check in the mirror, she rummaged through her purse until she found her lipstick applying the red to her lips. Snapping the lid shut, she met my gaze. Her eyes were liquid pools in which I would happily drown.

"Thank you for coming with me."

"I'm here for you." I would still have her back, even if she never loved me.

I stepped out and met her at the driver's side. If clothes were armor, Val dressed for battle. Her tall black heels made her legs seem endless, and her red toenails sparkled through a little cut out at the toe.

The crimson dress hugged every curve and swished around her thighs. My palms tingled, wanting to slide my hand under the hem to check out her panties. No doubt they'd be showstoppers.

"You're beautiful," I whispered in her ear, taking her arm in mine. She shivered, and I pulled her close. "Chilly?"

She laughed. "Stop leering at me, Evan. You're making me horny."

I snorted. "Never, gorgeous. When you dress to kill, I need to appreciate it."

"You look pretty great yourself."

I'd opted for black dress pants and a fitted purple shirt. I shrugged into the black blazer I'd draped across the back seat while Val undid another button on my shirt, exposing the lines of the tattoo underneath.

I gave her a wink. "Let's get 'em, gorgeous."

She snorted.

I could devote my life to making her laugh because it was my favorite sound in the universe. If she'd let me, I'd spend hours tickling her or telling her jokes. It would be my full-time occupation.

A physical sensation exploded from my heart. Unsteady on the steps, I groped for the railing with my free hand as realization hit me.

I loved her.

"Are you okay? You're turning a little green." Val peered up at me, interrupting my thoughts.

"Yeah. Sorry," I muttered, hoping she couldn't read the emotion that burned through me. Rocking me back onto my heels, leaving me dazed.

I loved her, but holy shit, my timing was terrible.

The door opened, and Val's parents stepped out. It surprised me to see them meet us. I'd half-expected a butler.

Val kissed each of her parents on the cheek. Matt shook my hand. He wore a blue polo and green and blue plaid golf pants that reminded me of the 1970s.

Aurora offered her cheek, and I gave her a quick peck. Her white dress flowed around her thin body, and she smelled of lilacs and lavender. A scent I associated with old ladies.

"Welcome. I'm so glad you're both here." Aurora led us into a room off the foyer.

The room tastefully decorated in shades of black and gray, left me feeling cold. Leather armchairs and sofa were set atop a gray and black rug. Huge black and white photographs of a dark, foggy forest hung on the walls, creepy and unsettling. The vibe reminded me of a Mythology class I took in college. The professor had this place in mind when he described the Underworld.

The only splash of color was a portrait of Val over a sparkling clean fireplace. She might have been sixteen or seventeen. She wore a fluffy white dress and held a bouquet of pink roses. Her smile was soft and wistful, but her eyes were sad. Was it titled *Persephone in the Underworld*?

Her parents claimed the armchairs, so I sat next to Val on the sofa. "That's a wonderful portrait of Val."

Aurora smiled. "It was painted before her debutante ball."

Val studied the painting. "I went with Arnold Chin, and he didn't talk to me the whole night."

Aurora nodded. "He's very shy, but his family is richer than Midas."

I squeezed Val's fingers. "He was probably left speechless by your beauty."

Matt snorted. "Our Val was an ugly duckling. She loved getting dirty and making a mess." He grinned at Aurora. "Remember how her nose grew faster than her face?"

"You wanted to take her to the plastic surgeon."

"I was ten," Val said quietly.

What kind of shit was this? They couldn't even reminisce without sounding like assholes. "I'm glad you didn't. I'm very fond of her nose."

Matt took this opportunity to glance up from his phone. "Can I get you a drink, Evan?"

"I'll take a beer. Do you want anything, Val?"

She nodded. "Sparkling water, thanks."

"I'll have a glass of rosé," Aurora added.

When the drinks were poured, Val said, "I need to speak with you both."

"Well, that sounds serious." Matt had his eyes glued to his phone. His lack of respect irritated me, and the temptation to rip the phone out of his hand grew with every scroll he took.

Val took a deep breath. "As you know, I've removed you from my bank accounts, insurance, and the trust Gran left me. You are no longer my beneficiaries or joint owners."

Matt peeled his eyes up. "You're so dramatic. I was just making a point."

For a moment, she seemed flustered and unsure, and I debated stepping in, but then her hands relaxed and the tension left her face.

"I never should have left you on those accounts."

Pride blossomed in my chest as I watched her take steps toward independence.

Aurora lowered her eyes, and a tear rolled down her cheek. Was she crying for the loss of her daughter or because she couldn't force Val to do as she wished?

"You're upsetting your mother, Valentine."

"You both have upset me countless times. But you've pushed me too far. I'm not playing games anymore."

She met her father's stare without blinking, challenging him to explain himself. He checked his watch just as the doorbell rang.

Matt rose to answer it. Voices came from the foyer. Male laughter filling the silence of the house. I sought Val's gaze. Worry filled her eyes and creased her forehead.

When Logan sauntered into the room, his black jeans and button-down shirt made him resemble like a country music singer.

Or the devil.

Logan kissed Aurora's cheek. He turned to Val, ignoring me. "Hello, Valentine."

She glared up at him, refusing to stand. He reached down, taking her wrist and pulling her up into his arms.

"Stop, Logan." She pushed her hands against his chest.

Ready to punch him, I stood, my eyes narrowed. Rage flooded through me. I stepped forward, my hand reaching for his shoulder.

Val leaped back; fury etched across her face. Her palm met Logan's smug face with a smack. His head snapped to the side, a red mark blossoming on his pale skin.

Logan laughed. "Stop flirting with me in front of your parents." He turned to me. "I'm sure you know; she loves it rough."

Matt put his phone down on the coffee table and offered Logan his chair. "Valentine, apologize. Logan is a friend."

Rubbing the red mark on his face, Logan laughed as Val sat back down on the edge of the sofa. Reaching up, she grabbed my hand and pulled me down next to her.

Scooting close, I stretched my arm up and across her shoulders. "You should applaud her. A woman should defend her dignity."

Logan smiled, oozing condescending charm. "It's all right. Valentine loves me."

Simmering rage burned under my skin. The only thing keeping me from ripping him apart was Val's clenched fist on my thigh.

Aurora attempted to smooth over the situation. "It's been so long since you visited. Have you been busy?"

"Business is fantastic," Logan said. His voice pure wealthy, Southern landowner. "It keeps me hopping."

Every muscle in my body tightened, screaming for me to pound him into the dust at his smug tone. Could her parents be deaf?

Matt leaned forward eagerly. "I'm investing in a Japanese start up that I think you might be very interested in."

"We should talk next week, Matt." Logan crossed his leg over his knee and winked at Val. "Maybe your boyfriend would like to join us."

I counted to ten before replying. "I try to keep all my investments within the US."

"I own a small tech company based here in Richmond. We develop apps for companies and are always searching for new people."

"Logan makes millions," Aurora interjected.

"It keeps me in Armani and Louboutin, but it is a niche business. Probably not something a small-town contractor would need."

"Don't be rude." Val's voice was low and full of warning.

Thinking about my dad's business, I said, "An app could be helpful in any business. In carpentry, people could type in the dimensions of their project and see the options available. It could provide them with order tracking and be a point of contact."

Logan grinned, his white teeth reminding me of the movie *Jaws*.

Duunnn dunnn... duuuunnnn duun.

"I could develop it, but what's the point?" he asked.

Duuunnnnnnnn dun dun dun dun dun dun dun dun dun dun dunnnnnnnnnnnn dunnnn.

And he finished with, "You're not a contractor."

"What do you mean?" Matt said, his tone innocent. But his smile told me he already knew.

Val shrank back against me, her face twisted in horror.

I braced myself for impact as Logan puffed out his chest like a tattling schoolboy.

"I did a little research. Evan doesn't own a business. He teaches middle school shop classes and makes birdhouses with teenagers. He's nothing but a grifter, trying to weasel into the family for money."

Val's laugh turned brittle. "Who would want to be a part of this dysfunctional family? Evan is too good for all of you."

Matt blustered. "He lied to us. He's after your Gran's trust."

"No, he isn't," Val said firmly. "He's only pretending to date me because I begged him."

Aurora gaped at Val. "You lied to us?"

"Of course, I lied." She leapt up, breathing hard, her face pink with frustration. "What choice did you give me? You treat me like an inanimate object. I'm something to possess and do your bidding. But that's over."

Matt stood, raising his voice. "Don't talk to us like that. We raised you better."

Val shook her head. "What happened to my mom and dad? Look at yourselves! You've changed so much."

Matt crossed his arms over his chest. "I see what you mean now, Logan. She's a harridan."

Aurora gasped, her shoulders shaking as she dabbed her eyes with a tissue.

Val stiffened her shoulders. "Keep your arrogant bullshit away from me. Don't call me. Don't come to

Marchfield. If you continue to harass me, I'll get a restraining order."

"Valentine—" Aurora started.

But Val was beyond listening. She pivoted, her red dress swishing around thighs. Her long hair swept to the side, covering her left shoulder. "I'm leaving."

I stood, too.

Tears flowed down Aurora's cheeks, the handkerchief wet and useless in her palm. "I'm so sorry."

"You should be. Neither of you were nurturing parents, but I loved you. Now, I wonder if you ever loved me back."

Aurora scurried out of the room. The sounds of sobbing followed in her wake.

"Get out," Matt ordered Val. "Don't come back unless you're ready to apologize."

Hell hath no fury like a woman scorned. I'd heard the quote all my life, but I'd never expected to see beauty amid such rage. Her red dress danced around her like flames, her eyes lit by a fire from within.

Her voice was cool and dismissive when she spoke. "Goodbye, Father."

Head high, she glided gracefully from the room. The tap of her heels loud but unhurried on the foyer floor. The front door opened and clicked closed behind her.

Logan and Matt faced me, and for the first time in an hour, I almost laughed. Matt's absolute confusion met Logan's look of irate frustration. They had no idea what had happened, and it was my pleasure to inform them.

"Your daughter is honorable, creative, and has the biggest heart. I've never met a more brave, loyal, or compassionate person. Can't you idiots see these things in her?"

"None of this is your business," Matt growled.

"I don't care. Neither of you see Val as a person. She's something to control, so you did everything in your power to destroy her spirit. I'm guessing for money or connections."

I saw the truth in their eyes. My fists clenched at my sides and kept going.

Logan's eyes narrowed. His pale face, a hateful mask. "You're no better, bringing your lies in here."

I stared Matt in the eye. "What does that say? Your daughter trusted a stranger, a fake boyfriend, more than you."

I dared Matt to say something. When he remained quiet, I continued. "She gave you an ultimatum. I'd respect it."

Matt sank down into a chair, tipping up his beer and draining the glass. Logan turned his back on me and stalked to the window, staring out.

As much as I wanted to rain hell down around their heads, it wouldn't change anything. And I couldn't protect Val from a jail cell.

Turning on my heel, I let myself do what Val had not, and slammed the door

Chapter 21
Val

After grabbing fast food at a rest stop, I dropped Evan off at his house. He'd been sweet, trying to distract me, and inviting me to stay, but it hadn't felt right. The events at my parents' left me feeling out of sorts and in need of chocolate and alone time.

But as soon as I drove away, loneliness and anxiety flooded over me. The fiasco at my parents' place shattered any hope for reconciliation and destroyed any illusion of compromise. The fact my own parents weren't willing to listen to me left a gaping wound in my heart. The water gates opened, and I cried for hours.

By the time the sun rose, I'd eaten two pints of Ben and Jerry's *Americone Dream* and watched a solid six hours of *The Ozarks* on Netflix.

It soothed my soul that money-laundering, drug-running Marty and Wendy Byrd were worse parents than my own. However, I was pretty sure even they wouldn't throw Charlotte into the marriage mart.

When Audrey arrived in the afternoon, I was still in my jammies.

She surveyed the crumpled tissues and empty ice cream containers that littered the floor. "I see you had a party without me."

"I'd have invited you, but you need your rest."

"Do you want to talk about it?"

No, I didn't want to talk about my fucked-up life. Or how I'd threatened my parents with a restraining order. We definitely shouldn't discuss how I was a spoiled brat who didn't want to share my bestie with her fiancé.

"I'll pass."

Audrey nodded. "Then you'd better shower and get dressed. We need to leave in 40 minutes for Cloverfield Farm."

I tossed a throw pillow at her. "Do I smell bad?"

"Since you asked, be sure to use the vanilla and jasmine soap I like."

My stomach growled as I drove Betty Boop toward the outskirts of town. "I'm so hungry, I may gnaw on my arm. Can we stop somewhere for a sandwich?"

"There will be plenty of food when we get there."

"And cake?"

Audrey sighed with impatience. "Yes, and flowers."

"You can't eat flowers." I snickered.

She laughed. "Remember that girl we had years ago who ate the green fundraiser carnations she got on St. Patrick's Day?"

"How could I forget, Toni Simpson. She threw up green petals in my trashcan an hour later."

Audrey's hand rose up to her throat. "Oh, don't say that. I'm sensitive to smells, tastes, and apparently thoughts of vomiting."

I grimaced. "Let me know if something triggers you today."

"Thanks," she said, then continued. "Can you believe I'm almost eleven weeks pregnant? And in four, I'll be married?"

I could and it made me feel a little sick. Everything was happening so quickly for Audrey while my life was stagnant.

A big part of me envied her happiness while small parts shouted to be cautious. I'd spent months reacting to the mess happening around me. I dodged punch after punch, but never threw one of my own. Caution had gained me nothing. If I wanted a life like Audrey's, I'd have to follow in her footsteps and throw caution to the wind. I needed to change the narrative and go on the offense, but how?

In the passenger seat, Audrey sighed. "I had this perfect plan."

"Face it, your plans always work out for the best. You wanted a fling, but instead you've found your soulmate."

"I'm not ready for a baby."

Slowing for a traffic light, I said. "From what I've heard, no one is, but you're going to be a great mom."

My emotions gathered in my chest, forcing their way up my throat. I let out a soft whimper as the first tears fell.

Audrey's eyes immediately filled with tears. "Why are we crying?" she asked.

"I'm going to miss you, Aud. You'll be married and a mom, and I'm already the third wheel."

Audrey's tears fell faster. "You and I are a team. You're my bestie for life."

"It's just so hard right now, Aud. I feel trapped and I don't know how to break down the bars."

She handed me a tissue from the box I kept in the car. "Are we talking about Evan now?"

I let out a gurgly chuckle and blew my nose. "Yes. Somehow, our fake dates felt more real than not, and it scares me."

The light turned green as Audrey said, "We'll figure it out. Let's think about it and come up with a plan."

Lighter and more optimistic than I'd felt in weeks, I drove out of town and into the country. We rolled down the windows, the cool breeze soothing our flushed faces.

The road twisted through farmland, by small ponds, and newly planted fields. Spring was popping out.

We got closer to the farm, pulling onto an even smaller road that zig-zagged past farms and woods. I glanced over to see Audrey's face was white and clammy.

Taking my foot off the gas, I asked, "You, okay?"

"Pull over."

I barely made it to the side of the road before she flung open the door and vomited in the grass. Rubbing her back, I worried. This wasn't morning sickness. It was two-thirty in the afternoon.

Did she have a stomach bug? Selfishly, I didn't have time to catch a virus. My classes had a test on Thursday, and the play was in its final weeks.

Swallowing down anxiety, I focused back on my friend as she leaned back into the car. Resting her head back, she closed her eyes.

"Here," I said, passing her a cold bottle of water from the cup holder. "Should we reschedule?"

She sipped water. "No. I'm okay. It'll pass."

An orange Subaru Cross trek slowed to a stop beside me, with Bobby behind the wheel. She leaned out of the passenger seat. "Y'all good?"

I bit back my lingering panic. "Yeah. We'll meet you in a second."

Bobby's brow wrinkled, but she said nothing, turning onto the dirt farm road.

I turned to Audrey. "Is this normal? Should we call the doctor?"

Audrey held the cool bottle against her forehead. "Unfortunately, this is common. I'm fine."

Breathing out a sigh of relief, I said, "If this is normal, they really should come up with a cure for it."

Audrey grunted. "Oz and I should tell Bobby about the baby."

"If you tell Bobby, everyone will know within six hours."

"I know, but if I'm going to be prone to vomiting, everyone will suspect."

A white Toyota Corolla pulled up next to us. This time Oz was behind the wheel with his mom, Diane, in the passenger seat. Audrey's mom, Ellie, sat in the back.

"Everything okay?" Oz asked.

Audrey grinned weakly. "We're good. Hi, Moms."

The women waved, but concern wreathed their faces.

I forced a smile onto my face. "We're the welcoming committee. Everyone's here now, so I'll follow you guys to the farm."

Oz narrowed his eyes. He pulled the car off the road in front of us and jogged back to my car.

"Switch with me."

"Sure." I left the keys in the ignition and jumped out.

Getting in the car with the moms, I said, "I guess they need a minute."

Diane chuckled. "He's so smitten. He can't stand to be away from her for a second."

Ellie frowned. "Is Audrey, okay? She was a little green."

"Just a little motion sickness," I assured her as I put the car in drive.

"Whose car is this?" I asked as we turned onto the farm road.

"It's mine," Ellie said. "Diane's spending the night with me and hopping a train back to Delaware tomorrow."

"How fun."

As I drove down the bumpy dirt road, we took in the rows of budding fruit trees. They grew along the road as far as the eye could see.

Coming around a curve, a white farmhouse came into view. A wide porch wrapped across the front and side, supported by thick columns.

We drove under two huge live oak trees and parked beside a rustic red barn. Its massive white doors were wide open in welcome. Bobby sat on a bench outside in the sunshine, waiting for us.

We walked down a wide slate path toward her, and she wrapped Diane in a big hug. "Where is the happy couple?"

"They're coming." I nodded toward the car creeping down the road.

Bobby watched the car's slow progress. "Is Audrey, okay?"

"She's fine. I got overzealous driving the country roads and made her a little queasy."

Before long, Audrey and Oz walked over, hands entwined.

A tall, thin woman approached. "Welcome to Cloverfield Farm. I'm so glad you're here. I'm Mel's friend, Shan. I own this place with my husband."

She showed us around the party space. Thick wooden beams crisscrossed high above us, strung with thousands of tiny, white fairy lights that would add beauty at night. Expansive skylights brought in the sun. Windows overlooked the orchard.

"Do you like it?" Ellie wrapped an arm around Audrey. She whispered something in her daughter's ear. They both smiled dreamily.

I couldn't remember a time when my mother showed such heartfelt emotion toward me. She exhibited a certain amount of caring, usually through shopping sprees, but the only time she whispered in my ear was to scold me in public. Wistful sadness spread through me, and I yanked my eyes away.

Two busy women set out trays of hors d'oeuvres, cakes, and samples of flowers. Identical in every way, they were both short and plump, with brown hair streaked with gray. They even wore identical outfits and aprons.

Doors stood open at the far end of the space. An industrial kitchen sparkled with stainless steel appliances. Shan led us over to the tables and pulled comfortable chairs up.

One of the women said, "Welcome. I'm Jenna and this is Jemma."

"Are y'all twins?" Ellie asked.

"Yup." Jemma answered. "We both coming running when you shout, Ms. J. We started a catering and floral business about ten years ago after retiring from education."

Bobby beamed. "Some of us are teachers, too."

Jenna and Jemma answered together. "We offer a ten percent educator discount."

Shan interjected, "Before we get into all of that, though, you should sample."

Both J's nodded. "Tell us what you like and don't like."

As soon as Jemma and Jenna began passing the tasting trays, I lost track of who was who, but it didn't matter. The food became the new star of the show.

One of the J's pointed to the food options. "These are stuffed mushrooms, grilled vegetable skewers, beef pot sticker spoons, and soup shooters. We can adjust seasonings or fillings to your tastes."

Audrey and Oz tapped shot glasses of soup. "Cheers."

"We also have pesto crostini and mini quiche tarts for you to try."

Audrey's stomach, now made of cast iron, ate a bit of everything. "I love it all."

"Oz, what do you think of these wings?" Diane asked.

"Almost as good as yours," Oz said, enjoying a second one.

Ms. J Number One laughed. "Now there's a smart man."

"These crostini are awesome," Bobby mumbled with her mouth full.

"The pot stickers are my favorite." I moaned as I dipped another in spicy sauce.

Ellie complimented the chefs. "It's all amazing."

"You guys are so easy." Ms. J Number Two smiled. "Try these pork or chicken BBQ sliders and spicy chicken wings."

"I'm going to pass out voting sheets so you can choose your favorites. Don't worry, Audrey gets the final say."

"What about me?" Oz pouted.

One of the Ms. J's patted his hand while the other smiled. "Darlin', we all know who's in charge.

I noted my favorites, enjoyed seconds, and tasted everything. When we finished, Shan collected ballots while the twins brought out trays of pastries.

Bobby clapped like a little child. "I've waited for this all week. Cake testing is the best part of getting married!"

Oz coughed. "What would Mel say about that?"

"If she hears about it, I'll know who to blame." Bobby gave us the stink eye before grabbing the cake.

Samples with a variety of fillings and frostings were passed around. "As you can see, we can mix and match, combining tastes and colors to suit your vision."

Audrey moaned. "Try the strawberry. It's amazing."

Diane closed her eyes, savoring her cake. "This chocolate ganache is so rich."

We sighed over flavors and textures. "It sounds like we're having an orgy." Audrey laughed, sobering suddenly. "Not that I have ever heard an orgy, Mom."

Ellie giggled. "Whatever you say, Audrey."

"I hope your orgy days are over." Oz chortled.

Audrey smirked. "You'll be invited if I ever have another one."

Shan passed out new voting slips. "As far as design, just because it's a small wedding doesn't mean it has to be boring."

"Small? Who are we kidding here?" I snickered. "How many people are you inviting?"

Audrey sighed. "A hundred?"

"Oh, Honey." Ellie winced. "I saw your list during spring break. Try almost two hundred."

Shan nodded, making notes on a clipboard. "Okay, so maybe not small, but not huge, either. Give me ideas of things you and Oz do together."

Bobby laughed. "Make out at school."

"Coach soccer," Ellie added.

Diane snorted. "Dance in drag."

"Travel," I suggested.

Audrey's soft smile grew. She glanced at Oz, and he nodded. "Make a baby."

All joking screeched to a halt.

"Oh my God. Way to go, Dude." Bobby launched herself at Oz, hugging him.

Shan clapped. "Congratulations."

True happiness blossomed in my heart. I hugged Audrey, knowing that no matter what she'd said, everything balanced on the precipice of change.

Nothing lasts forever. My feelings, whatever they were, for Evan would wane. We were opposites. In fact, I couldn't even think of one meaningful thing we shared except teaching and a few extracurriculars. His family knew how to love each other.

His greatest qualities were rescuing people and supporting them. He truly cared for people.

What were my greatest qualities? Shopping for bargains and ... I couldn't think of anything else. I had nothing to offer him except toxic dysfunction.

"Hey, you, okay?" Bobby asked as Jenna and Jemma led Audrey, Oz, and their moms away to study photos and decide on designs.

"No," I mumbled, tears streaming down my cheeks.

She herded me out of the barn to the bench in the sunshine.

"I've fucked up everything."

"It can't be that bad." She patted my shoulder.

"It can. It really can." I sighed.

"Lay it on me."

I wrestled with lying to her. But the longer I sat there, the more I knew running away wouldn't solve anything. I needed to deal with things head-on.

Wiping my eyes, I told Bobby about Evan's parents and mine. About my suspicions that Dad and Logan were after my money. I told her how my emotions were impossible to label and control. About the deep fear I had of being alone once Audrey married.

She listened, never interrupting as I blathered on. And at the end, when I blew my nose on the last tissue in my purse, she hugged me.

Bobby rested her arm across my shoulder. "Let me call my friend, Kelsey. She's a private investigator in Richmond. I bet she can dig up the shit on Logan and your dad."

I shook my head, ready to turn the offer down, when she said, "Turnabout's fair play, Val. Logan investigated Evan."

Was I reluctant because of my ethics or because I feared what the investigator would discover? I swallowed hard. Their abuse had to end, and I needed to know what they were up to.

"Okay," I agreed, and Bobby squeezed my shoulders.

Audrey came out of the barn with Shan. "What did we miss?"

"I'll tell you later," I promised, hoping she'd forget, and I'd never have to repeat it all.

Oz joined us with a mom on each arm.

"I love this venue." Diane grinned. "I can't wait to dust off my cowboy boots and dance."

"What a great idea." I gasped. "What if we had a Western theme? Bolo ties and cowboy boots?"

Shan nodded. "We could emphasize the theme with decorations from around the farm."

Audrey gasped. "Can I wear cowboy boots under my dress?"

"Heck yeah," I said before turning to Ellie for her opinion.

She grinned. "Only if I can wear some, too."

"Bolo ties aren't my style, but I could go for cowboy boots." Oz chuckled. "Can I wear jeans?"

Audrey punched him on the shoulder. "No."

"Let me know what you decide." Shan waved and headed back to the barn.

"Ellie and I better get going," Diane said.

"We're having a mother's sleepover tonight," Ellie announced.

Oz hugged them both. "Have fun."

Ellie added, "We're watching *Bridesmaids* and *The Hangover* for wedding research."

Audrey's mouth dropped open. "No puppies."

Oz slapped his palm to his forehead. "And no tigers in the bathroom."

A bolt of wistfulness struck my heart. Why couldn't my mom be more like these two?

As Ellie backed out, Diane rolled down the window. "By the way, we're also going to binge *Sense8*. I hear there are orgies, Audrey."

Ellie hit the gas, and they drove off cackling.

"I can't believe my mom said she was excited to watch orgies," Oz groaned.

"And *The Hangover*." Audrey hung her head.

"I wouldn't mind watching *Bridesmaids* again. Anyone up for a movie tonight?" I asked.

"Oh, hey, I almost forgot," Bobby interjected. "I know it's a school night, but I got a special invitation to an Open House at Polar Vortex. They're having a DJ with a dance floor and the poles. It's five bucks to get in." Bobby shook her hips. "Wanna go dancing?"

"Maybe we could invite Evan." Audrey winked at me.

Before I could protest, Oz said, "I'll text him."

Oz's phone binged almost immediately. "Keith and Evan are at Barrel playing pool. They can meet us in half an hour." He wiggled his eyebrows at Audrey. "Will you pole dance for me?"

I snorted. "Pervert."

"I might get sick spinning." Audrey rubbed her belly.

We walked over to the cars. My stomach tightened in anticipation or dread. I couldn't tell. The thought of seeing Evan made my heart lift and my stomach lurch simultaneously.

I was coming down with something.

Audrey pulled her phone out of her bag. "I'll text Rachel and see if she wants to meet us, too."

"One step ahead of you," Bobby grinned. "Rachel's picking Mel up, and they're coming together."

"I get tired early, but we can go for a while," Audrey said, gazing at Oz with her heart on full display.

He smiled back. "Just let me know, Red."

"You're coming, right Val?" Audrey glanced over, her eyes imploring.

"I'll hang out for a while, but as Bobby said, it's a school night, and I still have to write my learning goals for tomorrow."

Chapter 22
Evan

I lined up my shot as Keith hovered nearby with his hands on his hips, tapping his fingers on the billiards table.

"I'm serious. Wrap it up, so we can meet everyone at Polar Vortex," he urged.

When Keith called me, bored and out of sorts, wanting to play pool, I jumped at the chance to get out of the house and away from my schoolwork.

The ecology club wanted us to make ten bluebird nesting boxes for the rain gardens outside the school. I knew it would be a quick, fun project, but my heart wasn't into planning it this afternoon.

"Isn't that the pole dancing place?" I asked, taking my time. I had ten bucks riding on this game.

He threw his hands out impatiently. "All the more reason we should go."

I sank two and moved to line up my next shot.

"What if I give you my ten bucks now?"

"What's your rush?"

"Number one, pole dancing, dude." He hit his forehead with his palm. "Number two, Rachel is there."

Setting up a shot, I sank another ball before turning my full attention to him. "Are you into Rachel?"

He folded his arms across his chest, leaning against the table. "What are you? CIA? The faster you finish, the sooner we can go."

Picking my angle, I cued up the shot. "It sounds like you're into her."

"*Pfft.* She's fun to hang out with, but not my type."

I scoffed, unable to swallow a chuckle. "What type? You've slept with all kinds of women."

"I like women who keep things simple. Rachel is as complicated as it gets."

Straightening, I lifted a brow. "You and Val could be twins. You're both allergic to strings."

"Can we discuss this later? Finish the game, so we can get out of here."

Missing the ball on purpose, I grinned as Keith groaned. He jabbed his cue at the table without even lining up.

I laughed, then sank the next three balls with one shot. Keith didn't notice because he was busy texting.

Putting his phone in his pocket, Keith snapped, "You're driving me crazy. Let's go."

"Just let me drown the last ball," I said, planning to accidentally miss at least twelve times before I managed it.

"Did I mention that Val will be there?"

"You should have led with that." I slapped the cue down on the table, not wanting to waste any more time.

He passed me ten bucks for giving up the game, and I followed him out of the bar.

He grinned as he slid into his truck. "You were having such a good time goading me. I didn't want to take that away."

"Oz just told you, right?"

"He texted me that detail exactly sixty seconds ago."

I climbed into the passenger seat and barely closed the door before Keith floored it and pulled out.

"What exactly is Polar Vortex? A Gym?"

Keith shrugged. "I want to say it's a classy strip club, but I know Audrey would punch me."

I put my tongue in my cheek. "How about a strip club for the rapid empowerment of women?"

"What is that acronym?" Keith laughed. "SCREW?"

"I'm gonna go with the dance studio, so Val doesn't kill me."

"Wise choice."

The place was packed, so he circled around to park across the street. Before getting out, Keith popped a mint into his mouth. Despite all his bluster to the contrary, he was into Rachel.

I could relate. A sense of anticipation grew inside me. I couldn't wait to see Val.

After the confrontation at her parents', I hoped that laying down the law gave her peace. And when she turned down my offer to stay over, I wasn't that surprised. She had a lot to process.

But I'd missed her, and the thought of running into her today sent excitement racing through me. My heart bounced when Val bumped into me.

Inside the studio, a disco ball splashed rainbow hues across the walls. In the dim light, dozens danced to music pumped out by a DJ. In the main room, talented women in shorts and t-shirts spun on the poles, twisting, and twirling through intricate poses.

Val caught my attention immediately as she danced near the DJ with her friends. Her dark skinny jeans clung to her shimmying butt, and her pretty green blouse slid off one shoulder, exposing her neck and upper back. Her long brown hair swung loose around her shoulders as she moved to the music. The light splashed across her as she twirled, making her appear to move in slow motion.

Keith gave me a wave and bypassed the line, strutting over the group. Rachel shimmied over to him; arms raised. He grinned, spinning her as they danced together.

After paying the entrance fee with my ten-dollar winnings, a cluster of women inside the main room eyed me like caged tigers. I hustled away from them, keeping Val in sight as Grace Jones' *Pull Up to The Bumper* pumped through the space.

"Hey there, Hon." An older woman in neon yellow spandex stepped in front of me. "Wanna dance?"

"Thanks for the invitation, but I'm meeting someone." My heart skipped a beat when I saw Val approaching.

"Hi." She wrapped her arms around me briefly, stepping back before I could catch her. "I'm glad you're here."

Offering a friendly wave to the woman, who could easily be as old as my mom. Val and I made our way toward the rest of the group.

Part of me wanted to drag her away from the crowded room and ask her how she was, but I cautioned myself not to take this invitation too seriously.

When *Naughty Girl* by Beyoncé, Val and Audrey shrieked like middle school girls.

"Dance with me," Val demanded.

Shuffling my feet and swinging my arms to the beat, I drank in the sight of her dance with abandon.

"Is that all you've got?" She shouted over the music.

I leaned into the teasing tone of her voice, reciprocating. "Since you didn't ask nicely, this is what you get."

She smirked. "Will you cut a rug with me?"

Her sense of fun felt contagious. I pretended to consider, tapping my chin. "Hmm, still a bit lacking."

She rolled her eyes. "Please, Evan, will you boogie down with me?"

Responding with my best moves, I threw myself into the dance. She moved close, her hips swaying until we were dirty dancing.

The darkness of her eyes simmered with raw energy, and my heart responded, pounding to the beat of the song. The scent of jasmine and vanilla teased my senses as we gyrated to the music, ignoring everyone around us.

After three songs, she confessed, "I need a break and a drink." So, we threaded our way through the sea of people to a table stocked with water.

Winding our way back through the crowd, we passed out water to our friends, but had two left over. Keith and Rachel were gone.

"Did Keith come with you?" Oz asked.

"Yeah." I searched for his blond-brown hair. "But I don't see him now."

"Rachel just texted me." Audrey said, putting away her phone. "Keith took her home."

"Ooh." Bobby grinned. "Somebody's knocking boots tonight."

Mel shushed her. "They're just friends."

"Friends turn into lovers, my sunshine." Resting her forehead to Mel's, Bobby stared into her eyes.

Audrey sighed. "This is so much fun, but I'm tired and my back aches."

Oz leaned toward me. "We're pregnant."

"Congratulations."

"Thanks, Evan." Audrey glowed with happiness.

I hugged them both, but my eyes wandered to Val. She watched us with a serious expression and her lip caught between her teeth. All this change must be hard on her.

Bending to speak in Val's ear, I asked, "Are you okay?"

"Of course." Her lips twisted into a little smile that did nothing to reassure me.

Oz tugged Audrey closer. "Before we go, can you show me your moves on the pole?"

Audrey patted her belly. "Showing you my moves is what got us in this predicament."

"Please?" He begged.

Audrey glanced at Val, who nodded and wrapped her arm around her bestie. "Come along, boys, and prepare to be wowed."

They kicked off their shoes and chose poles side by side. Grabbing the metal high above her head, Val hooked one knee over the pole and did a slow spin. She arched her back, hair flying out behind her.

When her feet touched the mat, she turned, pressing her back to the bar, and sliding to the floor with her knees bent.

Her demure eyes lowered, and she bit her lip. Staring up at me through her lashes, she gave me a shy smile.

The attraction was like a bolt of lightning that set my cock on fire, and I shifted my stance, uncomfortable in my jeans. My eyes glued to her form as her back arched, grace and strength melding together. She brought me to the point of pleasure and pain simply by watching her.

Lifting off the floor, she swung around the pole again before landing with her feet together, hands in the air.

"A perfect ten, gorgeous. Even the Russian judges are too turned on to deduct points." Tugging her to me, I whispered in her ear, "You are seriously on fire, Val. Super-hot."

She blushed. "Wow. Keep those compliments coming."

I hissed like steam was coming out of my ears. "You blew my mind."

Nearby, Oz cheered as Audrey finished her dance with a round of twerking moves with her hips and then bowed. "You're amazing, Red."

A tall woman strutted over in towering heels, her eye make-up sparkling under the lights. "Sweethearts, you make me proud."

"Thanks, Starlight." Audrey giggled. "We were showing off for the guys."

"They seem impressed, but I wonder if they would be brave enough to try?"

Val raised an eyebrow at me. "I dare you."

Audrey pointed to Oz. "I double-dare you."

"It's not that hard," Oz said, tugging off his shoes.

Val narrowed her eyes at me like she thought I'd wimp out.

Toeing off my sneakers, I grabbed a pole.

Starlight cackled, "You've got yourselves two gorgeous and brave men, ladies. Let's see what they've got."

She showed us how to hook our legs around the pole and use our body weight to swing around.

We were drawing a crowd, but I could only focus on Val cheering me on. I tucked the mental picture away to examine later.

Starlight clapped, "That was an excellent back hook spin, men. Now, let's try a carousel."

Following her directions, I spread my arms wide along the pole. Pulling myself up, I wobbled through half a turn.

"Bend your knees," Starlight advised me as I tried again.

The crowd grew, clapping to the music. Encouraging us. The older lady from before waved dollar bills over her head and hoped she wouldn't try to stuff them in my waistband.

Val stood in front; her face lit up with humor and something else mixed together enhancing her beauty and driving me to show off.

Starlight smiled broadly. "Excellent. Now, strike a pose for your ending."

I placed my hands at the base of the pole and did a handstand with my back against the cold metal. Loud cheering erupted from the crowd when my feet touched the mat.

Starlight fanned herself. "Thanks for the fun time, and the free advertising. I bet half of these women sign up for classes tonight." She sauntered away to help others brave enough to try the poles.

Val approached and patted me on the butt. "I loved your dance." She hooked her arm through mine, sending a possessive glare to the few women who lingered. "I've never seen anything so sexy."

I snorted, making a face to show my disbelief.

She leaned up, her lips close to my ear. "It's pretty close to the expression on your face when you're inside me, though."

Capturing her chin, I kissed her. She tasted like warm sugar donuts, and I was ravenous. I could never get enough. Love flooded through me. I broke the kiss, hauling her close, hugging her while seeds of emotion took root and grew. The urge to say the words ached in my chest. I tilted my head down, ready to tell her how much I loved her.

But the words stuck hard in my throat.

I imagined myself yelling the words over the beat of the music in front of her friends and dozens of strangers.

What if she didn't hear me? The exchange played out in my mind:

"Val, I love you."
"What?"
"I love you!"
"I'm sorry, did you just say caribou?

No, I wouldn't spring it on her in public. There was too much at stake. She might go on the defense or run away.

Val deserved romance. I'd buy her flowers, candles, and excellent food, then whisk her away somewhere quiet. And when the mood was right, then I could tell her.

Chapter 23
Val

When the classroom phone hanging on the wall by the door rang in the middle of class, I rushed over to answer it.

"Hey, kiddos, I need to take this. Read the article in Part Two, and I'll be right with you."

"Who's in trouble now?" Maria Shelling called out in a judgey tone as I picked up the receiver.

I flashed a wide smile at the pretty girl, who had a sharp tongue and a heart of stone. "It's the President of the United States calling to ask how my students will do on the Executive Branch test tomorrow."

Addressing the whole class, I repeated, "Read the information, please."

Forcing a smile into my voice, I answered the call. "Hello, this is Ms. Bellini."

"Hi, Val," Rhonda, the office admin, spoke in a hesitant tone that gave me anxiety. "I have your mother on the line. She says she tried your cell, but you didn't answer."

I wanted to curse, but twenty-seven pairs of ears in the room were listening.

Mom had left me several voicemails and a half dozen text messages since I'd walked out. They all had the same theme. "Call me back."

"I'm in class now. Do you think you could take a message?"

"Oh, are you sure?" Rhonda sounded flustered. "I just figured you'd want to take it since your mom is ill."

Mom had played this card before, but I didn't have time to explain that Mom's illnesses disappeared as soon as she got what she wanted.

"Tell her I'll call back after class."

"But, the lab reports and the doctor's message, Val. You should take the call."

I sighed, rubbing my forehead to ease the tension. "Okay, put her through."

Glancing over my shoulder at the class, I saw their curious eyes drop away. "I'm sorry, kiddos, I need to take this. Finish the reading and sit quietly. I'll just be a moment."

I opened my classroom door and stepped into the hallway with the phone. I cracked the door so I could monitor the students.

"Valentine," Mom said, her voice higher than normal. She sounded both relieved and stressed, and I braced myself for the worst.

"Mother, I don't appreciate you bullying the school staff into getting your call put through."

"I didn't lie. I feel wretched about what happened at dinner. I know we haven't seen eye to eye, well, ever, but lately I've been..."

At her pause, I filled in the blank. "Demanding? Difficult? Pushy?" Honestly, I had more, but they weren't allowed in school.

"Yes, all of that," she admitted. "There's so much I need to tell you, but the most important is how sorry I am."

"Um, hold on." I opened the door wider and peeked in.

Class clown, Sebastian Zapita, froze with his arm lifted mid-air, a paper ball in his fist. I narrowed my eyes, sending him racing back to his seat.

"Thanks for apology," I continued, scanning the rest of the students for instigators. "But I have to get back to my class."

Mom took a deep breath. "Can we meet up later? I have something important to share with you."

"Mom, I told you. I'm done."

"Val, please." Her voice cracked with emotion. "I need to see you."

I eased back on my heels in shock. For the first time in my life, my mother had shortened my name.

Was it the desperation in her voice, or her use of my nickname that changed my mind?

"I don't get off work until 4:15."

"Oh, thank you," she breathed out in relief. "That's perfect. I'll drive down and pick you up. I know a darling boutique near you that sells the most adorable shoes."

"Sole Fusion? They're very expensive."

"I have my American Express. We can have dinner after. It's all on me."

I shook my head, trying to make sense of her words.

"I've gotta run, Mom. I'll see you soon."

I returned to the classroom to face the curious eyes staring up at me.

"Who's ready to play a game about the information in that article?"

No hands went up, and every child in the room groaned.

***

When classes ended for the day, Mom's cream-colored Bentley waited for me in the visitor's lot. I stowed my school bags in the trunk of my car and joined Mom in the backseat of hers.

The chauffeur smiled and waved. "Hi, Leo. How's your family?"

"We're all well. Thanks for asking, Val."

"Send your wife, Penny, my love." Sliding back into the buttery leather seats, I reminded myself not to get too cozy.

"Leo," my mother called. "Will you take us to the boutique we discussed earlier?"

As the car pulled away, Mom asked, "Would you like a drink, Val?"

I helped myself to a hard lemonade from the fridge between the seats, wondering if the ax would fall now or during dinner.

"How are you, Mom?"

"Oh, I'm well." She twisted off the cap to a bottle of water. "Better than I have been in months, years, really."

Turning my attention on to my mother, I noticed her demeanor seemed carefree and content. Her blond hair wisped softly at her jawline, and she wore designer jeans and a loose-fitting red top with wide flowy sleeves that surprised me. She'd even kicked off her expensive red Manolo Blahnick heels.

I slid my feet out of my Miz Mooz Mary Jane heels and sipped my drink, wondering what was going on.

"You seem relaxed."

"Patrick, my psychologist, suggested I take time to remember what it was like to be young. Can you imagine? I'm only fifty-five."

"Why did he suggest that?"

"To better understand your viewpoint."

"You went to a psychologist to discuss me?"

"I've been seeing him for a while. But recently we uncovered something I'd repressed. I remembered how your grandfather treated me when I wanted to marry Sam."

"Hold on. Who the heck is Sam?"

"He was my first love. The only love now that I think about it. My father didn't like him. He wasn't rich enough, polished, or sophisticated. His mom was a teacher, and his dad," she hesitated, then whispered like she said a bad word, "was a plumber."

"Didn't he know plumbers make a ton of money?"

Her eyes welled up, and she sighed despondently. "He didn't think it was the right kind of money, and father put his foot down. He threatened to cut me off and disown me if I married Sam. He told me to marry Matt, so I did."

How come she'd never shared this with me? "I never knew."

"Why would you? You never met your grandfather since he died before you were born. By then, I'd buried my anger and regrets so deeply, I didn't even realize your father and I were doing the same thing to you."

She flipped her short hair. "Close your mouth, Val, you're catching flies."

I snapped my mouth shut, clenching my fingers around the glass. "What about Dad?"

"What about him?" She shrugged.

Mom had lived her entire life pleasing Dad. She bought his clothes, ran his house, and hosted his parties. She always considered him first. But now? She was acting on her own?

"Does he feel the same as you?"

"Your father and I haven't spoken since that disastrous dinner. He's staying in a hotel and has been in meetings with Logan all week."

"Meetings?" A shiver of apprehension ran down my back. "What kind of meetings?"

"Oh, something to do with the business," she scoffed. "He tells me I'm not smart enough to understand all the ins and outs."

"What does Logan have to do with it?"

"He's loaning your father money. I'm not sure." She broke off. "Oh look, we're here."

Sole Fusion was a high-end shoe and accessory boutique in nearby Norfolk, Virginia. Unlike The Shoe Box, which dealt with overstocks and previous collections, Sole Fusion catered mostly to brides and wealthy women.

The shop was part of a remodeled street of late nineteenth-century townhouses. The shoe store was sandwiched among a jewelry store, a haberdashery, and a bridal boutique.

The shop was beautiful inside. Once a three-story townhouse, it was entirely gutted and redesigned. Glass shelving made the Betsey Johnson, Prada, Louboutin boots, pumps, and stilettos seem to float in the air. My palms itched to try some on as we browsed, chatting.

"I'm sick about not helping with Audrey's wedding. She's like a second daughter to me."

That was news to me. She'd met Audrey quite a handful of times and had bought her some fabulous shoes, but daughter?

"The wedding will be at Cloverleaf Farm. It's rustic, but also a beautiful location. She's thrilled."

"What are her colors?"

"You know Audrey. She's picked pink and green."

"I hope she let you pick out your own bridesmaid dress."

"I'm wearing the pink Helesi Alejandra dress with the applique flowers you bought me years ago."

Mom considered, a little furrow in her brow. "You'll look lovely."

A compliment? My soul lit up like the sun even as I tried to let it roll off my back.

Memories of shopping excursions crept forward from the recesses of my mind. Mom and I shopping at the mall, bringing home bags and bags. I'd have fashion shows for Gran, who would clap and cheer as I stalked down a runway of towels.

When did we stop having fun together?

Mom picked up a silver Jimmy Choo and motioned to the hovering salesperson. "Do you have this in a size eight and a half?"

A saleswoman in a black suit and classy Louboutin stilettos nodded and disappeared into the storeroom.

Mom sat in a plush gold chair in front of a wall of mirrors, like a Queen awaiting her court. Her expression softened before she said, "Does Audrey have a dress?"

I nodded. "It's a Princess cut, off the shoulders with sparkles all down the bodice. It's white with a hint of blue ice."

"Not your style, but perfect for her." Mom gestured to a blue sequin pump with a chunky heel. "Does she have shoes?"

"Not yet. It's changed to a Western theme, and she wants cowboy boots."

I forced my face to remain blank, waiting for her negative comments about Audrey's poor taste.

The willowy clerk returned with the shoes. "I apologize for overhearing, but we have some beautiful, handcrafted boots upstairs."

I blinked when Mom said, "We'd love to see them."

Leaving the heels behind, the woman led us up a wide staircase to the second floor. More glass shelves held boots of all shapes and colors with a dedicated corner to western boots fashioned from soft leather and in an array of pastel colors like delicious little cupcakes.

I stopped in front of the display, admiring the intricate patterns stitched in the buttery soft leather. The backs had delicate lacing at the calf, which reminded me of Audrey's dress.

"These are perfect." I breathed the words, afraid to ask for the price, but decided to text a picture to Audrey, anyway.

"Size seven in pink and eight in blue, please." Mom waved to the woman, who disappeared into a storage area.

Two months ago, Dad to cancelled my credit cards, and now Mom pushed expensive boots at me? I wasn't sure what to say.

"These boots are at least five hundred dollars, Mom. Audrey and I can't afford them."

She took my hand and squeezed it. "It's the least I can do. Consider it a wedding gift for Audrey. And an apology gift for you."

My heart melted and tears gathered in my eyes. This was the mom I remembered. The one who'd slowly disappeared over the last six or seven years. What had happened to change her, and how had she found her way back?

My phone vibrated with Audrey's text, showing a series of hearts and fireworks.

The saleswoman helped me try on the pink boots while my brain churned with questions. Did I even want to know the answers?

When I stood to get a better look in the mirror, the boots hugged my calves, ending below the knee. They were sassy and fun with my school dress, and perfect for dancing late into the night at my bestie's wedding.

"I love them, Mom."

"Excellent, we'll take both pairs. Can I also see those yellow ones in an eight and a half?"

"Certainly." The elated woman hurried off to get them.

I smirked. "Why do you need cowboy boots?"

"I called Audrey's mother last night, and she added me to the guest list."

My mind reeled. All the warmth drained away as cold reality settled over my heart. Today had been just one big act to get me back into the fold.

Of course, she'd weasel back into my life at the expense of my best friend. I'd set down boundaries, and Mom hadn't thought twice about disrespecting them.

"Mom, no. This isn't a good idea."

She whirled from the mirrors where she'd been admiring the yellow boots on her feet. "But they're so comfortable, and my butt looks amazing."

Was she deliberately misunderstanding me? "No, Mom, listen. I don't want you and Dad to come to the wedding."

"You know your father is too busy to attend. It'll just be me."

I shook my head, backing away. "I don't want you there."

"But, why not?" Her lower lip trembled as if she held back tears as she pulled the shoes off and put them back in its box.

"You've treated me horribly. I won't let you bring that drama to Audrey's wedding."

"But I apologized, Val. I thought you'd forgiven me."

I threw my hands up. "You can't erase years of degrading me with boots."

Mom turned her attention, thrusting the box of boots at the hovering saleswoman. "I'll take all three. Could you go ring them up? We'll be right behind you."

The woman nodded, her trained expression blank. How much family drama had she witnessed over the years?

Mom reached out as if to pull me into a hug, but I shrugged her off, feeling like a sullen teenager. "I refuse to let you manipulate me anymore, Mom. You need to go home."

She tilted her head to the side as if I were a riddle she needed to solve. "Val, I apologize for everything I've done to hurt you."

I wanted desperately to believe she'd changed, and things would be different going forward, but I forced myself to harden my heart. There were too many transgressions.

"It's hard for me to know if you mean it. I need time."

She and Dad had hurt me. They'd tried to use me. This is exactly why I set the boundaries in the first place. To protect myself from this kind of casual attempt to cross the line. If I let her attend Audrey's wedding, then a door would open for more issues to flare to life.

I couldn't let that happen. Not again. I stiffened my shoulders and hardened my tone.

"I need you to leave me alone."

Chapter 24
Evan

Cocoa met me at the door with a scrabble of claws on the wooden floor. She jumped up, resting her front paws on my shorts, her tongue darting out to lick any skin she could reach.

"Hey, girl." I petted her for a minute, then took her out before settling into my routine.

Grabbing shorts and a t-shirt, I went into the bathroom to shower off the day's grime. It felt radioactive—part sawdust, teenager germs, and sweat.

It had been days since Val and I had danced at Polar Vortex, but I was no closer to telling her I loved her.

She'd been busy with dress rehearsals and the daily grind of teaching. I heard she was helping Audrey with wedding invitations and other details.

I considered my options. Though the guys at school ribbed Oz about his grand gesture, he'd danced his way into Audrey's heart during their final soccer match. I considered asking him for advice, but there was never a good time.

In the end, I figured I'd just play it by ear and take a chance when the moment was right.

Back in the kitchen, I tossed the salad I'd picked up from the school cafeteria with vinaigrette and put a big pot on the stove to boil. Spaghetti always made me smile. Mom called it Da-sghetti because it was the only thing my dad cooked regularly.

Headlights swept through the front window and across the ceiling, followed by the sound of a car door opening and closing. I walked to the front door to greet Val.

"Hey, gorgeous," I said, catching Cocoa's collar before she could launch herself at her with fits of joy.

"Hi, Evan," she said softly. "May I come in?"

"Sure," I said, stepping back. "I'm making spaghetti. Will you join me?"

She turned to face me. "Oh, I don't want to interrupt your dinner. I just need to ask another favor."

The lines around her mouth and eyes hinted at her level of exhaustion. "Can I get you something?"

"Water, please." She sank into my recliner. Cocoa jumped onto her lap, and she patted my pup absently.

Turning the heat off on the stove, I retrieved two bottles of water from the fridge. I passed one to her and took the other with me to the sofa.

"How can I help?"

Her lips pursed. "I don't know why I rushed over here. It's not anything imminent."

"I'm glad you're here. Tell me what you need."

"I saw Mom today." Her eyes darkened. "She apologized."

Pigs do fly, and it's cold in hell. To say I was surprised would be an understatement. I'd tagged Aurora as one of those rich, entitled people who believed their shit didn't stink.

Val took a long drink of water before continuing. "We went shoe shopping. It all seemed so normal before it all went to hell. I actually thought we could work it out. At least for a minute, it seemed like we would."

She paused again, twisting the bottle in her hands. "Then she dropped the bomb on me. She'd called Audrey's mom and finagled an invitation to the wedding. I knew then that nothing had changed, and she was manipulating me."

I left the sofa and knelt at her feet. My hand found hers.

She took a deep breath, clinging to my hand. "I planned to ask you to Audrey's wedding as my date."

She wouldn't do that if she didn't have feelings for me. My heart raced, making it hard to hear her over the rapid drumming.

She continued, "A real date, Evan. Not this fake whatever I've been hiding behind, but my mom ruined it, the same as she always does."

"What do you mean?"

"I need you to help me stop my parents. They would ruin the wedding and continue to harass me if they attend."

It took me two seconds to decide. "Of course, I'll help you."

"There'll be a standoff because they can't take no for an answer. My mother bought shoes for the wedding."

She clutched my hand in her lap as if it were a life preserver.

I tried to follow her logic and failed, but it didn't matter. "I'll help. Whatever you need."

"Thank you. You're a good person, Evan."

Maybe it was the expression on her face, or that she had tears in her eyes, but this seemed like the right time. I wanted her to know she could always come when she needed help. I would be there for her through the good and the bad.

A door opened in my heart. "You don't need to thank me. I love you. I'd do anything for you."

Time stood still while she stared at me, into me.

I'd rushed it and bungled the whole thing.

"I-I don't know what to say."

"You don't have to say anything. I just thought..."

"Of course, you did. I said I wanted to ask you on a date, and I did—I do. I like you, Evan, but I'm afraid—"

"Of me?"

"Afraid of loving you. Of being vulnerable. My heart's trampled, and I can't risk it again."

A crushing weight sat on my chest. She spoke of me breaking her heart while she pulverized mine. A sad laugh erupted from my lips.

Her expression was unbearably sad. She opened her mouth to say something, but her cell phone rang in her bag.

She let it go to voicemail.

I stood, pulling her up in front of me, and wrapping my arms around her. "Your life has been out of your control for months, but I promise that between us, you can make all the rules."

She lay her cheek against my chest, her arms coming around me. Somewhere in the distance, the phone rang again. I shifted away. "You should get that."

"Whoever it is can leave a message," she replied.

"Okay." I bent my knees and picked her up in my arms, carrying her to the sofa.

She curled up on my lap, her head on my shoulder. I stroked her soft hair, wishing I hadn't put more pressure on her.

When the phone rang a third time, she left me to answer it.

Chapter 25
Val

As I sat on Evan's lap in his living room. I could barely hear myself think over the chanting in my mind.

He loves me. He loves me. He loves me.

He said I had all the power. The control. Nothing would change if I didn't want it to, but his declaration made everything different.

I'd known he liked me, but love seemed so huge, and I didn't know how to react.

My phone rang a third time. I couldn't sit here all night ignoring it. I slipped off his lap to answer, and a chill ran through me. I already missed his body heat and the smell of his cologne.

"You can take it in the office," he said with a gesture down the hall.

"Hello?" I answered as I closed the office door behind me.

"Hey, V." Bobby's cheerful voice thundered in my ear, so I jerked the phone away from my ear.

"Hey." My voice sounded steady, even though it was scratchy from crying. "What can I do for you?"

"My friend got back to me. I thought you'd want to know the details right away."

I sat down at the small desk and saw the framed picture of his family propped up on the surface. In the photo, the sun shone, and everyone smiled. A tiny voice whispered that I'd never fit in with them. I was too different, too fussy.

"Val? You still there?"

"Yeah. What did she find out?"

"Logan and your dad pass money around. Your dad pays Logan a regular installment of three thousand a month, and Logan has given your father almost twenty thousand dollars this year."

The words echoed in my head. "What does that mean?"

"It could mean they are doing work for each other."

"I doubt that."

"My friend thinks your dad could be paying blackmail. Also, considering that Logan wants to marry you, the twenty thousand might be..."

"What? Buying me?" Betrayal and denial fought inside me. Whatever was going on wasn't good.

"I'm sorry, V. Let me know how you want to play this. I've got your back."

"Thanks, Bobby. I'll let you know." I disconnected the call clumsily. My cold, stiff fingers almost dropped the cell.

I sat there, replaying the conversation in my head over again. Wondering what to do with this information.

When the phone rang again, I jumped. Assuming it was Bobby calling back, I answered.

"Hi."

"Valentine," Mom said, her voice shaky.

"Mom, I can't do this tonight. I'm hanging up."

"I'm leaving your father."

My mind whirled. I'd often thought Mom and Dad might be better off living separate lives, but I never thought she'd leave him. "Wait. What?"

"I was going to tell you during dinner, but I didn't get the chance. I know I ruined everything by being pushy, but I needed you to know." Her voice trembled, but she didn't cry.

Despite what I said, I couldn't hang up on her. "Are you okay?"

"I'm fine. I'm staying at the Hilton." She paused. I braced myself. "Did you know that Gran left me money, too? She saw how your dad chased one scheme after another. She wanted to protect me, so after my father died, she organized trusts for both of us."

For weeks, months, I begged her to explain what happened and why things had changed. And now I knew. My Gran was controlled by her husband. Grandad had forced Mom to marry a man she didn't love, but Gran had taken the power back with the trusts.

"I loved Gran so much. I'm glad she thought to take care of you."

Mom sighed. "Over time, I made investments. Now I have enough money to live well for the rest of my life. I never let Matt touch the money, not once, and he hates me for it."

I waited, not sure what to say. I knew Dad had a temper. Was he abusive?

She continued. "I overheard him speaking to Logan last night. They have a business agreement with a

Japanese investment group. Your father siphoned money from his hedge fund investors to buy in, and now he can't pay them back. They devised a plan for Logan to marry you to gain control of your trust."

My mind was busy connecting the dots with what Bobby's friend said. There was still one glaring question, though.

"What about the grandchildren you had to have?"

She sighed. "I made a mess of my life, Val. Your father didn't make me happy, and neither did having a baby. Garden club, the volunteering with the D.A.R. and the historical society left me more depressed than anything. When your father decided you needed to marry Logan, he convinced me to push for a grandchild. It's not an excuse, but I was lonely. I won't lie and say I don't want grandchildren. Edith and Meryl are always bragging about theirs. I've made mistakes as a mother, but I think I could be a good granny."

A good granny? I wanted to laugh. I'd always imagined any children I had would have to call my mom Mrs. Bellini.

Silence grew across the phone line. I knew she wanted me to say something comforting. To forgive her. But my lips wouldn't form the words. "Mom, I don't know what to say. I need to think about this."

"Your father and Logan are meeting at their pickle ball court tomorrow at ten. I'm going to do what I should have done years ago and confront them.

The steely resolve in her voice told me all I needed to know. She would do this for me and for herself. The least I could do was support her.

"I'll pick you up in the morning, and we'll go together.

***

As soon as I'd hung up with Mom, I texted Audrey.

6:30 PM
Me: Help.

6:33 PM
Audrey: Oz and I are on our way out to dinner. Wanna meet?

I walked out of the office, calling Evan. "Want to meet Oz and Audrey for dinner?"

Entering the kitchen, I found Evan in front of a boiling pot of water with an empty spaghetti box in his hand.

Evan gestured to the stove and raised an eyebrow. "Maybe invite them here?"

6:36 PM
Me: Come to Evan's house. He's making spaghetti.

6:37 PM
Audrey: I love it when men cook. Is he wearing an apron?

6:37 PM **Me:**
Are you coming over to find out?

6:39 PM
Audrey: See you in seven.

Evan took a plastic bag of sauce from the fridge. "Mom's homemade tomato sauce." He poured it into a saucepan and turned it on low heat. "You can compare it to your Gran's."

"Your mom is a fabulous cook. I'm sure it will be wonderful."

When we were seated at the kitchen table, I told them about the phone calls.

Evan's brow furrowed. "So, your dad is embezzling money from his hedge fund to invest with another company and wants to use your trust fund, too?"

I nodded; twirling noodles coated in chunky, spicy sauce. The meal was delicious, a balm on my soul after the last forty-five minutes. Relaying the conversations with Bobby and Mom had depleted my energy.

"And your mom told you all this because she's leaving him?" Audrey asked, patting Cocoa's head in her lap.

"I don't know." I shrugged. I'd wondered the same thing. What was Mom's motivation? I wanted to believe her contrite tone on the phone, but I'd been burned before. "Maybe she feels bad."

"She ought to," Evan muttered. "She ran you through the wringer."

"Agreed." Audrey nodded.

I finished off the last of my pasta. "I'm worried it's all an act. I'm going to show up tomorrow, and she'll handcuff us together until I produce an heir or something." I chuckled at my joke, my friends joining for a second.

"I'm not sure you should confront them without backup." Oz cautioned me.

"I'll be fine," I assured him. "I took a personal day from school, but y'all have to work."

"Text me every hour, so I know you're okay," Audrey demanded.

I snorted. "Kinda hard if I'm handcuffed to my mom, but I'll do my best."

Munching on a carrot, Audrey asked, "Are you sad about your parents' separation?"

"I'm not surprised, really. They never had much in common. She told me about a lover she'd hoped to marry, but her dad disapproved and made her marry my dad."

"I wonder where that guy is now," Audrey mused. "Maybe he's out there, single and lonely, and they'll find each other again."

Oz winced. "You've watched too much Hallmark Channel."

She shrugged. "It relaxes me."

Evan grinned. "My sister, Gennie, says she watched Hallmark movies during pregnancy, so she could remember the Happy Ever After."

I giggled. "Aud, you should see her husband. He's Adonis reincarnated. All I wanted to do was stare at him."

When we finished, Evan and I cleared the table and made quick work of cleaning up. After bumping into him so much, I hoped we'd do it again.

But we made a good team, moving around the small kitchen without crashing into each other.

"Do you have any cookies, Evan?" Audrey called from the living room.

Evan opened a cabinet and pulled out a box of sandwich cookies. Opening the flap, he turned the box over. "I'm all out."

"Do you seriously have an empty box in your pantry?"

"It's a great weight control strategy. I never buy more 'cause I think I still have a box."

She gaped at me like I had two heads, but I noticed a tiny curve of her lips.

Oz poked his head into the kitchen. "We've got to go. Audrey will have a craving meltdown if we stay, and you don't want to see her like that."

Audrey rested her hands on her hips. "I will not."

Oz rolled his eyes. "Last night, you cried when we didn't have chocolate ice cream."

The two of them were so sweet together. I could only hope that someday, I would have that kind of relationship.

I glanced at Evan, only to find him staring at me. The heat of his gaze met mine, and it traveled straight to my heart, kick-starting something I thought was long dead. Dopamine and oxytocin flooded my body, triggering my desire to strip Evan naked. A purely physical reaction not triggered by love, only gratitude and lust.

Oz coughed, and I startled, breaking eye contact. How long had Evan and I locked eyes?

"We're gonna go. Thanks for dinner. Be safe tomorrow, Val."

Shaking off the sensations coursing through me, I hugged Oz and then Audrey. "I will."

"Text me," Audrey demanded. "And kick their asses."

"I will," I repeated as Evan and I walked them to the door. Like a couple.

Warmth crept through me. Did I want this? The whole package?

Evan said he loved me, but did that translate to moving in together? I pictured us cooking and working side by side. Snuggling on the sofa and lying in bed tangled together. I imagined planting a garden in the backyard, flowers tumbling out of planters, and candles lighting the night sky on warm nights.

My mind swirled with possibilities. My body overloaded with sensation. The hairs on my arms stiffened, and my breath came out in short pants.

Did I love him?

Evan and I stood together at the door, watching their car lights disappear down the road.

My brain and body separated.

One urged me to turn into Evan's embrace, to kiss him, hold him, revel in him. I didn't need to think at all, just lean into the emotions.

The other begged for time to think, to examine my feelings, place them under the microscope, and see how this new paradigm worked.

I turned to Evan, and the flash of his dimple turned my insides to liquid heat. His hands circled my waist, and he urged me close.

I sighed, resting my head on his chest. "I'd love to stay, but it's late. I need to write sub plans and be up early tomorrow."

"I understand," he said. His hand tipped up my chin to give me a kiss.

I shuddered as our lips met, my body going up in flames, but my willpower tossed ice water on the fire. I pulled back. "When all of this is settled, I'd like to..."

"Me too."

I nodded, running my hands up his chest before stepping back.

Chapter 26
Val

Mom charged into the Richmond Heights Golf and Pickleball Club like she was ready to take on the social elite and bring down capitalism. Her red dress showed off her thin frame, and the sky-high heels made her look powerful, sexy, and ready to kick butt.

I still wasn't sure this sneak attack was the best plan, but I fell in behind her, in my sleeveless emerald sheath. I'd chosen chunky, black heels, perfect for grinding men under them.

No one stopped us as we made our way to Pickleball Court Two where my father and Logan were playing. We stormed down the hallway, following the grunt and thwack of men batting a ball around.

Logan's voice carried through the open door of the court. "Your women are out of line."

The ball whacked against a racquet but went out of bounds. My dad responded, "I have it all under control."

"You're staying in a hotel. Aurora isn't answering your calls, and Valentine threatened us with a restraining order."

Dad snarled. "All you needed to do was marry Valentine, but I don't see her running to you, begging for marriage."

"If you had your house in order, she and I would already be married," Logan spat out. "Serve, would you?"

The sound of the ball echoed back and forth as they played for a bit in silence. When the next shot bounced out of bounds, footsteps approached. Mom and I pressed our backs against the wall.

"I need a drink," my father panted.

Logan walked closer too, his voice loud and clear from where our hiding spot. "How much more is this going to cost me?"

"I'm waiting for Valentine's bank to call me back. Just keep sending the payments to Akari."

Anger thrummed through my body. I struggled to reconcile this greedy, horrible man with my father.

"I can only do so much." Logan's frustration was evident. "We're running out of time."

"Both of us will be stinking rich soon enough. You can divorce Valentine, and I'll leave Aurora."

"Will you marry Kerry?"

Wasn't there a Kerry in Mom's book club? No wonder that name sounded familiar.

My mother bristled; her outraged gasp sounded loud in the empty corridor. She clutched the strap of the bag on her shoulder tightly as her body vibrated with fury.

"I'm never marrying again," Dad said. "I'm going to play the field. There's plenty of women who'll let a rich man do anything."

Mom marched around the corner before I could stop her. "You're a filthy liar!" she bellowed, lunging at Dad, whose head jerked in her direction.

She hit him over the head with her heavy red Prada bag in a vicious swipe.

"Aurora, stop it!" Dad yelled, fighting off the attack in his flimsy white towel.

I grabbed my mom, pulling her back. "Mom, don't hit him. They'll call security."

My father growled, stalking toward the phone mounted on the wall. His face was beet red with anger and embarrassment. "Fantastic idea, I'll call them and have you both removed."

"You are a cheating bastard!" Mom shrieked, breaking away from me and rushing after him. "Go ahead and try to throw me out. It's my money that pays for your membership."

Logan circled my parents as they snarled at each other, issuing threats and ultimatums.

His jaw was tight as he glared at me. "How much did you hear?"

"All of it. You're in over your heads and decided to use me to solve the problem."

A muscle by his eye twitched once, twice before he spoke. "I'm only trying to help your dad. His business is bankrupt. He would've lost it all years ago if it wasn't for me. I've been taking his money and investing it."

I crossed my arms over my chest. "Did you know he's embezzling his client's money?"

Logan could lie without any tells. His straight face was legendary, so I smiled when he blinked. A year ago, I might have believed that blink meant he hadn't known, but not now.

"You're up to your neck in it with him," I said.

"I thought we could pay them back before they even caught on, but—"

I stared at him. "How would marrying me have solved anything?"

He met my eye and glanced away. "I thought we'd suit one another."

"Stop lying!"

His face tightened menacingly as cold light entered his eyes. "The truth is your mother is very wealthy and all their assets are in her name. I planned to trick you into giving me access to your trust. I'm good at making money. It would have benefited both of us."

"You are an accessory to all the crimes my father has committed."

"Why do you think I'm trying to save him and his company?"

"To save your ass," I said. There was no surprise, anger, or disappointment in my voice. Only realization.

"You're beautiful, Valentine." He twirled a tendril of my hair around his finger, leering at me. "If it weren't for your fucking stubborn streak, I might have enjoyed the perks of marriage with you."

I jerked away from him. "You're disgusting. Stay away from me. I'm getting a restraining order immediately."

His fingers grasped my upper arm like claws. "Your father owes me close to a million dollars."

I tried to wriggle out of his grasp. "If that's true, you were an idiot to lend him the money. Now let go of me."

He tightened his hold brutally. "Make me."

Reeling back with my other arm, my hand balled into a fist as swung a right hook into his nose. Pain shot through my knuckles as I felt the cartilage crunch on impact.

He let go of me as blood ran down his face. "You broke my nose!" He grabbed for a towel, trying to staunch the crimson flow.

Dad growled. "I only did it because you wanted grandchildren."

Mom reeled back and slapped Dad. The sound echoed off the rafters. "You asshole!"

He held his hand to his cheek, and I imagined a red mark bloomed between his fingers.

"I'm changing the locks on the house. When you want your things, call my lawyer."

"You can't do that!"

"Yes, I can. That butt-ugly house you love so much is in my name." She pulled a business card out of her bag and threw it in his shocked face.

"Aurora," Dad begged. "Let's go someplace and talk about this."

"No!" I'd never seen my mother more assertive in my life. She turned, taking in the fresh bruises on my arm and Logan's blood-soaked face and towel.

"Honey—" Dad tried again from behind her, but she cut him off.

"My lawyer speaks for Val and me from now on."

She took my elbow. We left with our heads held high, marching through the crowd that had gathered outside the door.

Chapter 27
Val

"I can't believe I ever trusted that lying idiot." Mom sniffed, dabbing her eyes with a tissue. Her make-up was smeared, and thick smudges of mascara gathered under her eyes.

Anger, frustration, and relief mingled inside me. I was furious with Logan and my father, and I wasn't sure I could ever forgive them, but I finally had the answers I'd sought.

The events of the morning swirled through my mind. My father ... sleeping with other women, embezzling money, and using me to dig himself out of the hole he'd dug. Greed had torn my family apart.

I patted her hand while keeping my eyes on the road.

"It'll be okay," I said, hoping it was true.

She gasped. "What if he gave me an STD? I'm going to kill him."

"You can get tested, Mom."

She was beyond hearing me as her mind flipped to another issue. "I am so sorry, Val. I tried to marry you off to Logan. They would have used your money and ruined your life. I wouldn't blame you if you never forgave me."

She burst into tears, sobbing uncontrollably.

"I forgive you, Mom," I shouted over her wailing cries. "They used you too."

I turned into the driveway, waiting while she gathered herself. "I hate this house. I know you won't believe it, but I wanted something smaller, but your father wanted to show off, make a statement, so I went along with it."

"I'm sorry. I never liked this house either."

She sniffled. "I made too many concessions for him. I compromised because that's what I thought I had to do." She blew her nose and stuffed the tissue into her purse. "But that ends today."

She exited the car, climbing the stairs to the house, her back ramrod straight despite her red face and swollen eyes. Whipping out her phone, she marched inside.

I turned off the engine and texted Audrey.

10:48 AM

Me: Back at Mom's house. Dad and Logan are greedy assholes.

10:49 AM

Audrey: Glad you're safe.

I left the car and followed Mom into the house.

She was in the living room on the phone with her lawyer. "I want a divorce as soon as possible, and I want to sell the house. He can have what he wants out of it, and I'm selling the rest."

Leaving her to finish her call, I wandered into the kitchen and pulled two bottles of water from the fridge, carrying them back. I handed one to Mom when she hung up.

"I'd rather have wine," she said sullenly.

"Hydrate first, Mom."

She drank the water, the adrenaline seeping out of her body as she slumped on the sofa.

"There's so much to do," she said wearily. "I'm not sure where to begin."

I wasn't sure either. Did they have lists for this situation on the internet?

"You've spoken to the lawyer; I think that's a good start. Maybe you should lie down for a while."

A panicked expression flashed over her face. "Not here. He's everywhere here. It makes me feel slimy. I can hardly breathe."

I didn't blame her. I wouldn't want to be alone in this depressing place. "You could go back to the Hilton…"

Her sad eyes met mine, and she shrugged.

"There's not really another option, Mom."

Her lips opened, and she said the six words no adult child ever wants to hear. "I want to stay with you."

Thankfully, my phone buzzed. Motioning for her to give me a minute as I stepped back into the hallway.

11:32 AM Audrey:
Is everything going okay?

11:33 AM Me:
Help! My mom wants to come live with me.

11:34 AM
Audrey: Yikes, like forever?

11:34 AM
Me: I don't know. Pray for me.

"Mom," I said as I returned. "I'm not sure you'd be happy in Marchfield. And my apartment is so small. I don't know—"

"I promise, you won't even know I'm there."

That was a full-blown lie. My mother was a category-five hurricane kind of guest. The kind that made you want to evacuate to safety before they even arrived. I needed to set some boundaries, or she'd run all over me.

"It's just that I have to work, and with the play performances coming up and Audrey's wedding, I'm not going to be home that much."

"Leave the wedding planning to me. You know how good I am at throwing a party."

Part of me leaped with joy at the thought of Mom taking over the wedding details. I had a list of things to do in the next two weeks that would take a miracle to complete.

On the other hand, Mom's parties were flamboyant. Audrey and Oz wouldn't want her adding a tablespoon of crazy to the mix.

"This isn't just a party. It's Audrey's wedding, Mom. She wants a fun, Western-themed wedding, not a three-ring-circus."

"Of course, it is, and I promise not to overstep. I just need time away from all of this." She gestured to the house. "To clear my head before I tackle the rest of my life. Please, Val."

I rubbed the pain throbbing in my temples. Living with Mom would be a challenge from beginning to end, but she is a refuge. How could I refuse?

I lifted my chin, resolved to help. "How long will you stay?"

"Just until the wedding, I promise. I'll help you with the wedding, find a new place, and get my head on straight."

How would Audrey feel if I pawned my mom off on her wedding? "I need to talk to Audrey first, Mom, but you can stay with me."

I tried not to groan.

***

Seven hours later, I hauled three large suitcases into my apartment and down the hallway to my guest room.

"You're only staying two weeks, Mom. Why do you need all these bags?"

"One for each week. The third is cosmetics, accessories, and shoes."

She frowned as she glanced around the small room. When I'd moved out, I'd taken my childhood bedroom furniture before I'd bought a bigger bed and moved the full-sized bed in here. I added a dresser I'd bought at a yard sale and end tables and lamps. It was clean and tidy, but it wasn't close to the Hilton.

Before she could complain about the room, I said, "I'll let you unpack and get settled while I figure out something for dinner."

"I'd love to have Thai tonight."

"Marchfield doesn't have a Thai restaurant. How about Chinese?"

The frown was larger this time with an added put-upon sigh. "Alright."

"Take your time. I need to check over my lessons for tomorrow."

I hurried into my bedroom, shutting the door behind me. Kicking off my shoes, I flopped down on my bed. Closing my eyes, I tried meditative breathing, but even that felt stressful.

Unlocking my phone, I called Evan. It went straight to voicemail, so I left a message.

"Hey, it's me. I'm alive. Call me, or I'll call you back in a bit. My mom is here, and I need to order Chinese. Bye."

Hanging up. I put my phone down, only to have it ring. It was Audrey.

"Hey, I thought I'd call since I'm not sure if you heard. Evan had to leave early today. Yona had an emergency, and he went to help."

A tiny seed of anxiety dropped into my gut.

"What kind of emergency?"

"I don't know. He took off as soon as they found a substitute around ten. You haven't heard from him?"

"No. I just tried to call him, but it went straight to voicemail."

The seed expanded. He should have arrived in Asheville by now. Why hadn't he answered his phone?

"I'm sure he'll call you as soon as he can. How are you doing?"

"I'm exhausted, my face hurts from forced smiling, and my knuckles ache."

"Why are your knuckles sore?"

"I broke Logan's nose when I punched him."

There were three beats of silence before she cheered. "Way to go. You're a beast."

It did feel pretty good to come out on top for once.

"One last thing. My Mom wants to help with the wedding."

"Anything for you, Rocky. Give her my mom's number, and they can discuss it."

"I owe you one," I said, gratitude making my eyes well up.

Changing the subject, Audrey said, "I missed you at school today. We had a fire drill, and I had no one to roll my eyes at."

We chatted a bit longer and hung up. A little of the weight had lifted off my shoulders until I remembered Evan and Yona.

Two hours later, I still hadn't heard from Evan. I'd called two more times, been sent to voicemail, and hung up instead.

Mom and I went to bed early. I lay in bed with my phone on my chest, hoping Evan would reach out.

***

I must have fallen asleep because the vibration of an incoming call woke me. The sky was still dark behind my curtains, so I knew it was early.

I squinted at the bright screen, reaching for my glasses on the bedside table.

It was Evan.

"Hello," I croaked, my voice rough from sleep.

"Hey, gorgeous. Sorry to call at the butt crack of dawn, but I wanted to talk to you before I hit the road."

I slid up against the pillows. "Are you driving home today?"

"Yeah. There's nothing else I can do here."

"What happened? Audrey said Yona had an emergency, and you had to leave school."

He sighed, and I imagined him running his hand through his dark hair. "Yeah. A toilet on the second floor flooded while they were all at school. The water got into the walls, and the place is uninhabitable."

It was rotten luck, but why did Evan have to drive six hours to save her? A spark of jealousy ignited in my heart. There had to be people closer who could help.

"That's terrible. Where are they going to live?"

"They moved in with my parents temporarily until school's out for the summer in their district at the end of the week. I'm not sure what they're going to do after that."

Dread joined with the jealousy. "Is she still considering moving to Marchfield?"

He was silent for a moment, and I wondered if he had heard the emotion in my voice. "Yeah. She wants to come down this weekend and search for a rental."

Emotions swamped me. I wanted to hate Yona, but I couldn't. She'd lost her husband and had two teenage daughters to raise with very little support. I understood why she would want a fresh start in Marchfield, closer to her found family. And yet, I wanted Evan all to myself.

It didn't seem fair, I'd just realized I loved him, and now I'd have to share him.

"What happened with your dad?"

"Mom's lawyer contacted the police. He and Logan will be called in for questioning."

"I'm sorry, Val." His deep voice was filled with regret. "I wish I was there yesterday when you called."

I grappled with my feelings, refusing to cry. How had I ended up in this shamble?

"It's okay. Mom's here, and I'm trying to support her."

"Are you going to school today?"

"Yeah. I can't take off any more time before testing."

"I should be home by two. Can I come over? Bring some dinner for you and your mom?"

"I don't know," I said. The weight on my shoulders seemed too much to bear. My emotions were a hindrance. I needed to put my head down and plow through the next few weeks. Then, maybe...

"Actually, Evan, I am beyond busy right now. The play is this weekend, and the wedding is the next. And with my mom here, I just can't deal with anything else."

"What can I do?" Evan's voice was almost pleading. As if he knew what was coming next.

"I'd like to pause whatever this is between us for two weeks. We both have things to sort out, and it'll be easier if we don't have more hanging over our heads."

"Are you sure this is what you want?"

Was I?

"Yes..."

The logical part of me agreed that this was for the best, even while the emotional side of me wailed.

The silence stretched, neither of us wanting to hang up, but not knowing what to say.

"I'll miss you, and I'll talk to you at the reception."

"Miss you, too," I whispered and hung up before I changed my mind.

Chapter 28
Evan

The last act of *Villains Incorporated* the student actors worked hard to give the audience the best show possible.

I sat a row behind Audrey and Oz. She held a bouquet of flowers in her lap that I assumed was for Val. Rachel and Keith were next to them. After intermission, Keith had tucked his arm around Rachel, and she snuggled close and was whispering something in his ear.

The plot reached its climax. The dialogue became fast and furious, and the audience roared with each punch line. The main characters were all back on stage and the villains seemed mostly reformed.

A tiny sixth-grade girl, ironically playing the loudmouth principal, whirled around to point at another character. Misjudging her distance from the set piece beside her, she crashed into it.

The three-sided wall structures toppled like dominoes, the first whacking a second, which fell into a third. Kids dodged the pinned fabric and plywood pieces, and everyone on stage froze, not knowing how to continue.

Val appeared with the backstage hands, a cheery smile pinned to her face. "Did someone call for maid service?"

The audience laughed, clapping as she strode across the stage. Lifting a piece back into place, her muscles flexed in her black sleeveless dress. A faded green and yellow bruise on her arm drew my attention.

She gracefully helped the crew reposition the rest. After whispering encouragement or directions to the actors, she smiled widely in the audience.

Finally, she announced, "Thanks for bearing with us. On with the show." And ran off the stage.

On the stage, Val bowed, her neck arched. My mind conjured an image of her in bed, riding me, her back bending as she bent to kiss my lips. I shifted in my seat.

The show resumed, but I couldn't get my mind back on the play. I hadn't seen her in seven days. It was torture being in the same school and not seeing her. Every night I reached for my phone, wanting to call just to hear her voice and make her laugh. But I held back. If she'd asked for time, and I'd give it to her.

After the show ended, the standing ovation finished, and the pictures were taken, Val popped out from behind the curtains. Rachel and Audrey met her with hugs and flowers, celebrating the achievement.

I longed to jump up and join them. The protector in me wanted to check out those bruises on her arm and know she was all right.

Aurora materialized. I hadn't seen her in the audience, but she must have been in the back. A man hurried behind her, carrying a flower arrangement filled with orange birds of paradise and salmon-colored roses the size of a small tree.

Val jumped off stage and into her mother's arms. I remembered her saying her parents had never attended her shows, and I was glad she had this moment.

Oz and Keith turned to talk with me.

"What's up, big guy?" Oz asked.

Before I could answer, Keith said, "Must be hard having Val's mom living with her."

"It's temporary," I said hollowly.

Oz laughed. "Audrey says Aurora's a blessing and a curse. She's taken over the wedding, and I heard Val and Ellie had to talk her out of bringing in a rodeo show and a bucking bronco."

I chuckled. "Sounds like fun."

"If by fun, you mean fucking chaos. You're spot on."

Keith chimed in. "Rachel told me Val's parents are divorcing, and her dad and that Logan guy are being investigated."

Oz kept his eyes on the women, but added, "Her dad may do jail time."

How would she handle the court case? Would she testify against him? There were still so many questions up in the air.

And yet, Val came to school every day with a smile on her face and got the job done. Perhaps she walked a little slower and laughed a little less, but she showed up for her students.

"It must be killing her." Oz winced.

"V is stubborn as hell," Keith said. "She could be dying and none of us would know."

Oz agreed. "She tells me she's fine, but in that tone."

The three of us nodded. "The one where you know it's not fine, but you also know you might be murdered if you ask too many questions."

I'd heard that tone often. Fala pronounced every apartment we'd toured as *fine* in a way that sounded as if we were killing her soul by asking her to move.

Right now, Jacy, Fala, and Yona were camped out at my house. Since none wanted to come to the play with me, I'd left them with pizza and cupcakes.

Wanting to change the subject, I said, "How's imminent parenthood going?"

"It's fucked up watching Red go through it and not be able to do anything."

"You're doing lots of stuff. Getting her pillows and feeding her cravings. Not to mention marrying her in less than a week." Keith assured him with a pat on the back.

"Do you know what babies do to women? She and I watched one of those real birth videos together. It's like *Alien*. There's blood and shit everywhere, tons of screaming in agony, and this thing comes out."

He shuddered, his face so horror-filled, I had to smother a laugh. "My sister says as soon as you hold the baby, it's like it never happened."

"That's bullshit," Oz muttered, shrugging his shoulders.

"I guess you'll know this fall."

Oz sighed and stood. "I'm heading over to congratulate Val. You guys coming?"

I considered it. I'd love to hug Val, feel her body pressed against mine, and hear her voice in my ear. But I also knew that walking away would be hard.

I'd promised to be patient. The remaining week would be an eternity of cold showers and loneliness, but it was a blink of an eye in the long run.

I stood and edged out of the aisle. "Tell her the play was fabulous, and I'm nominating it for a Tony Award. Ask her to save me a dance at the wedding."

I clapped a hand on Keith's shoulder and walked up the main aisle and out into the warm May night.

***

At home, Cocoa snuggled up on the couch with Fala and Jacy as they watched *Twister.*

A cow flew in a raging storm across a highway, and Jacy looked up at me. "Are there tornadoes in Virginia?"

I sat on the edge of the sofa. "Sometimes. Although, I've never heard of one hitting Marchfield."

"You just jinxed us. One will hit as soon as we move here," Fala muttered.

Jacy jumped up, threw her arms out, and spun around. "I think it would be fun to be that cow."

Fala rolled her eyes at her sister. "You're an idiot."

"I am not! Right, Evan?"

I sighed. I hated being pulled in between the two girls. Since Fala had turned into a surly teen, nothing I said appeased her or helped the situation. "Where's your mom?"

"Taking a shower," Jacy said. "Do we have any donuts?"

"How about a cupcake?"

"We ate them all," she giggled.

"We can get some donuts in the morning."

"Duh." Fala drew out the syllable.

"Uncle Evan, tell her donuts are for dessert too, not just breakfast." Jacy threw a pillow at her sister.

Fuck. Parenting was hard.

"I'm going to take Cocoa O-U-T-S-I-D-E. Either of you want to come?"

Cocoa's ears pricked up, and she leaped off the couch, racing to the door.

"When did she learn how to spell?" Jacy asked as I picked up the leash.

"The same way you did." I answered, opening the door before they could say anything else.

I slipped out after both girls declined the offer.

Outside, the quiet of the night soothed me. Cocoa and I walked past houses lit with glowing lights. The sweet smell of wisteria drifted on the wind. A mockingbird ran through his repertoire, starting with a crow, then moving into a car alarm.

Cocoa smelled everything along the sidewalk, giving me time to settle into my skin. Going to the play and seeing Val awakened a deep ache inside me. I missed her.

Heading back to the house, I saw Yona come outside and sit on the porch, her dark hair shadowy around her shoulders.

"How was the play?" She asked. Something in her voice tipped me off that she was getting ready to ask something more important.

"It was funny. The kids did a great job."

She paused. "Did you see her?"

Despite all the years Yona and I had been friends, I'd felt a change happening between us, as if she were yearning for more. Now she seemed almost jealous of Val.

"Yeah, but we didn't talk." I sat down on the rocker beside her. Cocoa lay down in the grass and rolled on her back.

She straightened her shoulders. "I'm not sure how to say this," she said softly. "I think you and I could be happy together. It might not be romantic, but we could be a family."

I'd known something had changed after I'd seen her in March, but I hadn't wanted to face it, to hurt her.

"I know," I said. "Noah wanted me to take care of you and the girls, and there was a time before I moved to Marchfield that I'd considered..."

Her eyes searched my face. "But not anymore?"

I spread my hands wide. "I love Val."

Yona scoffed. "And she treats you worse than a dog. Cutting you off and ignoring you."

"You don't know her or her reasons." My patience frayed around the edges.

"I know it's hurting you." She stood, anger clouding her face.

"I'm sorry, Yona, but I can't be that man for you."

The anger drained from her, and we sat in the dark together until she stood. "I know, Evan. I just want you to be happy." She paused before she said, "Will you come inside and help us make a plan for tomorrow?"

"You still want to move to Marchfield?"

"I do. It is the right move for the girls and for me, even if it's not how I envisioned it."

She opened the door and slipped inside. The second woman to leave me alone in the dark in a week.

Chapter 29
Val

The days leading up to Audrey's wedding were a blur. Virginia state tests would begin after Memorial Day, so my classes were busy reviewing.

After school, Mom and I were off to the races on last-minute wedding preparations. I made a million calls confirming details. We'd stuffed goody bags, printed maps, and picked up Bobby and Oz's suits from the tailor. By Thursday, Leo and I were both chauffeuring out of town guests around.

Plus, I was living with my high-maintenance mother, who expected coffee in bed each morning and wanted to stay up until midnight talking.

I should have fallen into bed every night and passed out from sheer exhaustion. Of course, lying in the dark, my thoughts turned to Evan. Tossing and turning, my heart ached as I imagined his smile.

While I appreciated that he was doing what I asked, I also hated it. Secretly, I wished he'd turn alpha and beat my door down. Grunting out his need for me and carrying me off to his house.

Finally, the day of the wedding arrived, and Mom and I got up early to drive out to the farm to decorate. Diane and Ellie met us there, and the four of us scurried like Cinderella's mice.

By the time we got home, we had just enough time to shower and head to Curl Up and Di for hair and make-up.

The owner, Di, snapped her fingers and her team of beauticians got to work.

Sitting under the hair dryer, I felt my nerves amping up. It was only three hours until I would see Evan, and I couldn't get him out of my mind. I had so much to say to him, and I wasn't sure how to begin.

"You okay, honey?" Oz's mom slid into the chair beside me.

I jumped, so wrapped up in my thoughts I'd missed her approach. "I'm fine. Just a little tired."

"You look like you have a man on your mind."

"She does," Audrey commented from her chair.

Rachel laughed. "Evan."

Ellie smiled. "Don't you miss young love, Diane? The racing heartbeat and delicious shivers?"

Diane nodded. "Those were precious moments."

"And anxious ones," Ellie continued. "So many worries ... Does he love me? Do I love him?"

"I remember," Diane said wistfully. "Liam, Oz's father, was a handsome man. My friends and I were having dinner before going out to a concert, and he was at the bar. I lost my breath just staring at him."

"The first time I saw Jerry in his Navy dress uniform," Audrey's mom fanned herself. "My insides melted."

"Oz's shoulders blocked out the sun," Audrey said, "And I thought the world stopped spinning."

Their spicy meet cute stories filled my weary heart with joy, but... "How did you know he was the one?"

"Liam had a wicked wit," Diane said. "He kept me laughing."

"Audrey, your dad wrote songs for me. He took care of people and was a great father." Ellie hugged Audrey. "He loved you so much, honey."

Audrey fanned her face. "Don't make me cry, Mom." Di grabbed tissues and rushed to touch up Audrey.

Alone with my thoughts again, I admitted Evan and I had sexual energy and compatibility. He could make my heart race and my panties damp with just a look, but he also made me laugh. He was patient, caring, loved kids, and truly listened. He was different from the other men in my life.

Was that enough?

Before I could ponder that question, Leo arrived to take us to the farm. We dressed in the beautiful bride's room full of light and flowers, and when all the moms left, Audrey, Rachel, and I slipped on our cowboy boots and drank icy cold champagne.

Jemma arrived to lead us to the barn. The chorus of *A Thousand Years* by Christina Perri swelled to a crescendo as Rachel walked down the aisle. I followed.

Delicate pink mini roses and white lilies artfully strewn in every nook and cranny and filled the air with sweetness. Tiny fairy lights glowed by the thousands, suspended from the ceiling like a cloud of fireflies.

A bubble of joy surrounded the bride and groom. Audrey resembled a Cowgirl Princess, in her beautiful gown, white lace cowboy hat, her blue boots peeking out under the hem. She glowed from the inside out at Oz in his blue Armani suit.

The ceremony began, but their vows blurred into the background when I couldn't find Evan. Had he lost interest in the two weeks we'd been apart?

At the end of the service, I followed Audrey back down the aisle, trying not to hyperventilate. My bestie was married. Things would never again be the same.

Anxiety flooded through me, and a hollowness filled my chest. Close to a panic attack, and I took in shallow breaths as I searched for a place to hide.

People moved around me. The farm staff whisked by with trays of drinks and appetizers.

I'm okay, I thought, even as the room shrank and my eyes blurred with tears.

Mom's voice came from behind me. "Would you like some champagne?" I took the glass with shaky fingers. "Thanks."

Her head tilted, her expression growing concerned. "Are you okay?"

I took a deep breath and burst into tears. "He didn't come, Mom. Evan's not here."

"Oh, honey." She led me into the bridal suite. Closing the door behind us, she pulled me into a hug that felt both wonderful and strange. "Maybe he's been delayed. Did you call him?"

I shook my head, trying to breathe in, but couldn't. She patted my back, rubbing between my shoulder blades until I could finally speak.

"He's lost interest in me. When I wasn't there for sex, he moved on."

"I'm sure that's not true."

"He's just like Dad and Logan, Mom. How could I be so stupid?" I felt sick. The room was spinning. Covering my head with my arms, I sank down into a chair with my head between my knees.

"You aren't. Listen, it's not the same thing at all. Your father and I should never have married. Neither of us loved the other, but I convinced myself to try. When I had you, Matt and I were happy for a while. Your father loved you, and because he did, I hoped he would love me, too."

Listening to her calm voice helped steady my breathing.

"By the time you were three, your father was bored, chasing one scheme or skirt after another. I asked for a divorce, but there was always a reason or an excuse why we needed to stay together. He benefited by having a stable family and clients trusted him. By the time you were five, I stopped asking."

A tear slid down her face. I scurried to a small table by the door to fetch the box of tissues. Mom dabbed her eyes, trying to save her make-up.

"I should have taken you and left, but instead, I started drinking. I ended up shutting out your father, and you too. I sent you to camp, enrolled you in dance and acting to keep you busy and away."

Her unhappiness had shaped my life for better and worse. "I wanted to be a teacher after all those summers in camp. I love acting and theater because of the lessons you paid for."

Real tears trailed down her cheeks. "You always rose above and found the people and things you loved, and you fought for them. I've always admired that."

Surprise rolled through me until I recognized the truth in what she was saying. She was right. I was tenacious when protecting the people I loved.

"I'm so grateful for these few weeks we've had, but it's time for me to deal with the mess I've made."

"You're always welcome here."

She shook her head. "You have no idea how much I love hearing you say that, but I like Richmond. I have friends there. I'll find a smaller, happier apartment where I'm close, but not a burden."

"I love you, Mom."

"I love you too, and I've seen how Evan looks at you. And I see how you look at him. When he gets here, let him explain. Trust your judgment, but don't walk away from a chance at happiness."

And just like that, the world shifted. The ground moved under my feet. Everything seemed brighter.

I turned to my mom with a question on my lips. "Do you think I love him?"

"What do you think?"

"I do." The words came out slowly, but with zero doubt. I loved Evan.

I just needed to find him and tell him.

Chapter 30
Evan

Audrey and Oz had a happy glow about them as they danced, and to be fair, it wasn't just them. Mel and Bobby danced cheek to cheek. Keith and Rachel snuck off ten minutes ago. Love was in the air.

And I was two hours late.

It'd been a miracle I hadn't received a speeding ticket on my way home from Asheville. Dad had woken in the night with chest pain, and he and Mom had gone to the hospital.

She called me in tears. I'd taken leave and headed home. I dropped Cocoa off with Dakota from the gym, and it wasn't until I was at the state line that I realized I'd left my phone on the kitchen counter.

When I arrived, Dad was in surgery. Gennie and Mom sat on hard plastic chairs in the tiny, drab waiting room. We took turns going out for food and coffee until Dad was finally in recovery.

By late afternoon, mom was exhausted. After a lengthy discussion, I offered to spend the night with Dad, so she and Gennie could rest. Three hours later he was stable and sleeping, and I dozed in the chair next to his bed all night.

When I woke at dawn with a crick in my neck, Dad's eyes were open.

"Son."

"Dad," I jumped over to take his hand. "How are you feeling?"

His lips curved slightly. "You look like crap. What have you done to yourself?"

I barked out a relieved laugh and took a deep breath. "Back at you, Dad."

He lifted his hand, bruised from the IV. "I'm alive. Tell me your excuse."

I could never hide anything from him. Even after a seven-hour surgery, he could read me like a book.

"Val and I took a two-week break. It's been hard."

"Do you love her?"

Cutting to the chase. "Yeah, I do. I've loved her since the beginning, but she's having a tough time with her family."

"I've seen the love in her eyes. You don't need to worry."

"Thanks, Dad," I said, squeezing his hand. Tears welled up in my eyes. I'd almost lost him.

He slowly reached toward the cup of water on the tray over his bed. "When are the two weeks up?"

"Today, but ..."

I passed him the cup, tilting the straw toward his mouth. He swallowed, and I took the cup out of his shaky grasp.

"Go. You should go."

Mom rushed in with her hair loose, like she had jumped out of bed and raced here without taking time to braid it.

"Go where?" She asked. She plumped the pillows, adjusted the covers, and gave Dad a big kiss.

"He has a date with Val tonight."

"But," Mom's gaze bounced between us. "You just got here, Evan."

It broke my heart to see Mom so vulnerable. "I'll call her later from the house. I'm sure she'll understand."

Dad shook his head. "Don't guilt him into staying, Deyani. Go, get your girl, son."

Mom's watery eyes met mine. She nodded.

I hugged them both, tears spilling over. "I'll come back soon. I love you both."

On the trip home, every mile felt like an eternity. A thousand scenarios, both good and bad, flitted through my mind.

Val, throwing her arms around me, kissing my lips, telling me she loved me clashed with images of her head bowed, walking away with tears on her cheeks.

Finally, back in Marchfield, I showered and put on my suit. I debated calling her, but nerves bounced around in my belly like jellyfish.

Back in the truck, I turned the radio on and then off. Music couldn't soothe the waves of anxiety crashing over me. I tried deep breathing exercises, but nothing helped. Whatever happened today, good or bad, would change my life. Damn, I hoped it would be good.

At the farm, I parked and jogged toward the venue. Inside, the band finished a cover of *Body Like a Back Road* by Sam Hunt and announced they were taking a short break.

Lights twinkled like stars overhead. The sweet smell of flowers mixed with the new wood smell of the refurbished barn. I searched the crowd for Val.

And then she appeared.

She paused on the threshold of a small room at the opposite end of the space. Her fussy pink dress reminded me of cotton candy, making me lick my lips from wanting to taste her.

At the front of the room, Bobby rose to give her toast as Oz's Best Bud. My friend's voice faded away as Val glanced my way, and I crossed the room to her.

"Sorry, I'm late. It's a long story, but I'd like to tell it to you."

"Evan," she whispered. "You're here."

I blamed myself for the exhaustion that rounded her shoulders and left her face pale. Her wide, red-rimmed brown eyes searched mine. Had she been crying?

She'd thought I wasn't coming. "I had to go to Asheville. My dad had a heart attack."

"Oh no," she reached for my hand. "I'm sorry. Is he...?"

"He had bypass surgery and has a long road ahead of him." The more I explained, the more I worried she wouldn't believe me. "He's awake and talking. I would have called, but I left my phone."

I searched her face for a sign, hoping I hadn't made a mess of everything. I couldn't read her expression. She wore a mask, and I couldn't see behind it.

Her lips pursed together into a little heart. Her quiet voice filled with doubt. "I thought..."

"I'm sorry, Val. I would never intentionally hurt you. You know that, right?"

Laughter and applause pierced the bubble around us. Bobby's speech was over, and she called Val to come to the dais.

"And now the maid of honor," Bobby introduced her.

"I have to—"

"Go, it's okay. I'll be here when you're done."

She hurried to take the microphone from Bobby, turning to smile at everyone.

"As Audrey's maid of honor, it's my pleasure to welcome Oz officially onto the team. When she first met Oz, the odds were stacked against them finding true love." She paused, grinning over at Audrey and Oz.

"Lust." The crowd laughed. "They were definitely in *lust*. But *love* took them both by surprise."

"I knew Audrey was in over her head when she thought Oz was sexy wearing a sack dress and shiny red shoes on the faculty cheer squad." She paused for more chuckles.

"He had moves and was the only one brave enough to wear size-fourteen women's heels."

"He sure did," Stella called out.

"But Audrey thought she had to choose between her career and love. It was hard for her, but Oz never gave up. He challenged her to see the world differently, and here they are happily ever after."

"To Audrey and Oz." Everyone toasted the happy couple, and Audrey came over to hug Val.

For a moment, the best friends whispered together. Audrey's red head nodded, and Val turned back to the audience. Clearing her throat, her eyes found mine.

"I hope you'll all forgive me if I speak for just another minute, but I'd like to tell you a story. I grew up thinking happy ever after was a myth. Like Audrey, I thought falling in love was a made-up fairy tale adults used to pacify little girls. As a result, I've lived a lie, denying my emotions, and pushing men away because I was afraid."

Audrey slid an arm around Val's waist.

"Let it out, girl," Mel yelled from the back of the room.

Her mom raised a glass to her. "I love you, Val."

Listening to Val bare her soul to the crowd made me lightheaded. I realized I was holding my breath. I let it out with a hiss, trying to make sense of her words in.

Was she talking about me? About us?

"When I met a man brave enough to take all of this on," Val laughed, gesturing to herself. "I thought I needed to protect him from the messy, twisty, dark parts of my life. But really, I was guarding my heart, holding back the emotions to keep myself safe."

My knees felt weak. Her speech gutted me. The crowd's eyes were on me, waiting to see what would happen.

She swiped a tear running down her cheek. I wanted to smooth my hands over her hair, down her back to comfort her. I didn't need a public declaration. I just needed her.

I took a step in her direction, but Bobby grabbed my arm. "Whoa. Let her finish."

So, I waited with love in my eyes and my heart on my sleeve for her to finish.

"Evan Shurden, I love you. I love the way you view the world with optimism. I love your humor, and the way you call me Gorgeous." The audience sighed in unison, sharing this moment with us.

"I love that you know my favorite color, and how I would kill for a chocolate donut and a hazelnut coffee. I love your family and your sweet pup."

"What about his ripped body?" Bobby yelled from beside me.

"And his best friends?" Oz exclaimed.

"Knock it off, guys. Let her finish." Audrey scolded in her best teacher voice.

Val bit her lip. More tears flowed down her face. "I know I hurt you, Evan, but I'll make it up to you every day if you'll forgive me."

Nothing could keep me from her any longer. I made a beeline toward Val, vaulting over the gift table to get there faster.

She sprinted toward me. Her face lit up with love. She was the most beautiful woman I'd ever seen in my life.

When she leaped off the dais, the band struck up Bill Medley's *Time of My Life*, and I caught her in mid-flight. Her dress fluttered as I swung her around before lowering her to the floor. Our friends cheered and joined us on the dance floor.

My lips found her cheek, salty with tears. "I love you, too, Gorgeous."

"I love you, Evan."

My lips met hers. The buzzing of the crowd buzzed around us as the sweet taste of strawberries and champagne flooded my senses. The frothy material of her dress sighed as she snuggled closer, and I knew I was never letting her go again.

Moments later, I lowered her onto the toes of her cowboy boots. My hands cupped her damp face and wiped her tears away.

She whispered, "I'm sorry I pushed you away."

"You're here now, and that's all I need."

I kissed her again and wanted more. My mouth moved to her ear, and I whispered the plans I had for her later.

I was delighted as her cheeks turned pink in response.

The band moved on to *Signed, Sealed, Delivered* by Stevie Wonder. I tucked her close to me to dance.

She sneaked a peek up at me. "Hold me closer, Evan."

Chuckling, I said, "Whoops. I forgot this wasn't a middle school dance."

Sliding my hands to her hips, I dragged her against my body, moving to the music with my best *Dirty Dancing* imitation. She laid her head on my shoulder, and I savored the feel of her. "Are you ready to add some strings to this relationship?"

I felt her smile. "I want to go on a real date."

"Excellent idea, Gorgeous. You busy later?"

She tapped her temple with her finger as if thinking. "I have to feed Audrey's cat, but otherwise, I'm free for the rest of my life. What about you?"

My heart thudded in my chest. Was she asking me to marry her? A collage of images flitted through my mind of the two of us living together. Happy, content, and naked.

"I'm not ready to get married." She read my thoughts like newsprint.

I pulled back, peering down at her. "Okay. I didn't realize I proposed."

M. Jayne LaDow

I would though, and soon.

Chapter 31
Val

The party wound down after Oz whisked Audrey off for a short honeymoon at the beach. After dousing them in birdseed and well wishes, the guests crowded into Ubers or rode away with designated drivers.

I hung back to help clean up, but Mel and Bobby beat me to it.

"Go home." Mel urged as she stacked chairs. "We've got this."

"Well, I guess I should go feed Audrey's cat."

Bobby smirked. "Is that what the kids are calling sex nowadays? Feeding the cat?"

"Hush," Mel admonished Bobby. "If you want to go bumper to bumper later, stop teasing."

Bobby glanced hungrily at Mel, then narrowed her eyes at me. "Go home, Val. Mel and I have plans."

I fetched Evan, who was stacking chairs by the side wall. Taking Evan's hand, we walked outside to where an Uber waited for us. In the dark backseat, I snuggled up close to him, tipping my chin up, so I could brush his mouth with mine.

"I'm sorry we have to stop at Audrey's, but Stevie is the world's hungriest cat."

The driver turned up Jamiroquai's *Canned Heat*. I hoped he knew how to get there because I was busy.

"What movie is this from?" Evan murmured as his lips explored the skin on the inside of my wrist, trailing up my arm to my neck.

I purred as his teeth closed on my earlobe. *"Scott Pilgrim vs. The World."*

He hummed lightly in acknowledgment, the vibration sending ripples of sensation over my skin. I reached up to cup his face between my hands so I could press his lips to mine.

He tasted like sugar, chocolate, and whiskey as I drank him in. The crisp, earthy scent of mountain air and pine swamped my senses. I angled my body against his, pressing my breasts against his chest.

"How long does it take to feed a cat?" His voice rumbled in my ear. His fingers tangled in my hair, tugging lightly as his lips danced over mine.

"Five minutes?" I rasped my nails across his neck, wishing I could wrap my legs around him.

"Too long." His fingers slid between us, crushing the small pink roses along the top of my bodice. The whisper-soft caress sent a shiver down my spine.

"Three minutes, tops." I promised. His fingers delved into the V of my dress's neckline.

Heat pooled in my belly and then lower. I clasped him to me, begging for more.

As the driver slowed to a stop in front of Audrey's house, I vowed to throw a can of cat food and a can opener at Stevie. He was a smart cat; he'd figure it out.

Lowering the volume of the music, the driver asked, "Should I wait?"

"Yes, please." I breathed in deep, steadying my pounding heart as I reached for the door release.

I vaulted up the steps and onto the front porch. Right on my heels, Evan steadied my landing. Was foreplay an Olympic sport?

I tipped up the planter full of bright red geraniums, and fumbled for the key.

Stevie's plaintive meowing picked up volume and urgency as I unlocked the door. He met us in the foyer and led the way to the kitchen with his tail straight.

Popping open a can, I dumped it on a plate and put it on the floor.

"Isn't that plenty of food for a cat?" Evan asked.

"Are we in a hurry or not?"

"Yeah, let's go." We hurried out, locking the door and replacing the key.

When we pulled up in front of Evan's house five minutes later, my skin flushed, and my panties grew damp. We stumbled out of the car, thanking the driver and hurrying up the stairs to the front door.

Dakota dropped Cocoa off at my house while I was out, so she met us at the door, tail wagging and tongue out. Evan sighed, hanging his head as she scrambled away to fetch her leash.

"I should walk her. Will you wait for me?"

"I'll come with you."

Evan slipped the leash onto Cocoa's collar, and the dog led the way down the steps to the sidewalk.

His big hand swallowed mine as we followed her. "She'll stop to smell every blade of grass if we let her."

"She wouldn't be a dog otherwise."

"This isn't how I envisioned getting you alone."

Cocoa stopped to sniff another shrub, and I leaned up to caress Evan's mouth with mine.

Shifting closer, he bumped my knees apart, inserting his thigh between them. I hugged him tight, pressing my core against him. His lips nuzzled my neck, and I groped for leverage, wanting to climb him.

"Hurry up, dog," Evan grumbled under his breath.

Skimming my hands over his broad shoulders, I stretched up to nibble his chin and neck. "Potty breaks are serious business for teachers and pups."

Cocoa dragged us from one scent to the next, and Evan groaned.

"Got someplace to be?" I snickered. Taking advantage of the dark night, I reached down to fondle his balls.

He bit back a groan. His voice was rough and gravelly. "Fuck, yeah. In bed with you, naked and panting, while I eat your pussy."

My heart skipped a beat and then hammered in my chest. My hand slipped up to stroke along his hard cock. The fabric of his pants frustrated me. I wanted to slide his zipper down and feel his steely heat.

I asked breathily, "What else will you do?"

He continued, low and husky, "After I make you climax, I'll flip you over onto your knees and fuck you so deep you'll see stars. I'll come deep inside you all while pinching your nipples."

His dirty talk was A+ in my gradebook. My lips molded to his, our tongues met and explored. My arms clung to his waist as the hardness of his body pressed against mine.

His hand moved to my upper arm, pulling back. The roughness of the leash brushed against my skin. "Cocoa's finished."

Stepping back, the cool night air cooled my heated skin. My knees were loose in my cowboy boots.

"Let's go, Gorgeous." Evan picked up Cocoa, tucking her into his side like a football with four legs.

He took five steps before he realized I'd stayed behind to admire his backside. He turned, reaching out his free hand. His dimple winked into sight.

"Are you coming?"

"I'm enjoying the view."

His warm palm swallowed mine. "Will you come with me, Val?"

I giggled, "I hope so."

"You have a naughty sense of humor."

"So, I've been told."

We hurried inside, and he set Cocoa down. She pranced around his feet as he grabbed a dog biscuit out of a jar by the door. He tossed it, and she scrambled after it.

Like a predatory animal, Evan pivoted, using his body to back me against the door. Pinning me, he brushed his knuckles across my cheekbone before gliding his mouth over mine.

Desire rushed through me. I gripped his shoulders and wrapped my legs around his waist. "I love you."

He trailed his lips over my neck, pausing to press his teeth and nip along my jawline to my ear. "I love you, too."

I nudged him, ready to get naked and move this party to the bedroom, but Evan was an immovable mountain.

Trapped between us, my dress cinched around my waist. He cupped my butt and squeezed. His index finger slid under the lace of my thong to explore along the crease.

"Mmm, yes," I moaned, pushing my hips against him, pleading for more.

He angled his lips across my throat to my ear. "I love you."

It wasn't fear that sent a tremor through my body, but resounding love. My heart swelled with longing, and I bathed his face with kisses.

I loosened his tie, tugging it over his head. Attacking the top few buttons of his shirt, I opened the collar wide and peppered the tan skin with kisses. Heat gathered in my belly. "I love you, too."

He growled against my neck, letting go of my bottom. I slid my legs down to the floor, my hands pulling the tail of his shirt from his pants.

The hiss of the zipper of my dress sliding down whispered in my ear. Sliding my dress off my shoulders, it pooled in a fluffy puddle around my feet, leaving me bare.

The heat of his gaze lit a fire under my skin. "Nice thong."

"They're my party panties. Wanna have a party?"

He grunted like a caveman, lifting me into his arms. Each step jostled us together. The frantic need to get him out of his pants and into my pussy inundated my very soul.

Dropping me onto the bed, he lifted my right foot and pulled one pink cowboy boot off. Palms running over my foot, making me giggle. I squirmed on the bed as he removed the other boot.

Kicking off his shoes, he tore off his clothes until he stood in front of me.

The sight of his long, thick erection caused me to suck in a breath. I sat up, reaching for him, but he refused to cooperate. Lying down on his side, he faced me, sucking my full, ripe breasts into his mouth.

My hips undulated against him, tempting him to hurry. But still he held back, torturing me with kisses and teasing me with the brush of his fingers.

Every nerve ending hummed. My abdomen clenched, my release imminent.

Pushing him back onto the bed, I straddled his hips. "Now, Evan."

"I have much more planned," he murmured as he buried his face between my breasts.

"Later. Come inside me now."

Taking the delicate thong in his fist, he tore it off me. Grappling for a condom from the box by the bed, he tossed the packet to me.

Lying back, he smiled. His dimple winked at me, and I was weak. How could one tiny spot turn my insides to mush?

"Since you're calling the shots, Gorgeous, you better take charge."

Ripping the condom open, I smoothed it over his foreskin. He clenched his teeth as I rolled it over him, trailing my fingers over balls.

Leaning over him, I kissed my way down his neck to his shoulders. His skin fascinated me, rough in places and smooth in others.

His fingers dug into my hips before trailing over my butt, slipping between the cheeks to my damp center. Dipping in, he found the spot that drove me wild.

Lowering my hips down over him, I pressed my opening to his rock hard cock, guiding him into me. My inner muscles clenched around him.

Arching his hips, he pushed deeper, filling me completely. "Fuck me, Gorgeous."

A giggle of delight escaped me. Gliding my body over his cock while his mouth claimed mine.

Moving together, my body arched over his. His fingers dipped between us, finding my sopping wet core. My body tightened inside, colors swirling behind my eyes.

"Come with me," I demanded. The friction left me blind with need.

And then I soared with pleasure as the powerful orgasm exploded within me and I screamed his name.

His body arched up as pleasure drove him until he shattered under me, and the world crashed down around us.

Sometime later, my body splayed over his, I whispered, "I love you."

"Say it again," He demanded. He rolled, tucking me into his body. His arms tightened around me, and our legs tangled together.

I sighed, snuggling in, his warmth making me sleep.

He loosened his grip, his voice low and slightly dangerous. "Gorgeous...?"

"Mmm hmm." I cuddled closer, pressing my cheek against his.

The muscles of his face moved against me as he smiled. "I asked you to tell me you love me, and you say, mmm hmm?" He wriggled a finger under my chin, tickling me.

"You can't coerce me. It's unfair."

He rolled me over, his body pinning me to the mattress. His fingers danced behind my knee, and I jerked, squirming.

"Stop." I laughed, trying to squirm away from him.

His eyes narrowed. "Say it."

"I love you." The dam broke and felt it in my soul. All this time I'd wasted pretending it was only sex, isolating my feelings, and not being honest with myself.

He kissed me, and I clung to him, breathing in his essence, the smells of forest and sunshine.

Cocoa's nails tapped across the floor, and she hopped up at the bottom of the bed. She licked my toes before sighing heavily and laying her head down.

"Will you stay?" Evan's lips skimmed along my hairline.

"I will," I promised.

"Every night?" he asked.

"Every night."

"Will you marry me?"

Snuggling in, content and happy for the first time in weeks, I wanted to savor it for a while before letting more change into my life.

"Someday," I smiled.

About the Author

M. Jayne LaDow is a playwright and author who leapt into writing romance after spending thirty-three years wrangling middle school English students—a challenge comparable to herding caffeinated cats.

Her hilarious teacher rom-coms draw from her years in education, where she regularly got pied in the face, belted out off-key classroom karaoke, and donned costumes to resemble book characters.

Now retired, she lives with her incredibly patient husband who undoubtedly deserves a medal, two brilliant yet snarky children who keep her humble, and three rescue cats who think they own the place. They are joined by a free-range rabbit who dreams of world domination, a toe-biting tortoise, and a bearded dragon who judges M. Jayne's life choices from behind his glass enclosure.

Stay in contact with me:

Sign up for my newsletter on my website: https://mjladow.com

Follow me on
Facebook: M. Jayne LaDow
Instagram: @mjladow
BookBub: @mjayneladow

Acknowledgements

Writing this novel has been a journey fueled by late nights, early mornings, and hundreds of cups of tea. First and foremost, thank you to my husband, Jim, who has put up with me for thirty-five years and still hasn't changed the locks. Your unwavering support during my long disappearances into the writing cave means the world to me.

To my children, Megan and Miles, your boundless creativity and humor inspire me. I love you both to the moon and back—and maybe even a little further on good days.

A huge thank you to my editor and proofreader, Erin Motta, whose insightful feedback transformed this story into something far better than I could have imagined.

To my fellow authors and beta readers—Suzanne Snowden, Tina Reeds, Lisa Warren, Dirk Valk, Joyce Palmer, Cass Bentleigh, and Rachel Anne Wallace, and Gabby Frantz—your belief in my work has been a guiding light through this process. Thank you for being my literary lifelines.

I'm also deeply grateful to my friend, Lauren Coulsting, who has been with me from the very beginning, reading every chapter and never hesitating to brainstorm with me. Your humor and wisdom are gifts I cherish.

Special thanks to Liz Lehrer for your endless encouragement, frequent check-ins, and razor-sharp wit. May your Mahjong tiles always align perfectly, and your canasta partner always help you make a winning meld.

To my big brother, Dave Hill, thanks for the support and for reading my books even the raunchy sex. You're a trooper.

Nancy Horner, thanks for keeping me up to date on all the school gossip, acronyms, and educational jargon. Your positive attitude makes every child in your class feel like a superstar.

To every teacher and student who ever stepped into my classroom, I learned more from you than you ever realized.

Finally, to every reader who picks up this book series, I am profoundly grateful.